Archangel

Archangel

fiction by

ANDREA BARRETT

W. W. NORTON & COMPANY
New York · London

For information about permission to reproduce selections from this book,
write to Permissions, W. W. Norton & Company, Inc.,
500 Fifth Avenue, New York, NY 10110

For information about special discounts for bulk purchases, please contact
W. W. Norton Special Sales at specialsales@wwnorton.com or 800-233-4830

Manufacturing by Courier Westford
Book design by Chris Welch
Production manager: Devon Zahn

Library of Congress Cataloging-in-Publication Data

Barrett, Andrea.
Archangel : fiction / by Andrea Barrett. — First edition
    pages cm
ISBN 978-0-393-24000-9 (hardcover)
1. Science—Social aspects—History—19th century—Fiction.
2. Science—Social aspects—History—20th century—Fiction. I. Title.
PS3552.A7327A73 2013
813'.54—dc23

                                            2013016958

W. W. Norton & Company, Inc.
500 Fifth Avenue, New York, N.Y. 10110
www.wwnorton.com

W. W. Norton & Company Ltd.
Castle House, 75/76 Wells Street, London W1T 3QT

1 2 3 4 5 6 7 8 9 0

for Cecile Pickart and William Bernhard

CONTENTS

We cannot part with our friends. We cannot let our angels go.
We do not see that they only go out that archangels may come
in. We are idolators of the old.

—RALPH WALDO EMERSON, "Compensation"
(Essays: First Series, 1841)

Archangel

The Investigators

(1908)

Early that June, Constantine Boyd left Detroit with his usual trunk but got on a train headed east instead of west. For the past three summers he'd worked at his uncle's farm in western Michigan, but now, just as he was becoming truly useful, his family had made other plans. Because a different uncle had requested the loan of him, he was being shipped elsewhere: like a harrow, or a horse.

He was twelve that summer of 1908, and he sulked all the way to Toledo, napped between Toledo and Cleveland, woke angry with his absent mother but then forgave her in Erie, when he found the cookies she'd slipped in beside the sandwiches. In Buffalo he passed a bank that looked like a castle, horses plodding along the canal, and a gigantic electric hoist moving grain from a ship into an empty boxcar. At the station where he switched for the train to Bath, he saw a motorized bicycle, one of the very sights his mother had promised, being chased by a terrier, and with that his bad mood slipped away. He was going someplace near water, he remembered. With new people, new things to see and do, away from the steaming city and his father.

In Bath, one of those new people carried Constantine's trunk to a dusty automobile. "It was made up the road in Syracuse," his mother's younger brother said, running his knobby hand over the hood. "I know the engine's inventor."

"My mother says you're an inventor too, sort of."

"More of an . . . investigator," his uncle said modestly. His hair was springy, almost wiry, brown strands mingled with surprising gray. "But I've made a few small things. Have you ridden in an automobile before?"

"Twice," Constantine said, doubling his one ride in Detroit.

"You're an old hand, then. Now"—the engine started with a clatter—"what shall we call each other? I'm not old enough for the whole uncle business. Why don't you just call me Taggart?"

In profile, and despite his hair and his bony forehead, he did resemble Constantine's mother. The two of them had grown up here, along with the older brother who owned the dairy farm where Constantine usually went. First Harry had headed west, wanting a bigger spread and land more suited to grain than vineyards. Then—this was almost all Constantine knew about this side of his family—his mother had gone to Detroit with his father. Taggart had stayed behind with their parents; later the parents had died.

His new uncle raced through the valley, showing off the engine's power as they passed potato fields, vineyards, farmhouses, a cemetery. Long low hills, like rows of dogs with their rounded backs touching, lined the flats on either side and seemed to breathe with the shadows sliding down their flanks. His uncle, following the shadow of another cloud, said, "What do you like to be called?"

"Stan," he said firmly. Why not try it out here? Stan was mature and experienced, not easily surprised.

"Stan," his uncle repeated. And then they turned left up one of the hills and followed the curving road along a ridge before stopping at a white house surrounded by fields. His uncle carried the trunk inside. From the porch, which wrapped around most of the house, Constantine could see the tip of Keuka Lake below, a few boats still moving about and the moon, already visible, sharing the sky with the setting sun. The little cluster of buildings and streets between the lake and the base of their hill was, said Taggart, the village of Hammondsport.

✣

CONSTANTINE SLEPT THROUGH that evening's milking, through dinner, and all through the night, missing the morning milking as well. When he woke, he followed the smell of cooking sausage to the kitchen but stopped in the door when he found, instead of his uncle, a girl standing over the stove and a large man fiddling with some papers at the table.

"Come in!" the man said. "You must be the nephew."

"Stan," he said faintly.

"Mr. Wyman," the man replied. "Or maybe"—he looked up at the actual uncle, who had just come in—"Uncle Ed?"

•

"I told him just to call me Taggart."

"Very modern," the stranger said. "Ed, then."

A blocky person, in all dimensions: square shoulders, solid square trunk, broad palms, forehead like a playing card. Twenty-seven, twenty-eight? The same age, Constantine calculated, as his uncle.

"You—live here?" he ventured.

The men turned to watch a cardinal flash across the window. "Ed's my lodger," Taggart said, turning back. "We went to Cornell together. And this"—he gestured toward the girl at the stove, who looked to be about eighteen—"this is Beryl."

She nodded, stacking sausage on a plate. Her hair was the same oaky brown as Ed's, although she was much slighter—his sister, perhaps? In this wandering house, where each room was two steps up or one down from the next and where doors opened unpredictably into bedrooms or a hall or a porch, there might be a whole separate wing where lodgers lived.

"Beryl comes in daily," Taggart said, moving behind Ed's chair and next to her. "To cook for us, and clean."

Beryl smiled and handed Taggart the plate. Three cheerful faces, perfectly unreadable behind their adult masks, smiling blandly at him. How were they all related? He had no idea what they were to each other, or how he was meant to fit in. Nor was the farmstead itself any more understandable at first.

Some things he recognized: vegetable garden, berry patch, fields of oats and timothy, horses and barns. An orchard, oddly arranged with many different types of trees. Corn, but instead of a big field with the stalks all similar, short rows interrupted by stakes and

.

4

colored tags. The vegetable garden was dotted with labels, measuring tapes, and scales. A pond, fed by a little stream, was marked by colored glass floats, gates at either end, nets on the grass at the edge; a long bed of scraggly stems turned out not to be a vegetable but evening primroses from which the flowers had been snipped. Even the animals were unexpected, no flock or herd of any one thing. Three odd-looking red chickens mingled with half a dozen frizzled cochins and a dozen bearded, cream- and coffee-colored birds. There were big ducks and small, grey geese and white, some small fowl he didn't recognize; a pair of Berkshire pigs but also Chester Whites and two breeds he'd never seen before. Goats, ewes, and—at last!—eleven milking cows, each golden brown and small but different in other ways. Where the Holsteins on his other uncle's farm had been similar in size and color and temperament, here—were these Jerseys, mixed-breed, what?

Taggart and Ed had bred them, Constantine learned, as part of a project to develop a more compact cow with a modest yield of high-butterfat milk. A spring balance hung on the wall, next to a chart with a column for each cow and rows for each morning's and evening's milking; Constantine was to weigh each pail of milk and note the result. Also to weigh the amount fed to each calf, and to measure the calves themselves daily. The pigs and goats and lambs and fowl all had their own measurements, charts, and scales. And then the plants had to be measured and inspected, some had to be hand-pollinated, fruit trees wanted grafting, seedlings in cold frames needed transplanting—too much work, Taggart said, for just the two of them. Especially this summer, when they were also involved with other projects.

•

"Which was why we were glad to invite you," he told Constantine, at the end of that exhausting first day. By then, Constantine had grasped that his tasks here were going to be as different from the straightforward round of feeding, milking, and mucking out as the rambling buildings were from his other uncle's big plain barns. Partly he was excited, and partly he wanted to throw himself under one of the massive old trees and sleep until fall came again. "Your mother said you'd been doing wonderfully at Harry's, so we thought you'd be perfect here."

This feed for these ducks, this mixture of grain for this cow; draw off this much milk from Susie's bucket to feed the bull calf with the star on his forehead and make sure to put the amounts in this notebook; his uncle, he could tell, half expected him to lose track of it all. But his uncle had no idea what he could do. After he milked his first two cows, Taggart brought over his own stool and sat down to strip the last, richest drops—then looked up, surprised, to find nothing left behind. Constantine knew, too, that his handwriting was tidy, his columns of figures straight and his sums correct; he was deft with the utensils and easy with the calves. Less visible, but more important, was what he'd learned at his other uncle's farm: an ability to keep working, without complaint, no matter how tired and lonely he really was. Here, the hours whisked by and the tasks were mostly pleasant. But what was he doing them *for*?

❖

AND WHAT WERE all the books for? One called *Variation of Animals and Plants under Domestication* next to the sofa, another called

The Mutation Theory out on the porch, the parlor table heaped with agricultural and horticultural magazines, seed catalogs and nursery brochures, issues of *Popular Science* and *Popular Mechanics*. A book about electrical circuits under one of the lamps and all the bookshelves spilling extra papers. At his school in Detroit, he shared a handful of torn textbooks with everyone else in that densely crowded room and seldom turned a page himself, but here Taggart and Ed always seemed to be reading or discussing what they read, a froth of words that made Constantine's head spin. He tried to filter out most of it, taking only what was directly useful to whatever he was doing at that moment.

Late on his fourth afternoon there, Ed gave him two fat books about the theory and practice of grafting and a twenty-minute demonstration, which he watched closely. He flicked through the books and set them aside as soon as Ed left; then went to work with a plum tree and the excellent little knife Ed had loaned him. Trimming buds from his bud stick, he cut his thumb twice—but finally he got three buds tied and waxed into the bark slits. When he straightened up, he saw someone he didn't recognize standing in the pond.

A woman, he realized, rubbing clay and beeswax from his hands as he walked over. And old enough to be his grandmother, with a creased face and gray hair knotted beneath a broad-brimmed hat. That, and her cotton work pants, had first made him think she was a man.

"Give me a hand?" she called. She was pulling on a rope attached to one of the floats.

He hurried to the edge of the pond, stripped off his boots and socks, and waded in, flinching as his toes sank into the muck. Something sharp nicked his left heel and he lifted it, before uneasily setting it down again: rock, glass, fishbone, wire, tooth?

"What should I do?"

"Help me lift this out."

Through the cloudy brown water he reached for a curved rim, tugging to the surface one end of what turned out to be a mesh cylinder the size of an apple crate. Inside were fish, flopping unhappily as he and the stranger towed it closer to the bank. "A trap?"

The woman nodded, pointing out the wire funnel while unhinging the opposite end. "Catfish, mostly." She reached inside, pushing the bodies around so she could examine them all. "But I was hoping to get at least one of the fish from Kentucky. No luck today, though." She retrieved her hand and shook the creatures into the water. "Thank you for helping. Are you working here?"

"Taggart's my uncle," he explained.

"Good to meet you," she said. "I'm your uncle's old high school teacher—Miss Henrietta Atkins." Her grip was shockingly strong and so warm, despite the water, that it felt electric. "Nice thing, to have a nephew," she added. "I have five nieces."

A fish, perhaps one they'd just released, broke the surface behind her and then disappeared again. "One's about your age. You'll be in school here this fall?"

But they were no longer alone. Taggart, who'd appeared from wherever he was working and now stood at the edge of the water holding a long tube, said, "Stan's visiting for the summer. He's helping us out with some projects."

How foolish his new name suddenly sounded! "Constantine," he said to Miss Atkins. Taggart looked at him quizzically. "I changed my mind."

"A person should always be able to do that," his uncle said. He waved the tube over the trap. "Anything?"

"Not today," Miss Atkins said. She stepped out, pulling the empty trap behind her and revealing bare feet below pants soaked from knee to hem. A little turn of her wrist unfurled a rolled skirt from her waist and concealed her legs. "But I brought fresh bait." She was slighter than Constantine had first thought and only an inch or two taller than he was.

"Do you think they're still alive?" Taggart asked.

Pushing into the conversation, wanting for once not to be left in the state of confusion in which he spent part of every day, Constantine said, "These fish—what *are* they?"

"Cave fish," Miss Atkins explained, dropping a foul-smelling gobbet into the trap. "*Amblyopsis spelaeus*, native to a cave in Kentucky. They don't have any eyes. They're flesh-colored, almost white, and when they're moving, they look like skinned catfish swimming on their backs. Smaller though." She measured out three or four inches between her forefinger and her thumb.

"But why . . . ?" Constantine said.

"Why are we interested?" Taggart said. He smiled at his old teacher. "We're both just curious about them—there's a lot of discussion about how they evolved. Why do *you* think a cave-dwelling species might lose its eyes?"

They were both looking at him intently. "Because they don't need their eyes in the dark?" he offered. How would he know?

"If they can find food by sound, or by touch, I guess it wouldn't hurt them not to have eyes, since the other animals around them couldn't see any better in the dark. Maybe eyes just disappear, if we don't use them?"

Taggart nodded. "Good guess—but when you really question the mechanism of *how* that happens, it's not so straightforward. Maybe some fish began exploring the outer parts of the cave long ago, and when they found food and shelter there, they moved back a bit farther into the cave with each generation, and as it got darker, those with imperfect eyes but more highly developed other senses were selected for, adaptations appearing little by little until finally those who made it deep into the cave had no eyes at all."

Constantine closed his own eyes for an instant, trying to picture this.

"Or maybe a whole group of fish were swept into the cave during a flood," his uncle continued, "and the ones with perfect eyes found a glimmer of light and swam out, but a few who already had imperfect eyes were trapped, and bred, and eventually lost their eyes entirely. Or maybe, outside the cave, some sport with no eyes appeared, the way a peculiar plant or animal pops up here— but then instead of that fish staying in its regular habitat, where it would have died, it fell or swam into a cave, where having no eyes wasn't fatal? And then somehow it found a mate, and then—"

Was this how adults thought? Maybe this, maybe that, and then and then and then.

"They're just *interesting*," Miss Atkins interrupted. "My friend Daphne asked if I knew anything about them—people writing

•

and arguing about evolution and Darwinism always point to these fish. So when one of Taggart's friends started studying them in Kentucky, we jumped at his offer to send us some. We turned them loose in the pond and figured we'd see what happened. If they're exposed to light, will their offspring develop eyes? If they breed with some other fish, will the offspring be blind, or not? Every now and then we drop in some traps, or run a net through part of the pond, to see what we find. So if you do see one . . ."

Constantine nodded and promised to let her know, suddenly overwhelmed by the sun beating down on his head, and his fierce concentration with the bud grafts and the beeswax, and this rush of words and ideas. Why not just keep the fish in a cage, or in a little pool by themselves, where they could be looked at and handled whenever you wanted? He backed away from the muddy pond, longing for the cool clear lake down below and the crowd of boys who swam there after chores and who, deep in their own pleasure, had let him splash among them yesterday without asking any questions. "Pete," one had said, and then others offered their names, Luke and Corey and Frank and the rest; all he'd had to offer was his own (Stan hadn't seemed so stupid then) and the phrase, "I'm visiting," and someone had held out a hand to pull him up onto the dock.

❋

HE SWAM THERE whenever he could get away; every day the heat grew worse and Taggart, who said they'd never had a June like this, asked Beryl to do all her cooking in the morning. That helped some, but beets had to be thinned regardless of the

•

weather, the apple trees needed spraying with Bordeaux mixture, and they ended up doing heavy chores first thing in the morning and then again after dusk. When the sun was at its worst they retreated to the porch, where Ed wrote articles and Taggart did paperwork, leaving Constantine to doze and consider all he'd already learned, and to imagine exploring whatever else lay within walking distance of the farm.

Before he could go anywhere, though, the cows had to be milked, the milk weighed and the data charted, his duties pulsing steadily through each day. Less steadily, but still several times a week, Miss Atkins came by to see a new flower or some freshly hatched chicks, or to show them a bat or a fossil she'd found in the Glen. Always she ended her visits by shedding her shoes and stockings, slipping on pants, and checking the trap she left in the pond for the blind white fish. Constantine, wanting to help, swept the water regularly with a dip net in her absence, but he brought up only the same minnows, catfish, frogs, and snails that made their way into the traps: never the *Amblyopsis*. Equally elusive were answers to his simplest questions about this place and its people. What, for instance, kept the farm afloat financially?

He could see money coming in from Ed, who in addition to his duties at the farm worked as the agricultural reporter for a Syracuse newspaper and paid Taggart room and board—but then it went out again to Beryl, paid to keep house. He himself worked for free, but he ate enormously and Taggart provided all his food, along with his work clothes, barn boots, and clean linen. Milk and eggs and vegetables were their own, but Taggart had to buy beef and grain and other supplies. The experiments they did in the orchard weren't aimed at increasing their yield of apples or pears but at developing new breeds; the same was true in the vegetable garden; they sold much of their milk to a local cheese maker but the point of all the weighing and measuring didn't seem to make the herd more productive.

One afternoon, when Ed and Taggart were busy with something in the village, Beryl emerged from the kitchen with a basket of laundry and caught him staring over the terraced vineyards below as he pondered these mysteries. "Are you homesick?" she asked.

"I'm not a *child*," he said, startled to have her ask something personal. Although she was there when he came in for breakfast and stayed until the supper dishes were done, they talked only about the tasks that needed doing each day. "I've worked away from home the last three summers."

"Your uncle mentioned that," she said. "And also said that your father . . ." She stopped, smoothed a creased shirt, began again. "Was it Taggart's older brother you visited?"

"Harry," he said, pausing to consider all the hours she and the men spent without him. "Do you know him?"

She shrugged. "Not really; I was a baby when he left, and not much older when your mother ran off with your father. I was wondering if he was like Taggart. Or if your mother was, for that matter." She prodded the heap of damp clothes with one foot. "You don't talk much about the rest of your life."

"Neither do you," he said, more sharply than he meant.

She carried the basket to the clothesline and pinned a shirt that might have been his. *Ran off*—what did she know? His mother said

•

she'd met his father, a stranger to the area, at the county fair and gone happily with him to Detroit when he found work. It was back there that he felt, not homesick but . . . some other thing. Wedged into a small flat with his three sisters and his parents, he longed for Uncle Harry's farm—as, he imagined, he would long for this place someday. Clean sheets on a bed his own, a room with no one else in it. Good food, time to himself, and a property that, although modest in size, continued to surprise him.

The dips and rises broke it into small fields and pastures; the trees pressed close and so did the neighboring vineyards; in sheds and outbuildings, benches bore tubs of peculiar substances. Balsam, he guessed of one, sniffing closely; lint, cottonseed, some kind of oil. Yesterday he'd discovered a room packed with wood, metal rods, glinting shavings, wires, lathes, chisels. Elsewhere chicks warmed beneath lamps, beans fermented, seeds slept in paper bags. Some days Taggart and Ed disappeared into one or another building after breakfast and didn't emerge until it was time for the evening milking; other days they sat on the porch for hours, arguing and drawing plans. Everything about the way they lived was new to him, including the neighbors who, on bicycles made by a local mechanic at the edge of the village, zipped past him as he walked down to the lake to swim. At home, his family was so far from being able to afford a bicycle that he'd never let himself want one. Here—maybe someone had an old one, a very old one, that he could have in exchange for work?

The mechanic, he soon learned, also built motorcycles: staggeringly fast, endlessly fascinating. Once, as he walked past the pharmacist's store, he was nearly run down by a thin man with a dark mustache, crouched low over the handlebars of a model with a particularly raucous engine. Other days, as he watched motorcycles dart past loaded wagons, annoying even the drivers of the automobiles already annoying the horses, he imagined himself as one of the goggled drivers. On the afternoon that Ed and Taggart tore out of the driveway on a pair of motorcycles he hadn't seen before, only his mother's orders not to ask for anything kept him from begging for a ride.

He did the milking and the data tabulation by himself that evening, finishing up before he heard the pair of engines tracing their way along the west shore road, through the village, up the hill to the house. Both men were talking happily as they made their way toward the barn and then, once they saw all the work was done, into the house.

"That," Taggart said, taking in the freshly washed pails and completed charts, "was very thoughtful." He swung his goggles from his thumb, white-rimmed eyes shining in a face caked everywhere else with dirt.

Two days later, Ed rode a used bicycle up the hill and offered it to Constantine for the rest of the summer. He learned how to ride it in an hour, and then—suddenly he could reach so many places! He pedaled for several miles along the same shore road Taggart and Ed had taken. He rode up and down the hills along the road toward Bath. He explored the Pleasant Valley, a stretch of bottomland extending back from the lake, and he found the farm owned by one of his uncle's friends, who bred and raced trotting horses. The oval track was sometimes loaned out for bicycle races, and he dreamed of being old enough to enter one.

•

He was sharpening a knife on the porch, a few days later, when he looked up to see a giant dragonfly rising from that same valley. Or not a dragonfly, but a mechanical version of one, guided by a man seated between its golden double wings. He dropped the knife, leapt the rail, and ran toward it across the field. The sound attached to the sight—*tik-a, tik-a, tik-a, tik-a. Tika tika tika*—brought his uncle to the door of one of the sheds.

"Do you see?" Taggart called.

The thing moved steadily, casting a slim shadow. As it sank, Constantine saw another figure watching from halfway down the hill, a girl with curly dark hair resting her hand on a wooden stake in the vines.

"That's one of G.H.'s aeroplanes," Taggart said. *Tik . . . a*, and it touched unsteadily down. "He and some friends have been experimenting with a double-wing design, using his lightest motorcycle engine."

"I, I, I," Constantine stuttered. "I want—can we go see?"

"Of course," Taggart said easily, and the next day brought him right inside the little factory he'd only walked past before. Bicycles and motorcycles, motors and frames, shelves and benches and then, in a separate shed, parts of a flying machine. The man who'd nearly run him down in the village—this was G.H.—showed him bamboo struts guyed with piano wire, a three-wheeled landing gear, hinged tips at the end of wings and the shoulder yoke that controlled them. An elderly man wearing a fez walked in holding a model helicopter, which was powered by rubber bands; over the winter he'd gotten a full-sized version three feet off the ground. A young mechanic suspended a model wing inside a long box

·

with a fan at one end and then invited them to view the swirling threads of red silk. Everywhere Constantine saw another marvel. He had no desire to emulate his father, who worked, when he worked at all, at a tool-and-die shop, but he loved the machines. The biplane he'd glimpsed was called the *June Bug*; it was kept in a tent near the racetrack he'd seen, and had already flown several times. Two other models had been tested earlier in the year and the light, powerful engines G.H. built, which had first powered motorcycles and then dirigibles, had meanwhile lured to the area other men interested in building flying machines.

As Constantine listened to the men talk, he understood for the first time that his uncle wasn't just a tinkerer or an amateur animal breeder: he *made* things. Something that helped bind the bamboo into a sturdy frame; a refinement of the varnish spread on the wings to seal the cloth. The little crook in the tubing controlling the rudder was his design as well. In the same way that Taggart tinkered with cows and fowl, cross-breeding and selecting until he'd improved some aspect, he joined inanimate objects—screws, oil, guncotton, rubber, parts from those tubs and bins at home— until something new emerged.

※

SO THE VILLAGE, which had looked so quiet, turned out to be just as mysterious as the farm. Now that Constantine knew to look, he found dirigibles parked in a hangar on the flats and others corralled, like whales in a narrow bay, in the same glen where Miss Atkins found her fossils. Beryl revealed, while serving dinner, that last summer she'd seen several of the strange,

·

lumpy shapes moving slowly between the hills. And in the spring, she said, a few months before Constantine had joined them, she'd stood on the swimming dock as a dirigible bumbled past like a gigantic fat bee, the pilot pointing the nose up or down by scuttling across the matchstick frame of the gondola suspended below. If she'd had a ladder, she said, she could have grabbed the pilot's foot. Constantine gaped, he envied her furiously; why had she kept this secret?

The nights were short now, as they neared the end of June; they milked a bit later but still it was light when they ate, light when they cleared their plates, light enough for a bicycle ride after supper, when the air finally began to cool. Unremarkable-looking strangers he'd earlier ignored were now revealed to be aerialists, drawn here by G.H.'s presence, many acquainted with his uncle. One experimented with a full-sized version of a helicopter, one had built a flapping-winged thing called an ornithopter, another worked on an experimental monoplane. He met stuntmen, engineers, an Army officer interested in dropping bombs from the air. Each gave him a different sense of Taggart but didn't help him understand more about Ed.

One night he rode down to the beach and stayed longer than usual with the splashing boys, looking up for a shape in the air each time his head broke the surface. By the time he dressed the sun was nearly gone, and the last part of his ride home was dark enough to be difficult. He steered by the light from the kitchen window, found the house empty when he entered, and padded barefoot across the floor, imagining Taggart and Ed working in one of the sheds and Beryl long since headed for home. A noise

•

from the porch drew him across the parlor toward the open door. In the dim light he saw someone—Ed, he realized, when his eyes adjusted more fully—standing very close to Beryl.

Both seemed to be looking at the sky above the lake. He backed up a few steps and then moved forward again, this time purposefully banging the doorframe as he passed. Smoothly the pair slid apart, greeting him with neither embarrassment nor explanation.

"Did you have a good swim?" Beryl asked.

"Excellent," Constantine replied. Were they . . . courting, then? That was the word his mother would have used. But if they were, where did this leave Taggart?

Ed began to fan her with a magazine he picked up from one of the chairs. Beryl lived with her father, Constantine knew by then, along with her brothers and sisters and a maiden aunt in a house not half a mile away. Her father worked with G.H. as a mechanic at the little factory but spent much of his pay packet on new gadgets; her wages supported the household. He'd begun to feel guilty for the extra work he caused her.

"Tomorrow," Ed said, swirling the pages enthusiastically, "we'll have a chance to see an eclipse, if it doesn't cloud up. Look." He held the magazine out to Constantine.

Popular Astronomy: what was he supposed to do with this? An eclipse was . . . he thought he remembered from school that it had something to do with the moon, but the article marked by a long piece of grass was no use at all, dense text framing an array of maps covered with curved lines and numbers. As he let the magazine fall to the chair, Taggart stepped onto the porch. Beryl seemed perfectly glad to see him.

.

"I was showing him Phoebe's calculations for the eclipse," Ed said, adding to Constantine, "We knew the person who made those tables when we were all at Cornell. Phoebe Wells, she was then."

"What time does our Phoebe predict?" Taggart asked.

Ed retrieved the magazine, found the right table, and ran a finger along one of the curved lines. "Just before ten," he said, and then, ignoring both Constantine and Beryl, began planning with Taggart what they'd need for the following morning. A few minutes later, Beryl left. The men were still talking intently when Constantine went to bed: and talking, still—had they even slept?—when he rose and found them in the kitchen, eating crescent-shaped pancakes that Beryl, who called them "partial-eclipse cakes," flipped on the griddle.

He ate three himself and they all scurried to finish the chores before gathering on the porch. Taggart produced pieces of smoked glass through which, he said, they could watch what was happening without damaging their eyes, and Constantine peered astonished through his as the moon's shadow bit its first curve from the sun. So this was an eclipse! Ten forty-five, eleven o'clock; the sun was a chubby crescent pointing toward the lake, then a slimmer crescent pointing down. In Florida, Taggart said, those lucky enough to be in the shadow's direct path would see an annular eclipse, a brilliant ring around the darkened sun. Here, as the eclipse peaked, a little more than half the sun was covered.

After a few minutes, Ed tapped his arm and pointed at the fluttering pattern of light and shadow under the big maple tree. "Take a look," Ed said. "An indirect view's as useful as a direct one—you can see the changing shape of the sun just as clearly there, on the ground. Each little hole between the overlapping leaves acts like a pinhole camera to project an image."

What was a pinhole camera? Later he'd ask for an explanation but for now he trotted over to the tree and saw what Ed meant; light filtered through the canopy and cast bright crescents onto the ground, each the exact shape of the sun at that moment and all of them trembling with the breeze. On the porch, the adults had set down their bits of smoked glass and, leaning over the railing with outstretched arms, had made themselves into trees. Ed, in the middle, held his left hand angled left, fingers spread, with Taggart's right hand lying perpendicularly across it. Beryl's left hand, angled left, similarly crossed Ed's right. Each set of intersecting fingers formed a cross-hatched pattern, which focused light like the leaves. On the ground bright slivers danced beneath their joined hands and the three of them laughed and laughed.

❖

ON THE THURSDAY after the eclipse, Constantine heard the sound of the aeroplane's engine while he was wading in the pond with his dip net, and again while he was tending the calves, but he missed seeing it. On Friday, while he was weeding the eggplants, he leapt up as soon as he heard the clattering whirr and ran to the rise, where he was rewarded with a glimpse of the varnished golden wings through the trees. On Saturday, the Fourth of July, the aeroplane was to fly in public, as part of the holiday celebration, and he planned to be as close as possible when it took off.

That night he was too excited to sleep and he rose and dressed in thick darkness the instant he heard his uncle stir. But although he and Taggart and Ed finished the chores before it was fully light, and Beryl packed a picnic basket before they'd even finished breakfast, everyone else had the same idea and they arrived at the Pleasant Valley field to find a crowd already there. Tromping the grounds of the Stony Brook Farm, pressing up near the tent where the *June Bug* sheltered, or grouped with blankets and baskets along the embankment, were hundreds of people who lived in the area and hundreds more who'd come from far away. Reporters and amateur aerialists and curious families, staff from the *Scientific American* come to assess the flight—this wasn't just an exhibition, Constantine learned. The magazine had offered a trophy for the first aeroplane flight of one kilometer—3,281 feet, Taggart said—measured in a straight line. Packed around the magazine men were a movie crew, hoping to film either the flight or an exciting disaster, and members of the Aero Club from New York.

All the best spots were already taken, and they would have ended up on the far side of the potato patch if Taggart hadn't spotted Miss Atkins waving at them from a prime spot under a tree just north of the red barn. As they crossed the damp field she rose to greet them and then introduced Constantine to the girls sprouting around her feet.

"Marion, Caroline, Elaine," she said: a girl nearly grown, one about his own age, and an elfin one with beautiful eyes who might have been seven or eight. Perhaps because there were so many strangers around, Miss Atkins was wearing an ordinary dress; two toddlers, chubby-legged and dark-haired and impossible to tell apart, clutched fistfuls of the sprigged cloth. "And these are the twins," she added. "Agnes and Alice."

·

"Your nieces?" Constantine guessed, remembering their first meeting. Her sister must be a good deal younger.

She nodded. "Their mother loaned them to me for the day."

But everything else seemed more important. The men from the city, with their fancy hats; the pair mounting movie cameras, which he'd never seen before, atop heavy wooden tripods; visitors on motorcycles or in unusual automobiles, many carrying umbrellas and all focused on the white tent sheltering the *June Bug*. Through an open flap, he could see one man doing something to the propeller while another fiddled with the tail section, and he began to inch closer. Beryl had headed off toward some friends her age, and Taggart was watching her rather than him, but he'd barely begun his move when Taggart gestured and said, "Stay here, for now. This is serious business."

Dismayed, he turned back to the nieces. The girl closest in size to him, Caroline, patted the blanket. "You're new here," she said, as he sat beside her. "Where are your parents?"

"Back home," he muttered. Only when she turned to take a muddy stick from one of the twins did he realize that she was the girl who, the first time he'd seen the aeroplane fly, had been watching from a spot lower down on the hill. Then he made more of an effort, adding, "In Detroit. Where are yours?"

"At home," she said. "Up the road. Sometimes Aunt Henrietta takes us out for a day, to give my mother a rest." Imagine, he thought, using Miss Atkins's first name! "She's sick a lot," Caroline continued. "And we're so many—" She gestured vaguely at her sisters.

"Are you all like your aunt?"

·

23

One twin was feeding grapes to the other, a process Caroline watched closely. Indeed, this seemed to be her job; her aunt was talking intently to Taggart while her older sister strolled away with a young man wearing a plaid cap. "Sorry," she said. "What do you mean?"

"You know—so interested in cows and fish and plants and everything."

"Oh, that." With a delicate little shrug, she said, "Some of us are, some of us aren't. Marion"— her tall sister was now laughing with her companion—"isn't interested at all. I'm not either, really. But Elaine is"—Elaine was reading a book, he saw then, although she seemed young for that. "It's too early to tell about the twins. Are you like your uncle?"

"I don't know," he said. He knew he wasn't like his father, although they shared deft hands, a gift for understanding machines, and a quickness with figures. But Taggart had those traits as well. His father drank until he was stupid and disappeared, returning enraged by everyone but particularly, peculiarly, by his son. Was he like his uncle, then? He enjoyed the grafting and pollinating and the handling of the animals. But the abstract ideas didn't interest him at all, and the charts and theories bored him.

"Halfway, maybe?" he said to Caroline. "I'm not that interested in the farm experiments, but I really like the flying machines."

"They're beautiful, aren't they? The first time I saw one up in the air—did you see the *Red Wing* take off from the lake in March?"

He shook his head. "I wasn't here then." How unfair that he'd missed not only all that Beryl had seen, but this too!

•

"The wings were red silk," she said, "and it had runners on the bottom. The builders loaded it on the steamer and brought it to the edge of the ice—it had already melted at this end—and lots of us walked along the shore until we reached the launching place. The men held on to it while the engine warmed up and when they let go it chattered down the ice for a bit, then rose up and . . ."

She described every detail rapturously, her face lit up even as her hands retrieved sandwich crusts cast aside by the twins, dolls dropped, shoes pulled off, and suddenly he found himself paying complete attention to her.

❦

WHILE THEY TALKED, rising occasionally to chase after one or another of the twins, feeding them and Elaine from the picnic hampers, the hours passed, the temperature rose, the wind increased, and the clouds piled up, flipped on their backs, tumbled over each other. The boys Constantine swam with thundered by in a herd, ignoring him. The crowd grew more and more restless as G.H. and the mechanics—"There's my father," Beryl said, pointing out a short, bowlegged man before turning back to Ed—kept stepping outside the tent to check the clouds and test the wind, to shake their heads and step back inside. Taggart and Ed walked over several times and returned, looking grave but still convinced the flight would take place. People left, but others arrived and the grounds were still crowded when, early in the afternoon, the rain began to fall. Miss Atkins, cleverly, had brought a large piece of oilcloth that she strung from the tree to a pole Ed made from a sapling. The winery opened its doors and many on that side of the field ducked inside until the cloudburst ended.

The sun came out, but then it was windy. Then the wind dropped but the clouds gathered ominously again. Miss Atkins caught a fat beetle flying heavily under the oilcloth and showed it to Constantine and the girls. A June bug, she said; it flew with its thick outer wings, which were called elytra, stuck out stiffly while the little underwings whirred below: rather like the busy propeller beneath the stiff wings of the aeroplane, which was how it had gotten its name. Constantine tried to look interested—it *was* sort of interesting—but Caroline laughed affectionately and patted the back of her aunt's hand. The dirigible man passed by, also the men experimenting with the ornithopter and the helicopter. A handsome young man in a white suit came over to talk to Taggart and Ed, who introduced him to Miss Atkins but not to the rest of them; after he left Miss Atkins said he was a famous plant explorer who'd helped his father-in-law design a massive tetrahedral-celled kite.

All afternoon the crowd milled about, each swirl and shuffle bringing new people past their little plot: some of Taggart and Ed's old professors from Cornell; men from the experimental station at Geneva; automobile makers from Rochester and Syracuse; reporters from Buffalo and Albany and New York. Constantine, now firmly cast in the role of Caroline's helper—he'd watched after his own younger sisters at home for so long that he couldn't help interfering with these—eavesdropped on their conversations as he dabbed jam from Agnes's hands and removed Alice's wet socks after an incident with a puddle. He heard gossip about the Wright brothers' aeroplane, which they'd so far declined to exhibit in public, and which launched from a track instead of rolling along on wheels. Twice more it rained, but only briefly, and still almost everyone stayed. Had there ever been such a long afternoon?

Elaine fell asleep over her book, the twins dropped their heads onto Caroline's lap, and Constantine gave up and stretched out on his back, looking up at the square of cloth and the bugs flying heavily back and forth. The cloth was the sky and the bugs were aeroplanes, crossing in stately procession so far above that from up there he was the tiniest particle, indistinguishable from the others in the field. Did he fall asleep? He couldn't remember. At one point he overheard Taggart and Henrietta Atkins discussing their families, one of them his.

"I invited my sister to come for the summer, with all the children," Taggart said. "But she wouldn't, she'd only send . . ." and Miss Atkins said, "My sister's just as bad with *her* husband." But maybe he only dreamed that, the way he dreamed himself as a June bug bumbling through the trees. Then, somehow, it was nearly six o'clock.

Taggart had gone home to do the milking, taking Beryl with him, and returned talking quietly with her; the wind had died down and the sky had cleared; men were pushing the *June Bug* from the tent! It was both larger and smaller than he'd imagined, the wings very long—six Taggarts end to end, he guessed; maybe seven—but the pilot's seat smaller than a kitchen chair, the nose not much longer than the pilot's outstretched legs, and the tail section, which two men were attaching now, no more than

.

a shape outlined by skinny poles. Some men ran off to measure out a kilometer—a little more than half a mile, Miss Atkins said, which was easier to imagine than Taggart's conversion—over the muddy fields. Before long G.H. settled in between the curved cloth wings, which from Constantine's angle looked like an open mouth in the process of swallowing a man. Someone spun the long wooden propeller and the engine caught with a familiar noise. Someone pulled away the blocks. Those holding on to the wires and the bamboo frame opened their hands simultaneously and the machine clattered along the dirt, picking up speed until it rose into the air, soaring over the clover and the potatoes and the vines. Ten feet above the ground, twenty, then thirty—

"Too steep!" someone called, and Constantine, running after the flying machine, could see G.H. struggling to bring the nose down. Before a minute had passed the *June Bug* landed bumpily, far short of the finish line, on wheels half the size of those on Constantine's bicycle. He trotted alongside the swarming men as they pushed the machine back to the official starting line. The tail section had drooped, the mechanics decided; they removed it, reattached it correctly, and pronounced it ready to fly again.

The sun had dipped in the meantime, pulling shadows like taffy over the field. Taggart and Ed joined Constantine, and then Miss Atkins came over with all five nieces.

"Home!" a twin—Agnes, Constantine thought—demanded crankily.

"Soon," Miss Atkins promised her. "But first you have to see this, something marvelous is going to happen."

And then, with all of them watching, and the cameras snapping and rolling, the aeroplane did take off again, this time rising smoothly and leveling and then flying as easily as a real June bug over the fences and stakes, making a gentle curve as it soared past the marker—Constantine, running behind it, heard the excited cheers of the spectators there—and continuing on before settling in a field twice the needed distance away.

❖

THAT NIGHT THERE were celebrations, and on the following day G.H. and all his helpers, along with the visiting Aero Club members, were feted with a banquet and a steamboat cruise on the lake. Later, articles and photographs showed up in the newspapers and then in the weekly magazines. In one, Constantine saw Ed and Beryl standing together; in another Taggart and Ed; in a third, himself and Caroline, staring openmouthed at the bow-winged bit of magic flying by. In the photos they were part of a crowd, noticeable only to themselves, but in fact the visitors had long since disappeared, leaving behind the beets and sheep and corn and cows, the frizzled fowl and the apple tree top-grafted so many times that it now bore twenty apple varieties and several sorts of pear. The plants and animals still needed everything they always needed, every day, and with Taggart and Ed occupied by the aerial crowd, Constantine was so busy that two weeks passed before he stepped into the pond again to check the fish.

The sky was an even, soft gray that day, so windless that clouds of tiny flies hung in the air as if set on a shelf, and the water was shallower than it had been during even the hottest June days. Gingerly he crossed the new rim of soft silt and watched his feet

·

disappear in the murky water. Quiet, quiet. He trailed his net back and forth with no expectation of anything unusual. When he pulled it up, two fish, dully pale, almost translucent, with nothing but blank, scaled skin where the eyes should have been, were caught in the fine mesh. Ghost fish, nightmare fish. He stared at them so long they began to gasp. Then, trying not to touch them, he dropped the net and ran to the barn, where Taggart and Ed were tinkering with a gear meant to improve the connection between an aeroplane's front landing wheel and the rudder.

"They're still alive, then!" Taggart said. He set down a wrench, hopped on his motorcycle, and buzzed off, returning a few minutes later with Miss Atkins riding behind him. By then Constantine was back at the pond along with Ed, avoiding the hovering clumps of flies and eager to show off what he'd found.

"It's a miracle they haven't been eaten yet by some other creature," Miss Atkins said, apparently thrilled. She patted Constantine's arm as she spoke. "And a miracle you didn't scare them off. I thought they'd be especially good at sensing any movement."

"I don't know," he said. "I couldn't help disturbing the water with my net."

"You were lucky, then," she said. She'd already put on her cotton pants, and now she rolled her skirt around her waist and stepped into the water armed with her own net. "Shall we try again? If we could see them, and see if they've changed . . ."

Not a word about what he should have done, suddenly so obvious: stow the fish in one of the traps before rushing off to find the adults. How could he have been so foolish? He flushed as Miss Atkins swept the water, bringing up minnows, catfish, newts, twigs, a swallow's corpse, a slimy horn, everything but the blind fish, who might never have existed, or never been caught by him.

"Maybe if you try?" she said, handing the net to him.

Obediently he stepped into the water and swept. If he were one of those fish, he'd be on the other side of the pond by now, hiding behind a root or sheltering in a hollow, every place invisible to him. The boy was a movement, his net was another; the boy was a set of vibrations that would reveal—what did he seem like, to the fish?

As Miss Atkins turned toward him, startled, and both Taggart and Ed shouted his name, he lay down in the water, head submerged and eyes tightly closed, concentrating on what he could feel and hear. Small currents, slight changes in temperature. Sounds, more than he'd imagined. Of course the fish could sense him coming. So too could his uncle; last week, when he'd asked if he could stay in Hammondsport and earn his keep by doing chores, go to school with Miss Atkins and train to work with the mechanics on engines for the motorcycles or even for the flying machines, Taggart hadn't been surprised at all. His face had gone completely smooth and whoever had been about to join them at the weighing station—Ed or Beryl, he couldn't be sure from the footsteps—had stopped and backed away.

"Your mother needs you," Taggart had said. Which meant that they'd talked, brother and sister, more than Constantine knew. And that Taggart might know something about his father's rages and the way that, on those boiling summer days when the sun refused to set in the sky, the wind refused to blow and the clouds wouldn't form, when the apartment steamed and smelled as badly

•

as the inside of the sweltering factory, his father turned on him. No one, his father said, could blame him for having a few drinks in a cool bar: and who was Constantine to look at him that way? What happened afterward was bad enough that, even his first summer at Uncle Harry's, he guessed why his mother had sent him away. But when the heat broke his father's rages abated, and then his mother needed him around. To help with the girls, he'd assumed. But also, Taggart had said, "It changes things, when you're there."

If he went home, his uncle had said, for just a while longer, until he finished high school and his sisters were older, he could come back to Hammondsport then and live at the farm and work wherever he wanted. Or maybe his mother and sisters would come as well. Either way would be wonderful. Faintly—he had years ahead of him, years and years in which to explore everything here—he heard Miss Atkins calling his name.

•

The Ether of Space

(1920)

✤

There was a lot of chitchat, to start. Some the usual—Owen's health, the weather in London, a tactful acknowledgment of the tenth anniversary of Michael's death—but some not: Owen's sister was heading to Russia with a group of Quaker relief workers, his nephew was working for her old teacher at Cornell, his paper on variable stars would be published in the spring. But where was the crucial news?

Across the ocean, at her desk in her bedroom in her parents' house in Philadelphia, Phoebe Wells Cornelius scanned the pages of her friend's letter impatiently. Last March, after the fighting had stopped, some British astronomers had quickly organized an expedition to view the eclipse. At two different stations along the path of totality, despite clouds in the Gulf of Guinea and a distorted mirror in Brazil, they'd photographed stars in the neighborhood of the sun. The results had been

•

presented in November, at a meeting in London that Phoebe had been in no position to attend, and since then—nearly two months; it was already January, not just a new year but a whole new decade—she'd been waiting for Owen to supplement the sketchy, sensational newspaper articles with some firsthand observations.

We were all squeezed into the meeting room at Burlington House; the pews were packed and there were people standing behind the last row and in the anteroom. The usual eminences from the Royal Society and the Astronomical Society—J. J. Thomson, Fowler, Lodge, Silberstein, Jeans, etc.—but also the philosopher Whitehead, several reporters, and many I didn't recognize: about 150 of us, so many the room was steaming despite the wintry day. Dyson spoke first, summarizing the work of the expeditions and then describing the photographs in the <u>most</u> enthusiastic terms, despite the lack of data. He claimed there was no doubt that they had confirmed Einstein's prediction: the sun's gravitational field had been shown to bend the rays of starlight in accordance with his law of gravitation.

But Dyson's words don't really explain it—it was more the tone, the <u>feeling</u> in the room. I wish you'd been there. Half of us sighed as the other half gasped, some thrilled and some appalled and some split between the two; the older members were really upset. I could feel— well, I'm not sure what that was. Something that shook me. I took notes as fast as I could, trying to get not only the Astronomer Royal's tabulated values but Dr. Crommelin's description of conditions in Brazil during the eclipse and Professor Eddington's comments on the difficult weather. I noticed that Eddington had discarded many

·

observations, but we'll see what's really there when the full report is published a few months from now. I do believe that Einstein's theory is correct, but I'm not sure these results support it as definitively as they're claiming.

The report on the meeting in the next day's Times *was typically muddled regarding the mathematics and said nothing, after these years of denouncing all things German, about the oddity of celebrating the work of a German scientist. In fact an article on the same page announced the King's call for two minutes of silence during the anniversary of the signing of the Armistice. I went with my sister to the cenotaph that day, and when eleven struck and the guns went off, the crowd fell silent. The traffic stopped too, and the trains, and the Tube, people stood still in the shops, stood up at their desks—I wept like everyone else and thought: I've never seen anything like this. Although later, I realized that, at Burlington House, I'd had a similar sense of being present at a—what do you call these? A discontinuity, a rift? In one case torn by grief and in the other by wonder.*

For some, the meeting itself was a kind of grief. In the midst of the questions, Sir Oliver Lodge stood up abruptly and rushed out without a word. Later, he told a reporter he'd left to catch a train, but some of the younger men have been a bit cruel, the old man running from the new theory and so forth. Not easy at that age, I imagine, to find that the world has just become a different place.

I have forgotten to thank you for your report on the Washington meeting, and to say that I read your chapter on "The Evolution of the Stars" with real interest. I hope the book is coming along wonderfully, and that you and Sam are both well.

•

An actual report, finally, from an actual witness: how pleasing, to glimpse a scrap of reality! The articles in the *New York Times*, based on cables sent from London, had been as muddled as those Owen described. *Men of science more or less agog*—oh, indeed. *Lights all askew in the heavens.* The articles trumpeted the impossibility of understanding the theory while at the same time suggesting that it had changed the world.

Phoebe rose from her desk, went downstairs, and stepped outside to look at the sky. Nine o'clock and freezing cold, the moon two days past new, the stars giving no sign that they were not as they'd once seemed. The sound of her father's viola waved down from the top of the house, bits of Bach easing through the old glass in the attic windows, spreading from her mother's garden, where in June the peonies flourished as if fertilized by the sound, through the tiny backyard to the neighbors on all sides. Always her father played at night, retreating from what to him was a world in which everything—business, politics, music, art—grew steadily worse. Yet the house hadn't crumbled around them; the house, in which first he and then Phoebe had grown up, and in which she was now raising her son, Sam, looked the same. So too—she checked again—did the stars above. Where you lived and what you knew determined what you expected to see. Once the moon was a smooth glowing orb, and then it had mountains and seas. Once Jupiter wandered alone, and then he had moons; once orbits were round, and the stars stayed still in space. In earlier books, she'd traced those changing perceptions. Now she was trying to write about the universe beyond the solar system. Who first thought those glowing specks were other suns, like ours? Or that some were island universes, far beyond the Milky Way?

Back in the dining room, her mother sat at one end of the table, doing something with a heap of cloth, while Sam, at the other end, frowned over his homework. Phoebe stopped in the doorway, next to the long crack that might have appeared to a stranger as part of the molding's design, but in fact had been made when Sam, in a fit of temper after they'd first moved here, had hurled his suitcase at the wood. "I had a letter today from London," she told her mother. "Michael's old student, Owen—"

"Do these look the same length to you?" her mother asked, holding up two white strips.

"She's been cutting out sleeves, for shirts to send overseas," Sam explained without raising his head. He turned the pages of a small notebook and with his pencil added a tiny number to a column.

"Homework?" Phoebe asked her son. Look up, she thought. Talk to me.

"Sort of," he said.

If she moved his way, she knew, he'd smile and close the notebook, say good night, and a minute later disappear into his room. Door closed behind him, books closed on his shelves, body— he'd suddenly sprouted six inches, and his hair had darkened to Michael's shade—concealed beneath long sleeves and long pants. Instead of reaching for her secretive boy she hung back and watched her mother shuffle paper patterns, pins and chalk, and a formidable pair of scissors.

"Russia?" she asked. "Owen said his sister is headed there with another relief committee."

.

"Arkangelsk," her mother said. "Way north, near Finland. There's been a lot of fighting there. Odette's doing the collars and Leila's working on the cuffs. We'll start piecing them together next week. What else did he have to say?"

Briefly Phoebe explained the meeting in London and the results Owen had described. Sam's pencil ticked down the numbers while her mother's scissors yawned and then snapped through the middle of a sentence. "That sounds important," her mother said.

"It is," Phoebe said. "I need to understand it better, for a chapter in the new book. In fact—"

"Of course," her mother said, snipping away. "Don't let us interrupt you."

⁂

BACK AT HER desk, back in her room, centered in the house like a plum in a dumpling. Her father above and her mother and Sam below—Sam, who for a couple of years after Michael's death had clung so closely that sometimes, if she stopped or turned quickly, she'd trip over him. He liked to balance on a footstool, one hand on her thigh and the other on the frame of the large painting hanging in their tiny rented house in Washington.

"Tell me," he'd demand, until she pointed out the figures that her great-uncle, Copernicus Wells, had painted on Pike's Peak during the eclipse of 1878. Then she'd name the instruments— telescope, spectroscope; your father had fancier versions of those—and finally note the flaring corona and the coincidence of her being born, far away, on that exact day. Copernicus had given her father the painting, which her father had given to her—

"Just after you were born," she'd add, pushing away the memory of Michael gazing at his new son, eyes wide beneath his reddish gold brows. "When you're grown up, I'll give it to you."

Adrift in Washington then, with no idea how to continue her life, she'd imagined that she and Sam would always be close and that when he was older she'd tell him how that painting, along with her love for mathematics, had helped steer her toward astronomy. How her father had bought her a telescope when she was twelve, while her mother, who came from a Quaker family with a long tradition of learned women, had encouraged her studies. Surely Sam would want to know what she'd done before he was born. She'd imagined telling him about her time at Cornell, where she'd been drawn not to the patient collection of data, nor to speculations about the nature of the universe, but instead to the long, complicated, orderly calculations of celestial mechanics. An observant professor had helped her find a job as a computer at the nautical almanac office in Washington, where she'd briefly imagined that she might be promoted. Instead, she'd met Michael Cornelius, an astronomer with the Smithsonian.

"We fell in love," she'd told Sam beneath the painting. A phrase that usefully hid everything, from the feel of Michael's leg against her own to the smell of his hair warmed by the bedside candle. "We got married, and—your father always appreciated the work I did—I kept my job until you were born. I helped him with his papers."

·

Sam, not quite four when Michael died, claimed to remember only his father's instruments and the scarred wooden desk where he'd bent over maps of the sky. What different images they'd kept from those few years! The bed she and Michael had shared, their passionate absorption in astronomy, and their companionable hours of work were invisible to Sam, who remembered only what he saw and heard, and what had to do with him. In the dimly lit room where they worked after supper, Sam would sit on Phoebe's chair, his back snugged against her side, tightly held by her left arm—but it was Michael, concentrating fiercely, whom he faced and whose smile lit Sam's eyes. So too had he faced the student visiting from England, a young man with an odd gait who delighted in clowning and liked chanting nursery rhymes to Sam. Tweedledum and Tweedledee: that was Owen, acting out bits from *Through the Looking-Glass* while she calculated results from the data he and Michael had gathered.

Owen was at Cambridge now, a rising young astrophysicist with everything before him. Whereas she . . . at least he was polite about her work. Books and articles for the interested ignorant—*Astronomy for the Young, Eclipses for Everyone*—mingling what she hoped were sufficient facts with artful descriptions and homely analogies designed to take the place of the mathematics she loved but knew her readers couldn't understand. The Milky Way is shaped like a biscuit. A nebula is like a cloud on the verge of condensing into rain. Donkey work, requiring a certain gift but not, despite what Owen was polite enough to pretend, a valuable one. She pushed herself to try something new each time. For her latest, *The Universe Around Us*, she'd promised her publisher a clear and interesting version of the complicated material often mauled in popular accounts. Until recently, when she'd begun this difficult chapter on gravitation and the ether of space, she'd thought it was going well.

She turned back to Owen's letter, struck again by that image of Sir Oliver Lodge bolting from the meeting. Only a few days earlier she'd seen an article about him in the newspaper. He was on a ship from London to New York, about to begin a big lecture tour. Some of the talks were already sold out, which wasn't surprising—unusually, for such an eminent scientist, Lodge liked to write for those who had no scientific training, and she'd sometimes turned to his books for help. Remembering that a list of lecture dates had appeared in the article, Phoebe rummaged through the stack by the fireplace until she found the right paper.

❖

ON THE EVENING of Lodge's scheduled talk, a crowd snaked out between the tall arches of the Academy of Music, and she learned that every seat was sold. Reluctantly, she bought a standing-room ticket and stepped into the moving mass, carried up the stairs and then up again to one of the galleries on the second tier, where she came to rest behind two women pressed against a fluted column.

"You can fit in here," the first woman said, moving her purse to make room.

"It's Phoebe, isn't it?" said the second. Her nostrils faced more out than down, giving her a slightly pig-like air. "Odette," she continued, tapping her chunky throat. "Jenkins—your mother's friend?"

•

"Of course," Phoebe murmured. One of the scores of well-meaning women who served with her mother on committees to educate the children of China or feed the starving people caught in Russia's civil war. Too many to keep straight. They'd cheered her decision to go to college, been delighted when she got her job in Washington, tried to conceal their disappointment when she married young and promptly had Sam.

"There he is!" the first woman said.

Phoebe craned her head but could see the famous old physicist only in snippets. One long leg, one big hand; he was enormously tall. A sliver of his forehead gleamed in the light of the chandelier before a woman's hat eclipsed it. He would speak, he said—he had a fine voice—on "The Reality of the Unseen."

She missed his introduction. His words floated up through the horseshoe-shaped tiers, interrupted when the crowd murmured or shifted in their seats, obliterated entirely when Odette whispered to her friend. There were things known to be real, Lodge said, but impossible to see: atoms, for example. Molecules. She strained to hear, hoping he'd describe the invisible but omnipresent ether. Instead she caught something about the vast distances between the stars and the contrast between that and the minuteness of the atomic world: also unseen, but also real. After a lost chunk that must have contained a vital transition, she heard next a sentence about the reality of mental events, such as thoughts and feelings, which were also invisible. She peered through the crack between the two women's necks.

"Likewise," Lodge said just then, "the human personality

·

survives death in a form we cannot see, but which makes communication after death possible."

She pulled her head back and jammed her hands into her coat pockets. What kind of science was this? She knew he was interested in psychical research—he was as famous for this, in circles she avoided completely, as he was for his work on the ether and electromagnetic waves—but she'd assumed his lecture would be about physics. Instead, he was explaining how great discoveries in science have reversed the evidence of the senses: the earth is not flat, but round, and it is not static, but whirls through space at inconceivable speeds. "So too will we come to reverse the evidence of our senses with regard to death," she heard. "Psychic research, the youngest science, deals, like astronomy, with phenomena that cannot be examined in the laboratory. Still, theories can be tested and refined over time. Science will eventually prove the existence, all around us, of former humans; they are not far from us; we are all one family still. To the mothers of boys lost in the war, I would say that they are only separated from us by a veil of sense."

In front of her, both women sighed, and Phoebe remembered that Odette's son had gone overseas to drive an ambulance. Had he returned? All around her, the audience—mostly women, she now realized—listened raptly, while Odette reached back to touch Phoebe's arm, as if they had something in common.

"We should not exalt the senses," Lodge continued. Phoebe drew her arm away. "They have been developed through necessity for the physical survival of the fittest. But if we did not dedicate ourselves so completely to the daily work of keeping our bodies alive, what organs of spiritual comprehension might we not develop? The space that separates you"—he stretched one hand toward the audience—"from me"—he pressed that hand to his chest—"is not empty. It is the purveyor of light, of electricity, of magnetism; and it may well contain our immortal souls, which persist after matter has disintegrated."

She stepped back before she understood that she was going to, ignored Odette's startled face, and pushed her way through the bodies and down the stairs. Wrong, so wrong. She hated when people spoke of communication with the dead, and it was worse when a scientist did so. Rappings and knockings, scribblings on slates, ectoplasm and all of that—ancient history, half a century old, most already proven fraudulent and the rest fit only for parlor games but still strangely persistent. When those superstitions had surfaced again, during the thrilling years when the discoveries of X-rays and radium, radio waves and electrons had made almost anything seem possible, she and Michael had simply ignored them, instead reading eagerly about light as waves, light as photons, energy possessing mass. The space between them, Michael said, was filled with energy, the ground of life itself.

She couldn't imagine what he'd have made of the ease by which, once the war began to swallow the young, those left behind succumbed to the resuscitated parlor tricks. The turbaned women cracking their joints in code or slipping their feet from specially stiffened shoes to write with their toes on slates—by then, left behind herself, she knew exactly how despicable they were. In 1909, not long after Owen returned to England, Michael had welcomed into the observatory a little boy who turned out to have measles. The boy recovered, but Michael's fever soared higher and higher until the morning he closed his eyes and sighed and—stopped, just stopped. In that instant she'd known she would never talk with him again.

The lobby stank of face powder; Phoebe pushed through the doors and into the street, where the snow flickered in the electric lights and a cat streaked by with something squirming in its clamped jaws. Michael had wanted to show off the wonders of the universe and now—she was walking so fast that her cheeks were hot and a woman in a short skirt stared at her—now, because a boy had given him measles, because she had a boy of her own to raise (the church bells chimed the hour; he'd be doing his homework), because, despite working all the time, she couldn't save enough to buy a house of her own, she was, at the age of forty-one, living with her elderly parents, and still, despite having published three books and innumerable magazine articles, orbiting so far from the center of the scientific world that she must turn to others for explanations that would, when included in her book, lend it the air of authority she lacked herself. She must go to a lecture where, instead of learning what she needed, she was forced again to confront the unalterable fact of Michael's death.

❀

I WAS ASTONISHED, she wrote to Owen a few days later.

Not to mention disappointed. How does a man like him—a man who has spent his entire life thinking and writing about physics—a

•

45

man who idolizes Clerk Maxwell and Helmholtz and the rest—end up like this? One thing to bolt from your meeting; Einstein's theories are so abstract that I sometimes wonder if anyone really understands them. But to refuse to accept them on the basis of insufficient proof, while at the same time contending that the survival of human personality <u>has</u> been proved: how does this make sense? The crowd was enormous, though, and seemed to glide right over the holes in his logic.

What, she thought as she took a new sheet of paper, would Owen have made of that talk? He'd been fresh out of university when he came to Washington, a slim boy with a high forehead, a clubfoot, and a calm faith in the triumph of true science. Not once had he acted surprised by her mathematical skills or questioned her ability to help him and Michael. He'd been Michael's protégé, not hers, but she'd come to think of him as a friend and an equal and still considered him her one stalwart colleague, although they hadn't seen each other since before Michael's death, and she could no longer picture his face. Always—almost always—he responded to her letters. Always, courteously, he asked about her son, although she knew he envisioned not this Sam but the eager, open toddler of their days in Washington. Sam's hair had been blond then, wisping pale curls she could never keep parted; no more like the springy auburn mat he now hid behind than her own sandy dullness was like the shiny chestnut waves Michael had loved. But then Owen himself might be halfway bald, no longer thin; perhaps with a stoop, still with a limp: wouldn't he have told her if he'd had his foot repaired? Maybe not. Ideas connected them, mathematical

.

symbols and diagrams, a disembodied thread of thought divorced from their daily lives. When she wrote him, she shaped her letters around pleasant anecdotes.

There'd been no point describing the details of those first harsh years after Michael's death, when she'd tried and failed to regain her old job and then found that she and Sam couldn't survive on the piecework calculations sent over by the Ephemeris staff. Skipping over the daily humiliations and petty miseries, she wrote lightly about the newspaper editor seated next to her at a dinner party—in her letter to Owen, a casual encounter; in fact, her rescuer—who, after learning about her training, had asked her to explain what caused the spring and neap tides. Pleased by her quick demonstration with an apple, an almond, and two bits of bread, he'd suggested she try writing about astronomy for the general public. From the column in his local paper (no examples of which she sent to Owen), she'd moved on to articles for the *Electrical Experimenter* and *McClure's*, then to her *Scientific American* pieces (which she did send), and her first books.

She liked the work; she was good at it and pleased when Owen praised her: but it was too painful to explain to him that, even writing all the time and as fast as she could, she could barely pay the rent, and she was sometimes short with Sam. Nor had she wanted to mention that Sam repaid her with temper tantrums, shrieking with anger when she tried to work on weekends, until finally her parents, after several worried visits, had convinced her to move back to Philadelphia—which move she'd presented to Owen as a pleasant choice. No mention after that, of course, of the way Sam at first ignored his teachers and balked at his

·

grandfather's attempts to discipline him; nor about the molding he cracked around the dining room door or the scene he caused, a few months later, that ended with a broken vase and a cut on his scalp. And so, thus, no need to express her huge relief when, after a while, something happened—a teacher was kind, his body changed when he turned eight, who knew?—and he settled down. And no need to admit, except in the most positive and praising terms—*Sam has grown very studious and stays late at school almost every day, working on special projects with his teachers; you'd recognize him instantly as Michael's son*—that now, instead of hanging around her, scowling and demanding her attention, he was completely courteous but as distant as Jupiter.

A SERIES OF short magazine articles on the night sky in winter kept her from tackling the chapter she should have been writing, and she felt herself falling farther and farther behind. Behind what? her mother asked, reasonably enough, when she found Phoebe fretting at the window. The same unambitious and pleasant publisher had handled each of her books, approving her rough outlines and then leaving her alone until she returned with a tidy pile of pages, which he exchanged for a check. It was hard to explain that the self-imposed schedule she'd laid out so carefully was as real to her as the demands of her mother's garden.

Weary of her own excuses, she was also embarrassed by the way she'd left Lodge's lecture, bolting from a disagreeable idea in the same way that Lodge himself, confronted with the evidence that his beloved ether might be in jeopardy, had fled the meeting in London. At the library, where she went to catch up with the astronomical journals, she instead took out a pile of his books. She read swiftly, voraciously, taking notes. What was she hoping to find? She could not have answered, she was glad no one asked. Nor could she have explained why she expanded those notes into pages describing material that she and Michael, years ago now, had once discussed. She wrote:

The whirling machine, the massive metal structure bolted into the bedrock beneath the lab: it's difficult for a modern reader to imagine without inspecting the illustrations from Lodge's 1893 paper, "A Discussion Concerning the Motion of the Ether near the Earth." Here you may see the steel discs, a yard in diameter, perched on the central pillar like an oversize hat on a woman's head. In a separate drawing is the optical frame, complete with mirrors, telescope, and collimator; a third illustration shows the whole assembly in action, a man standing beside the pillar, frighteningly close to the discs and caged by heavy timbers supporting the optical apparatus. It looks like a sketch for Mr. Wells's Time Machine, an utterly improbable device on which Sir Oliver Lodge made the experiments he has called the most important of his life.

During the 1890s, he performed a series meant to supplement the Michelson-Morley experiments, which he felt could not be right. Electromagnetic waves, including light, moved through the luminiferous ether; a wave must have something to wave in, and the ether, whatever its mechanical structure, was the needed medium. That medium must be detectable, flowing past the rapidly orbiting earth as a kind of wind, but the two scientists in Cleveland had failed to find it. Their results suggested that a layer of the ether must be carried along by the earth, but that hypothesis offered another set of problems. To test it, Lodge designed his pair of huge steel discs, clamped together with an inch of space between them, rotating at high speed while light traveled round and round between them with and then against the discs' motion, which might determine if rapidly moving matter could drag the ether with it. The machine was enormous, and very expensive. All the experiments failed. But he continued to define and extend the properties of the ether in his 1909 book, The Ether of Space, *and still defends his concepts despite the absence of confirmatory evidence.*

The Smithsonian's copy of that book was one of the last that she remembered Michael reading, and indeed the instant she opened the library's cheaper edition, poorly bound and smelling of pipe tobacco, she saw the gilt apples along the spine of the red morocco volume Michael had held. Clearly written, she remembered him saying; parts quite useful but canceled out by the odd sentences dropped here and there: *If any one thinks that the ether, with all its massiveness and energy, has probably no psychical significance, I find myself unable to agree with him.* He'd pushed the book aside, then, not derisively but with a dismissal final enough to keep her from reading it.

Nor would she now; she pushed it, palm flat as Michael's had been, away. What did she want from this, why did she care? What she'd written was already both too detailed for her book, and not detailed enough for a proper article. Yet that evening, back at her parents' home, she tried again, meaning to convey some sense of Lodge's fame as a teacher and scientist:

.

Sir Oliver Lodge, long a preeminent physicist, is only slightly less well-known than Marconi. At an early age he decided that his main business was with what were then called "the imponderables"—the things that worked secretly and have to be apprehended mentally. So it was that electricity and magnetism became the branch of physics that most fascinated him. Once, in London, at the height of his fame as a lecturer on popular science, policemen had to rearrange the traffic patterns outside the Royal Institution so that the cabs delivering his eager audience could fit in the street. Another time, giving a lecture and demonstration on "The Discharge of a Leyden Jar," he was as astonished as the audience to see the coating on the walls flashing and sparking in sympathy with the waves being emitted by the oscillations on the lecture table. From the basement came a man, shaken and pale, to report that the gas and water pipes were similarly sparking.

She stopped when her mother, walking the house restlessly long after she should have been in bed, leaned over her shoulder and read the last lines.

"I like the sparks," she said, resting her fingers on Phoebe's forehead.

As if the sparks explained how a man could move from the drudgery of his family's clay and chemical business to the heights of science, and then to an ardent belief in the possibility of communing with the dead. Or how a leading researcher into electromagnetism and the nature of light could end up being the most famous opponent of a radical new theory. If Einstein was right— but he was only *possibly* right; which meant Lodge was possibly

.

not wrong, or at least not wrong about the ether, although utterly wrong about the spirits *in* the ether ... Phoebe squirmed beneath her mother's hand.

"That's—for your book?" her mother asked.

"Not exactly," Phoebe said. "Maybe. I don't know. I went to hear him ..."

"I know," her mother said. "Odette mentioned." She traced the outline of Phoebe's forehead with two fingers, as if the friction might extract a clearer sentence. "Let me make you some tea."

Phoebe, pulling away, pushed her mother's hand toward the newspaper, open to yet another of the frequent pieces about Lodge. "Here," she said. "I'm not the only one who's curious about him."

The article, which her mother scanned quickly, offered an impression of Lodge as he'd appeared soon after his arrival in New York. A typical Victorian, the reporter had noted, "of the tradition of Darwin and Huxley, who still reads his Wordsworth and Tennyson, who still appreciates the poet's wonderment in those days at the marvels of science."

Three more columns followed, all meant, Phoebe thought while her mother finished, to drum up interest in Lodge's forthcoming lectures. His next scheduled talk was actually to be on "The Ether of Space"—his special area of expertise, and the material she most needed to review. Owen had gone to the meeting in London, to hear the results of the Einstein experiment. Maybe she should go to this in the same spirit and listen to Lodge expound what he really knew, taking from it what she needed. Wasn't science based on weighing evidence for oneself?

Surprising herself, she said, "I should try to hear this next lecture. I think I'll ask Sam to come with me." She imagined his quiet, sturdy presence at her side, his quick intelligence; he'd see things she didn't, and he wouldn't be easily distracted or upset. "He might find it interesting. And I could use the company."

"Since when," her mother asked, moving away, so rich herself in friends and colleagues that she might not have meant her question to pierce Phoebe, "do you want company?"

※

IT WAS TRUE that she and Sam seldom did things together anymore—he kept to himself, as she did, and he was busy, as she was herself—but to Phoebe's secret delight he said the trip sounded fun; she'd only brought him twice before to New York. Together they took the train and shared the sandwiches Phoebe's mother packed for them; together they rode the subway to the towering Woolworth Building and there took the elevator up and up, braving the last little climb on the spiral stairs for the sake of the view from the observatory. The entire island lay before them, the East River and the ships moving out into the harbor, Brooklyn stretching away to one side and New Jersey on the other. Pigeons wheeled and sank and rose again, seagulls floated on curved wings, radio waves poured invisibly from the windows. Marconi himself, Phoebe told her son, had sent a wireless message from his office across the ocean, announcing the opening of this building.

Sam leaned against the railing and pointed north, saying, "Look at the park! Look at the rivers! You can see the museum!" When he laughed and tugged his coat from her hands, she realized she'd been clutching it as if he were a toddler about to pitch over the side.

·

He teased her about that for the rest of the afternoon, as they ducked in and out of bookshops and took the subway back uptown. After a quick bowl of soup they headed to the theater, where they found seats high in the balcony, and Sam inspected the crowd streaming into the orchestra seats and up the stairs. Around them, coats migrated into seats and hats moved onto laps, until a curtain opened on Lodge's tall, white-haired figure, bowing into the wave of applause and then, as Phoebe studiously readied her steno pad and mechanical pencil, beginning to speak.

Sam brushed her arm with his—an accident? Turning to him, watching him, she missed Lodge's opening lines. Usually, when she reached to straighten Sam's collar or fix his hair, he stood so still it was as if he was willing himself not to flinch. But he bumped her elbow with his again, gently, almost playfully, as he had when he was small. "Thank you for bringing me," he whispered. "This is interesting."

Sam was glad he was here, Sam was interested; she focused her attention on the talk. What had she already missed? The ether, Lodge was saying, far from being beyond all comprehension, was in fact the most substantial thing in the universe. Why then had we taken so long to discern it? Just because it is so universal. If we were fish living at the bottom of the ocean, surrounded by water, so far from the surface that we had no sense of anything but water; if we were moving in water, breathing water—what is the last thing we would discover? The water itself. So it had been with the ether of space.

Now Phoebe listened intently; she could use this. "Hold your hand near a fire," he said, "put your face in the sunshine, and what

.

is it you feel? You are now as directly conscious as you can be of the ethereal medium. True, you cannot apprehend the ether as you can matter, by touching or tasting or even smelling it; but it is something akin to vibrations in the ether that our skin and our eyes feel. The ether does not in any way affect our sense of touch and it does not resist motion in the slightest degree. Not only can our bodies move through it, but much larger bodies, planets and comets, can rush through it at a prodigious speed without showing the least sign of friction. I have myself designed and carried out delicate experiments to see whether whirling discs of iron could to the smallest extent grip the ether and carry it round, with so much as a thousandth part of their own velocity. The answer is, no. Why, then, if it is so impalpable, should we assert its existence? May it not be a mere fanciful speculation, to be extruded from physics as soon as possible?"

So far, so good; she was glad to see the whirling discs again, but then . . . her hand was writing, words flowing smoothly and rapidly, but her mind had stopped catching hold. Was it that what he was saying didn't make sense, or that she wasn't concentrating? Action at a distance cannot take place, with the exception of mental action, or telepathy—she looked down at the paper; had he just said that?—and the actions of gravitation, magnetism, and electric force require some intervening medium. The nature of that medium is mysterious, but it might be thought of as a jelly-like substance filling all space.

"A body cannot act where its influence is not," her pencil wrote, but her wayward mind pictured a giant jellyfish, pulsing faintly, stretching in all directions. The pictures were *always* wrong; only

.

the mathematics conveyed the truth. "Another and perhaps a better way of putting it is to say that one body can only act on another through a medium of communication. When a horse pulls a cart, it is connected by traces; when the earth pulls the moon, it is connected by the ether; when a magnet pulls a bit of iron, it is connected by its magnetic field, which is also in the ether."

Here he reached below the podium, brought up a candy box striped in yellow and green, and set the box on a table beside him. "Would it be magic," he said, reaching for his cane, "if, by waving this, I caused the box to move?"

Sam was staring raptly at the stage—as indeed was the entire audience. Lodge passed his cane through the air, two feet above the box. The box slid sideways on the table.

"Hey!" Sam said, leaning so far forward that his chin would have brushed the hair of the woman sitting in front of him, had she herself not been leaning over the balcony rail. His own hair was a beautiful color in this light. Lodge raised the cane above his head and the box rose from the table.

After the exclamations from the audience subsided, he smiled modestly and lowered the cane. "When you see action of this kind," he said—the box settled back down—"always look for the thread."

What a showman. The thread was invisible at this distance, but he caught it between the cane and the box and suggested, by a tugging gesture, how it was connected.

"Always look for the medium of communication," he said. "It may be an invisible thread, as in this conjuring trick; it may be the atmosphere, as when you whistle for a dog; or it may be a projectile, as when you shoot an enemy. Or, again, it may be ether ripples, as when you look at a star. You cannot act at a distance without some means of communication; and yet you can certainly act where you are not, as when by a letter or telegram you bring a friend home from the Antipodes. A railway signalman can stop a train or bring about a collision without ever touching a loco-motive. A conclave of German politicians could, and did"—his voice rose here, making Phoebe look up from her pad—"oper-ate on innumerable families in England and slaughter their most promising members without the direct action of a finger."

She felt a small tremor, as if that finger had moved, miles away, through the water in which she floated. "No one wants to be deceived," he continued. "All are eager for trustworthy infor-mation about both the material and the spiritual worlds, which together constitute the universe. The ether of space is the con-necting link. In the material world it is the fundamental sub-stantial reality. In the spiritual world the realities of existence are other and far higher—but still the ether is made use of, in ways which at present we can only surmise."

Her pencil stopped, but he did not. She could feel him gather-ing up his thoughts, preparing for some final argument.

"Last May," he continued, "when astronomers measured the bending of a ray of light around the sun during an eclipse, they obtained data that when measured made Einstein's theory of gravitation appear to triumph. But what is the meaning of this triumph? Is it the death knell of the ether?"

Before Phoebe could frame an answer, Lodge surged on. "Must we now think in terms of four or even five dimensions to explain

·

this warp or curvature of space? In my opinion, we ought clearly to discriminate between things themselves and our mode of measuring them. The whole relativity trouble arises from ignoring absolute motion through the ether, rejecting the ether as our standard of reference and replacing it by the observer."

The whole relativity trouble—that simple phrase made Einstein's theory seem a piece of trickery as foolish as the thread. Caught in the smooth stream of words, Phoebe could question his logic only when she split her attention in two and set one part struggling against the flow. Yet even as she was giving up—he was now discussing the relationship between matter and the ether—he said something that made her write faster.

"Undoubtedly the ether belongs to the material universe, but it is not ordinary matter. It may be the substance of which matter is composed. If you tie a knot in a bit of string, the knot is composed of string, but the string is not composed of knots. The knot differs in no respect from the rest of the string, except in its tied-up structure; it is of the same density as the rest, and yet it is differentiated from the rest. In order to cease to be a knot, it would have to be untied—a process which as yet we have not learned how to apply to an electron."

There—that was why she admired him, why she'd come tonight. That was the kind of image she searched for in her own work and found, when she was lucky, with a sense of release that was almost physical. He was not a charlatan; he was a scientist who'd made real discoveries—he, as much as Marconi, had discovered the basic principles of the radio—and he'd drawn many to science through his lectures and his books. He might be old, and distinguished, and British, and a man; capable, as she had not been for years—had she ever really been?—of doing real science: but still they had more in common than just bolting from disagreeable ideas. How strange that what he seemed to care most about now was the possibility of communicating with the dead.

❖

THE LECTURE LIGHTENED something in her, or perhaps it was Sam's presence beside her; his arm next to hers, his mind engaged, however briefly, with something that absorbed her. The distance between them had grown, she would have said a week earlier, because he'd developed his own interests, which he didn't talk about much. On the train ride home, though, she considered how little she'd recently shared with him, so busy that she'd lost the habit of explaining her work. But as soon as she'd exposed him to Lodge he responded, which might mean that he'd be interested in the rest of the project; perhaps she could share other sections with him: perhaps the book would be wonderful! With a burst of enthusiasm, she began to draft her chapter on the ether.

First a bit of history: a quick glimpse of Descartes and his whirling vortices, and then the newer conceptions answering the need for a subtle medium, universally diffused, that could propagate the undulations of light and electricity while also transmitting the pull of gravity. Waves in the ocean travel through water; light waves must travel through a similar interstellar ocean, which we can neither see nor feel nor weigh. This is the ether, nowhere apparent but everywhere implied. The ether, which, until quite recently, most scientists had assumed *must* exist. How then might we conceive of this omnipresent, impalpable, invisible something?

She touched on Maxwell's ingenious models and the various arrangements by which wheels and rubber bands, gears and pulleys and springs had been set to represent possible mechanisms. Neatly she fit after those pages the sketch she'd made of Lodge's experiments with the whirling machine. Then on to the more recent and less mechanical conception of the ether as the ground from which both matter and energy arise. From Lodge's lecture— she pushed aside the tangle of upsetting digressions and disturbing assumptions—she lifted the image of knots on a string, matter as coiled-up ether: matter may be, and likely is, a structure in the ether, but certainly ether is not a structure made of matter.

And there the chapter crashed. She meant her tone to be judicious, sketching what had been believed when she was young, and what could fairly be believed now. To write something like: *Experiments performed during the recent eclipse suggest that Einstein's theories may be confirmed, in which case we may not need to postulate an ether to explain the transmission of light. However, spirited disagreement continues among scientists as to the meaning of these results, and it seems best, for now, to keep an open mind.*

But even as she wrote that, she knew she didn't believe it herself. No one could find the elusive ether; all the experiments had failed. Lodge and those who disbelieved Einstein wrote as if the ether were real but mysteriously unfindable, the experiments that had failed to detect it somehow defective, and she'd meant to give equal space to that position but—how could she? It wasn't just the lack of evidence; something was wrong with the logic too. How could the ether be composed of knots or vortices *in* the ether? Her brain stuttered, her mind balked. Her eyes burned and ached. The sentences crumbled as she wrote them, and when she thought again about Lodge's lecture, the tangle she'd pushed aside then snared her. The ether was a home for ethereal beings, the medium by which soul spoke to soul; perhaps God lived there: perhaps it was God himself?

She lay down and pressed a wet washcloth to her eyes. The ether was nothing and it was everything, it was whatever anyone wanted it to be. Writing about the ether was like trying to write about phlogiston. Although she'd explained more complicated models, and outlined concepts in which she believed less, never before had she tried to write something that taunted her with a sense of Michael hovering, just out of sight, in some gaseous form.

❖

THREE DAYS OF heavy rain trapped her inside. On the fourth day, a front blew through and cleared the air as completely as if a giant hand had sponged it dry. That night, very late, after everyone was asleep, Phoebe went outside and lay down on the flagstones bordering her mother's garden. Late March, the ground alive despite the cold air. There were the stars, circling above. There were the stars. Brilliant, blazing, bright against blackness, as beautiful as when she'd first stared at them so many years ago. White, blue, yellow, red. Once she'd gotten serious about the work to which the stars had drawn her, she hardly ever looked at them. She studied their motions, not them—when did she look at the sky anymore? Months passed when night meant her yard, her street,

•

a few blocks of Philadelphia: everywhere people, everywhere lights. Now the lights were out, there was no one around. With her back pressed against the stones, she smelled dirt and leaves and budding trees. Branches fringed her view of the sky, which was speckled everywhere—and wasn't it remarkable, really, that she should see the stars at all? Inconceivably far away, emitting light that traveled and traveled—how? through what?—and fell upon her optic nerves to form a picture in her brain: stars! She felt herself falling up into them, a feeling she remembered from her childhood. The space between her and the stars was infinite or nothing at all, it was empty or it was completely filled, it was, it was, it was . . .

The next afternoon she went looking for Sam, longing to talk about this. But Sam was gone; he was at a friend's; they were working on a project for school. Disappointed, she sat down and wrote to Owen, describing her struggles and the two lectures she'd attended.

> *Strangely, it was listening to Lodge that confused me. I'm not sure why, maybe that—how to say this? Lodge's conception of the ether is one of those models that, like an orrery or a gigantic watch, sets a nearly infinite number of pieces of something into motion, each affecting the other, until the actions are explained. But I don't think we can explain this mechanistically. Listening to him describe the survival of the personality after death as some element held in or made from the ether made me realize how completely attached he is to the ether as an actual physical thing.*

Interesting that she'd write that, but not a word about Michael. Not what flared through her mind at night: *Lodge must be wrong, he has to be wrong. If he's right, then Michael's been within my reach this whole time and I could have been talking to him. I could be talking to him now.* Not once had she even tried. She and Michael had held séances and spirit messages in such contempt that even to study the written accounts, never mind visiting a medium, would have felt like a betrayal.

Yet here was Lodge, famous and influential, perhaps even— was it disloyal to think this?—a better scientist than Michael had been, testifying to his beliefs before huge crowds. Either he was a liar, which he didn't seem to be; or she herself was the worst kind of fool. But Einstein's theories had also generated a similar confusion, especially here, as she wrote to Owen:

> *There's a lot of pressure here—far more, I think, than in England— not to accept Einstein's theory. People are so emotional—a promi- nent astronomer at Columbia started calling the theory "Bolshevism in science" as soon as the eclipse results were announced, and since then he's written a slew of articles disputing the evidence. Another, in California, repeats him, but more shrilly. They have alternate explanations for the advance of the perihelion of Mercury. They object to the interpretation of the eclipse data (you know these arguments, the discarded observations, the large margins of error, etc.) and in the next breath claim that even if the light from the stars <u>was</u> shown to be bent, the cause may well be refraction by the sun's corona, or a spurious displacement resulting from the chemistry of*

·

film development. They have plenty of supporters, working astron-
omers who place a premium on precise observations, and think the
data from the expedition is nowhere near as solid as claimed.

THE DAFFODILS PUSHED through the dirt; the trees budded
and the forsythia bloomed; the tulips came and went as she struggled with her chapter. Over breakfast one morning, she read about
a professor who'd been following Lodge from city to city, con-
tradicting everything he said about the dead and demonstrating
some of the fakery employed by mediums; apparently she wasn't
the only one disturbed by the mingling of physics and spiritualism.
She read the article to Sam, who set aside his toast to listen.

"That seems harsher than he deserves," he said, surprising her.
"I liked him, the way he seemed determined to think for himself."

But before she could encourage him to say more, her father
passed through the room, humming disconsolately, and Sam
rose and followed him, leaving Phoebe alone with her failures.
Here her father was, getting older and struggling: she *had* to earn
more money. She went back to work.

Her mother's obdurate peonies pushed through the dirt and
unfolded their leathery leaves as Sam finished school for the year.
The peonies budded, the buds bulged. Her mother, wrapped in
a green apron, her hands sheathed in canvas gloves, disappeared
into the garden, and her father retreated to the attic; Bach wafted
down from the windows. She picked up her notebook and wrote:
Sound is a wave that moves through the air, light is a wave in the ether . . . Then
she crossed that out and wrote to Owen again, enclosing what she

had so far. Owen didn't write back, and didn't write back, and then in late July he finally did, complaining about the shortages of food and coal and describing the weekend lectures he'd been giving to gatherings of miners and farmers. Only then did he comment on her draft.

Most of what you have so far seems fine to me, coherent and logical, if too heavily weighted toward the history. Too much context, not enough of the actual theory? That might just be my own perspective. Phoebe, I really am not sure about this—but haven't you fallen into that old trap of trying to make, from the symbols we use to reason about reality, pictures we can view in our minds? You know as well as I do that our ideas about space and time and molecules and matter aren't anything like the "real" universe, although they parallel it in some way; we make models because they help us think, but what we're really talking about here are mathematical statements that describe the relationships of phenomena. It's a mistake to weed out all the mathematics, even when you are trying to explain a theory we already understand to be outmoded. I think you could do this more succinctly. And that you could come down more firmly on the side of what we know now—not what we used to think we knew.

Since when did Owen talk to her like that? As if she were his student; as if she were a colleague's undereducated, amateurish wife. She stared at her draft, unsure how to make it better. Once she'd been able to write, clearly and even powerfully. Once she'd gone to her desk each day with the unthinking expectation that she would pick up her pen and begin, and that from the very

·

movement of pen across paper a train of thought would develop. Concepts would clarify themselves, sentences would flower into paragraphs; in this one small arena, she could do no wrong. She had lost Michael, she was at a loss with Sam, her parents were a mystery, she had no home of her own—yet on the page she could make an object that was shapely, and orderly, and on occasion helpful to others. She'd counted on this for years, without understanding what it would mean if it disappeared. As she'd counted on the sympathetic ear of a man she apparently no longer knew.

"You're so flushed," her mother said, when the heat drove them outside to sit stickily on the chairs they'd pulled into the garden. "Are you feeling all right?"

"I'm fine," Phoebe told her. "Just tired. It's been hard to sleep."

But what kept her from sleeping was not the heat. She tried to squelch the bitter thought that Owen did not, after all, regard her as his equal intellectually. For all her efforts to keep him from viewing her primarily as a woman—efforts that had cost a great deal in other ways—he still condescended to her.

Quickly, almost mechanically, she wrote over the next few days a magazine article about the implications of the red-shifted spectra Vesto Slipher had observed for a handful of spiral nebulae. Then, with her papers drooping moistly over open books, she returned to her chapter, still unfinished, still not right. She tried this:

> *If the ether exists as some sort of rigid jelly, then all of space is filled*
> *by it, everything in space is connected to everything else, a ripple*
> *here causes effects inconceivably far away—but space, however tied*

·

together, is all one thing, and time is something else. In Einstein's vision, etherless, space and time are tied together into one four-dimensional continuum, impossible to visualize but perfectly clearly expressed mathematically. Time is variable in that vision; time expands and contracts depending on the position of the observer, and it seems possible that the past, the present, and the future might all exist at once, so that everything we've ever done and been might be laid out, accessible.

Michael, she thought. The day they met, the moment their hands first touched, the day they were married, the moment when Sam was conceived. She scratched those lines out thoroughly.

❖

SEPTEMBER CAME AND Sam returned to school, still without Phoebe having completed what had once seemed like a manageable task. She gave up writing to Owen. She shut herself in her room, still far too warm, and she wrote and wrote, crossed out and wrote more. Then she fell sick for three weeks—the strain of working so hard, her worried mother said—and when she could rise from her bed she was more behind than ever. She'd lost weight, her hair was dry, and her periods had vanished; was it already time for that? Perhaps it was just from being sick. She made an effort to eat the meals with which her mother tempted her, and she put the chapter on the ether out of her mind. An acquaintance who taught astronomy at Bryn Mawr asked if she'd be willing to tutor three struggling students; she took them all. At the request of an elderly high school teacher in upstate New York, she also wrote an article detailing useful experiments, requiring little equipment, for youngsters.

She found herself, as the new year came and went, in roughly the same place she'd been when Owen's letter about the eclipse expeditions had arrived. Another year older, her hair more gray, still at her desk in her parents' house—except that now she was past the time when she'd promised to send in her book, and Owen had drifted away, and Einstein was hugely famous everywhere. One by one, essays attempting to explain his theory to the non-mathematically trained reader had been published in *Scientific American*. Across the ocean, *Nature* devoted an entire issue to the explanation and implications of the principle of relativity. In the library, dutifully at first but then with some excitement, Phoebe read through those articles.

She copied out phrases from the well-known physicists who examined different aspects of Einstein's theory but in the end agreed that it was right: all except for Sir Oliver Lodge, who declared stoutly that while the theory might appeal by its beauty and weird ingenuity to mathematicians lacking a sense of physical reality, it so oversimplified the properties of matter as to risk impoverishing the rich fullness of our universe into a mental abstraction.

Now that he and his psychic beliefs were safely in England, his recalcitrance seemed almost admirable. That steadfast insistence on common sense and the reality of a physical world in a physical ether: what did it cost him to maintain that position, now so unpopular? One afternoon, reading with her mother and Sam in front of the fire, she asked what Sam remembered of Lodge from the lecture last spring.

•

"He remembers it very well," her mother said. "Don't you?"

Sam nodded without looking up from the huge volume open on his lap.

"What are you reading?" Phoebe asked.

"A biology textbook," he said, spreading his fingers over the pages. "My teacher loaned it to me, for an extra project." When her mother said, "Sam?" he added, "I wrote something about Lodge, for an English class."

"Can I see it?"

He paused, looking down at his book, and then closed it on a pencil and rose. "If you'd like." He left the room and returned with a few sheets of paper, covered in his meticulous small script.

The essay, which he'd called "My Father, at a Distance," started not with a memory of Michael but with a description of Sam's evening at the theater in New York. Here were the rapt women, the box with the thread, the flow of Lodge's talk as she too remembered it—but these things, for Sam, had been only a beginning. Like her, he'd gone to the library and investigated Lodge's writings; but unlike her—she hadn't been able to stand more than a few pages—he'd actually read Lodge's book about his son, Raymond, who after being killed in the Great War had supposedly made efforts to communicate with his family.

I didn't expect to be swayed by it, Sam wrote. *But I was, although perhaps not in the way Lodge meant.* Sam described the letters Raymond had sent from the front, the photographs of him as a boy, the long transcriptions of Lodge's sittings with mediums after Raymond's death, the chapters of theory and exposition meant to help a reader interpret what Lodge presented as evidence for Raymond's continued existence in another form. What this was, Sam argued, was evidence of a different sort: evidence of love. When Lodge wrote, *People often feel a notable difficulty in believing in the reality of continued existence. Very likely it is difficult to believe or to realize existence in what is sometimes called "the next world"; but then, when we come to think of it, it is difficult to believe in existence in this world too; it is difficult to believe in existence at all,* what he meant was: *My existence makes no sense without my son.*

From Lodge's longing for his son had come, Sam argued, an entire theory of etheric transmission, which, if it wasn't true—he himself believed it was not—was still a marvelous example of how science was influenced by feeling. About the connection between that feeling and the construction and testing of any scientific hypothesis. Lodge had suggested in his lecture that Einstein's theory had been tested but not completely proven by the eclipse experiments. His book suggested that his experiments after Raymond's death offered a similar level of proof for the theory of survival of personality. Phoebe slowed down and read each word.

> *My father died when I was four; I miss him all the time. For years I was sure he was up in the air somewhere, among the stars he studied. I listened for him every night; I thought that from someplace deep in space he would try to contact me. When we moved from the house where I was born, I was terrified that if he sent a message it wouldn't reach me. Later, I convinced myself that he could find me anywhere, at any distance, and that the fault was mine; if I couldn't hear him, it was because I didn't know how to listen. If I stretched myself, broadened myself, I'd be like a telescope turned onto a patch of sky that before had seemed blank; suddenly stars would be visible, nothingness*

·

*would turn into knowledge. Across time and space, my father would
reach out to me.*

Here was Michael at last: she could see his face as clearly as
when they'd first kissed on the riverbank, under the starry sky.

*Eventually, I had to give up on this idea, but as I listened to Lodge's
lecture I fell back into it, and for a few moments, I wanted so badly
to believe him that I <u>did</u>. I understood the ether of space to be exactly
as Lodge described it, a universal medium that transmits not only
electromagnetic forces but also the thoughts and longings of the dead.
Only when I looked around at the audience and saw them all believing the same thing did I realize what was happening.*

*I don't understand the physics behind Einstein's theory, and I
don't believe in the existence of a spirit world, but my introduction
to Lodge's work changed the way I think. I don't know, and I don't
believe there is sufficient evidence yet to prove, whether the ether is
real the way the atmosphere is real, or the way the equator is real.
Whether Einstein's theory has been proven, or Lodge's theory of survival of the personality after death, or neither or both. I don't know
whether my father exists in some ethereal form or only in my heart.
What I do know is that the questions we ask about the world and the
experiments we design to answer them are connected to our feelings.*

Where had Sam learned to write like that? Upstairs, her
father's viola sang, dismantling troubles Phoebe knew nothing about. Across from her, Sam and her mother nestled back
in their chairs, each reading with such concentration that when

·

she finished Sam's essay, neither noticed for a moment. Then her mother looked up.

"It's good," she said. "Isn't it?"

"Lovely," Phoebe agreed. Her mother had already read it. Down the stairs, through the empty rooms, triplets rippled in sets of four: the prelude to the sixth Bach cello suite, transcribed for viola, which her father had been playing while she and Sam and her mother read, each of them deep in their own thoughts but sharing a room, the light from the lamps, the sense of piecing together a sequence of thoughts. Then—not a rift, but a discontinuity. How does a person end up like this? For much of her life she'd been listening, sometimes consciously, sometimes not, to her father play those suites. Until just that moment, with the triplets running steadily up and down, she would have told herself that the space between her and family wasn't empty at all but held light and music, feelings and thoughts, and a bond that could be stretched without breaking.

·

The Island

(1873)

The train trip took the whole day. Oswego to Albany and then the length of Massachusetts, orchards and mountains and rivers and fields, cities appearing then disappearing while the sky darkened steadily until, near Boston and the coast, the rain began. By nine o'clock, when Henrietta Atkins stepped down at New Bedford, it was pouring. Her skirt was spotted with mud before she was halfway down the block; her hair dripped over her shoulders; the two bags packed with notebooks, drawing pencils, boots, clothes, and the tiny stipend meant to cover her expenses for the next seven weeks sagged alarmingly.

This was on a Friday night in July of 1873, the low clouds trapping a smell—weedy, salty, slightly medicinal—that Henrietta, who had never been near the shore, thought might be the sea. She headed away from the station, searching for the hotel that the organizers of the natural history course had recommended to those coming from far away. Excelsior? Excalibur? She'd lost the letter with the details—but there at the end of the block was a gray building, four stories tall, marked with a giant E. She climbed the steps, set down her bags, and pushed back some wet strands of hair. Inside, she imagined, might be other students signed up for the course: girls who, like her, had just graduated from Normal School and were about to start teaching, older women who'd worked at academies for a while, men who taught at colleges and might give her advice. A shame to meet her new companions so bedraggled.

The hall was empty, but she followed the sound of voices into a sitting room, where two men stood before a fire. One, talking intently, was stout and young and cradled his round stomach with one hand. The other she recognized as the famous professor. In person he looked older, and less robust, than the portraits in the newspapers. When he caught her staring, she set down her bags again.

"If you have books in there," he said, interrupting his companion to gesture her way, "I hope you wrapped them in oilcloth."

"Of course," she said, mortified. She'd imagined meeting him in a classroom, where she could hide among a mass of other students. In a classroom, not here. At Oswego she'd studied his zoology textbook and read his work on glacial action, while long before that her mother, in response to a public plea for specimens, had proudly contributed to his study by sending him fish from Keuka Lake. His letter of thanks, matted and framed—a form letter but, as her mother always pointed out, personally addressed and signed—still adorned their dining room wall.

•

She offered her name, adding, "I'm one of your students, I think. I'm so looking forward to starting your course tomorrow."

"Tuesday!" the professor said genially. "We don't start until Tuesday."

"If then," the younger man added. "The buildings are barely halfway done and I don't see how we can finish in time. You may have to delay the course." He flicked at the newspaper lying on the table. "There's an article in here about it, so embarrassing . . ."

"We *will* start Tuesday!" the professor repeated. "We absolutely *must.*" He turned back to Henrietta. "But why did you come so early?"

She'd confused the dates, Henrietta learned then. Mocking, by her own stupidity, the award her teachers had given her at graduation, which would pay for this course; mocking her proud mother's twenty-first birthday gift of boots and a specimen box. For all her bee-like bustle, her endless lists and meticulous packing, she'd been so sure the course started on a Saturday that she'd failed to double-check the actual date. As she began to panic about her stipend, which wouldn't cover the extra nights in the hotel, not the extra meals or even an extra bar of soap, a woman in a green dress rose from an armchair across the room and called her over.

"You're one of my husband's students?" she asked. The professor's wife, Henrietta realized. Who had herself written several books, and joined many of her husband's expeditions. "What's happened?"

Abashed, Henrietta explained her situation. As she finished, the woman, who'd been nodding and smiling kindly throughout, glanced over at the men and then returned her attention to

·

Henrietta. "You'll travel with us tomorrow," she said. The skin around her small dark eyes was soft and crinkled. "It's not a problem, if you don't mind roughing it with us until the rest of the students arrive."

That night Henrietta slept in a tiny room, with a dormer window that leaked and a ceiling so low that she could press her palm against it. The sound of water dripping onto tin made her dream of the buckets she and her sister, Hester, set in the springhouse at home. The rain continued as she woke and dressed and trailed the professor and his wife to the waterfront, where at last she saw the sea—or not the sea, exactly, but a crowded harbor dense with docks and masts. At Oswego, schooners had also crowded against each other along the busy port. But that was a lake, not the sea, and there she'd been a struggling student, sharing sinks and bad food, washing her own clothes between classes with the other girls come from similar small towns and farms. Here— she grasped her bags more firmly—here she was a woman with a teaching certificate, about to start a course she couldn't have afforded on her own.

The boat awaiting them was bigger, but not by much, than the wooden sailboat her mother used at home. The professor and his wife sat inside the small cabin and she sat outside, across from a mound of packages, between two women in gray dresses, beneath a piece of canvas strung up as an awning. After an hour the rain stopped, and although she'd dreaded seasickness she felt fine. When the captain said, "That's it," she leaned over the rail and saw a small island, curved like a comma, completely unimposing.

At the dock she stepped from the boat and saw gulls, a mound of dirty hay, a huge pile of packing crates, and another, larger boat pulling away, half the workmen leaving, on this Saturday afternoon, for their weekend holiday. A man the age of Henrietta's father greeted the professor and said in a harried tone that he'd been there since early Friday and had rescued the newly delivered dormitory furniture. Fifty-eight beds and blankets and pillows, fifty-eight pairs of sheets and chamber sets—all, he said, as they moved along the sandy shore, piled into the barn that was meant to serve as their kitchen and lecture room.

The barn toward which he gestured, and from which the sheep had only just been moved, stood near an old house and a partly finished new building. Near it were planed boards, stacks of shingles, wheelbarrows, shovels, casks of nails—but not a sign of the microscopes or nets and dissecting trays which, Henrietta thought despairingly, the advertisements for the course had led her to expect. All night she'd fought the feeling that she'd made a terrible mistake. The boat's captain consulted with the women dressed in gray, who were hanging back uneasily. The older one, who had signed on to cook—she'd earlier mistaken Henrietta for another of the servants—now declared that she was going back to the mainland. Her younger sister, who had looked envious when Henrietta stammered that she was actually one of the students, agreed that she too would leave.

But the house was almost ready, the man supervising the site assured them. The situation was better than it looked. He gestured toward the figures picking their way through the planks, ferrying bedrolls like a line of ants across the sandy ground to the barn: those were the remaining carpenters, moving out of the

·

house and making room. The sheep were on their way back to the mainland and the workers would follow when they were done. At the news that there was a place off the pantry prepared for them, the cook and her sister decided to stay, while the professor nodded happily on hearing that he and his wife could settle upstairs as planned, along with the other teachers when they arrived.

"And you," the professor's wife said kindly, turning to Henrietta. "Until the rest of the students show up."

"Thank you," Henrietta said, trying to cool her burning cheeks. Soon everyone would be here and she'd be invisible. Near the tip of her boot a little black cricket popped into the air and the professor, sweeping his arm to include not only the cricket but the land, the house, the barn, the sand, the birds and oysters and eelgrass, said, "A rich man donated all of this to us."

How, Henrietta wondered, did one get given an island? The same way, she supposed, he'd been given a museum, a university department, a staff, a wife who seemed able to read his mind. Not once, either last night or this morning on the boat, had he mentioned where the students would sleep or eat, instead speaking rapturously about all they'd study. Taxonomy and paleontology, the embryology of radiates and the anatomy of articulates, the physiology of vertebrate fishes, techniques of microscopy, dissection and specimen preservation, the chemistry of the sea. Or some selection of those things: he didn't believe in a set curriculum. They would follow, he said pleasingly, where the book of nature led.

"You'll see," said the professor's wife, patting Henrietta's arm and pointing out the attractions of the buildings they passed.

.

The barn would be divided into a kitchen and a large dining hall, which would also serve as a lecture room. The empty dormitory, shaped like a giant *H*, would soon have on its upper floor twenty-nine sleeping rooms for the male students, lining both walls of one long wing, and the same number for the women in the other, with dressing rooms in the short connecting wing. Two enormous workrooms would fill the first floor, each lined with rows of tables and aquaria.

Would, would—but so far the dormitory had no floors at all and the barn floor was only half-laid, cartons and furniture trailing off into packed dirt. No walls had yet been built and there were no signs of either a kitchen or a lecture hall. The foreman explained that his remaining men would work for a few more hours and then leave in the morning for their Sunday holiday. For a moment Henrietta thought of joining them. Then she put down her bag, followed the cook and her sister into the house, seized a broom and, as if she were back home, cleaning up after a family gathering, began sweeping together the sand and tufts of grass and bits of tobacco left behind by the workmen.

The cook lit the stove, boiled water, found a frying pan and some eggs; her sister washed cups and plates. Sweeping the detritus out the door, Henrietta watched the professor, his white hair waving gaily in the breeze and his cuffs flapping over his wrists, convince the workmen of the importance of his summer school for the study of natural history. They would stay through Sunday and Monday too, the men agreed, giving up their day off in an effort to finish the dormitory before the students arrived.

"Aren't they kind?" said the professor's wife, coming up behind her. She'd found an apron, which she dropped over Henrietta's head. "Sacrificing their holiday like that? We'll follow their example."

What they accomplished during the next three days would later, when Henrietta looked back on it, seem simply impossible. The carpenters worked until it was too dark for them to drive a nail, laying the floors in the dormitory, finishing the barn floor and raising a partition that set off the lecture room, finally installing the big stove in the kitchen. In the dormitory they didn't have time to divide the long spaces into bedrooms, but they did enclose several dressing rooms and wall off the men's side from the women's. Henrietta, the professor's wife, the cook, and her sister unpacked and washed and put away hundreds of plates and cups and saucers and glasses and a clattering mound of silverware, then repeated the process with the chamberpots and basins and ewers. They unwrapped the furniture, organized the move across the yard, swept the shavings from the new dormitory floor, and had the men arrange the beds against the walls so that each had its own window overhead. Sheets, blankets, and pillows spilled from the crates and settled on those beds, which along with the chamber sets marked off imaginary rooms.

The clean white linens glowed against the pine and the windows offered squares of sky through which moved clouds, terns, gulls, geese, ducks, an occasional osprey, and, on the side facing the shore—Henrietta had chosen as her own the fourth bed, equally far from the stairwell and the dressing room—miles of Buzzards Bay. She slept there on the night before the rest of the students arrived, leaving behind the sofa where she'd been camped. The

•

building was so quiet that from her window she could hear the tips of the eelgrass brushing against the sand.

✳

OF THE FIFTY-EIGHT applicants the professor had selected, forty-two arrived on Tuesday, those who canceled—all women, he noted with surprise—apparently frightened off by reports of the unfinished buildings. But that was plenty, the professor thought, a strong group, young teachers themselves, come to be trained by him. Twenty-nine men and thirteen, no fourteen women: he'd forgotten to count Henrietta, who'd been working hard since Saturday and who, at meals, listened to him so attentively. When he pointed out an osprey's nest or the pattern the mussels formed on the pilings she seemed to register every word, and when she was sharing tasks with his wife she took direction easily, always an excellent sign in a student. Although he was tired, indeed he hadn't been feeling well for months, the sight of her made him eager to teach again. He had not had a real disciple in years, and the prospect of a young woman, as hungry for knowledge as his own wife had once been: what did he care if the lecture room wasn't finished? Brilliant sunlight outside, velvet shadow past the threshold; he stepped through the double doors, drawing deep, delighted breaths. He'd taught in tents, on glaciers, on boats, in basements. This was luxury, standing on fragrant new boards with twenty feet of air above him, the cool shade pierced by swallows swooping between the rafters, darting in and out.

The room grew quiet. He knew he was ready. Behind him, on the blackboard hastily mounted to the new wall and concealing

•

the sight but not the sounds or the smells of the cook and her helpers preparing lunch, were the first of the chalk drawings he'd use to lead the students to the truth. He opened his mouth and whole paragraphs leapt smoothly out, one suggesting the next, each familiar but delivered this time in a different order, a different context. The paragraph on the divine order of nature knitted gracefully onto the paragraph about how we could learn more from a single living grasshopper, closely observed, than from twenty dusty books. One paragraph came directly from something he'd written himself: *All the facts proclaim aloud the one God, whom man may know, adore, and love; and Natural History must in good time become the analysis of the thoughts of the Creator of the universe, as manifested in the animal and vegetable kingdoms.* Another paragraph spoke of the great tradition this school embodied, the lineage of Cuvier and Humboldt passing directly from them to him, on to all his earlier students, and now to those before him. Soon he'd spoken the paragraph of thanks to his supporters, and the paragraphs introducing the other teachers: the six former students, now his friends, middle-aged themselves, responsible for different areas of natural history. Then came the lines in which he instructed the students to stand and introduce themselves.

Two Johns, a Robert, Elias, Oscar, Katherine, Mary, Mary; Josietta, oddly rhyming with Henrietta, whom he liked. A Daphne, a Hazel, a Lily, a Rose, like a clump of flowers. The names flew past. Some taught at public high schools and some at normal schools or colleges, some were in their twenties while others were older—Benjamin, David, Claire—but all looked young to him, skin unmarked and eyes transparent. Later, he knew, the faces crowded around the three long tables and peering up at him would look less like rows of sea anemones. Later, as they asked questions or sat lumpishly mute, demonstrated a deft hand with a scalpel or botched the simplest drawing, he'd be able to distinguish some as individuals. For now they were like variations on a single underlying idea, their differences not uninteresting but in the end slight. Few, perhaps not even Henrietta, really grasped who he was. Some might know his books, others the museum he'd founded; a few might be familiar with his theory of glaciers; most knew he was famous but not exactly why. It was their parents who, a quarter-century ago when he could fill any city's lecture hall, had really appreciated him and his work. That moment on the boat when Henrietta confided that her mother had been one among the thousands responding to his call for specimens had pleased him, at first, reminding him of those glorious days. Then wounded him with the reminder of his age.

He leaned on his cane as they spoke. His knees hurt, one of his hips, the tips of his toes and his fingers; he was sixty-eight and his digestion was in shreds; he had cataracts in both eyes. Ahead lay weeks of morning lectures, afternoon demonstrations, expeditions, and conversations, day blurring into day and lecture into lecture. The nights would be his reward. On the beach, beneath the stars, near the soft hiss of water striking sand, he and his friends would relax at last, free to remember their own discoveries. The glaciers rolling down, reshaping the landscape; all year he'd been looking forward to these discussions. For now—he opened his mouth and from it poured a summary of the general

·

characteristics of the vertebrates, the mollusks, the articulates, and the radiates.

"Is this division of the animals into four groups," he concluded, "the invention of a great naturalist? Or is it simply the reading of the Book of Nature? Can the book have more than one reading? If our classifications are not mere invention, if they are not an attempt to classify for our own convenience the objects we study, then they are thoughts which, whether we detect them or not, are expressed in Nature. So then Nature is the work of thought, the production of intelligence, carried out according to plan, therefore premeditated—and in our study of natural objects, we are approaching the thoughts of the Creator, reading his conceptions, interpreting a system that is his and not ours."

Two swallows darted past as he spoke, headed for the rafters, and half the young people assembled before him looked up.

⁂

IN THE FIRST batch of mail for the students, delivered by the same little boat that had brought her to the island, Henrietta had a letter from her mother. After giving the family news, and wondering how Henrietta's journey had gone and how her boots were holding up, she asked about the professor:

> What is he really *like*? I imagine him sitting down with you
> individually, showing you the secrets of a turtle's egg or a minnow,
> but perhaps I imagine this wrongly and he doesn't spend that much
> time with you. Does he lecture, or does he leave that to the other
> teachers? If you do get to talk to him alone, please tell him how

much we treasure his books in our home, and how seriously we in
our small village have taken his work. Your father and Hester send
love, as do I.

She'd written, Henrietta imagined, with those very books
around her, her pen moving briskly while Hester, who had just
turned twelve, fussed over the brood of tawny hens she'd raised
herself. Already she dreamed of having a big family, while Henrietta had wanted only this. Because of the professor's books, she'd
sailed through the zoology questions on the entrance exam for
Oswego: *Give the names of the sub-kingdoms of animals. Give briefly the*
characteristics of each sub-kingdom, speaking particularly of the arrangement of
the circulatory, digestive, and nervous systems. What mental and moral powers
has the cat? Prove it. Describe your right hand.

It should have been easy to write to her mother about their
household god—but the truth, Henrietta thought as she folded
the letter away, was that she had little to say, despite her early
arrival at the island. During those three days of working like
one of the servants, she'd shared meals with the professor and
his wife and awaited his brilliant insights. Instead, he'd talked
about the money due to the carpenters and kitchen staff, the
price of coffee and sugar, the state of the sheets. He drank tea
without sugar, she learned. Stripped the meat from fish heads
and the marrow from bones. As his teaching staff trickled in, she
also learned that he greeted old friends with a kiss on each cheek.
Six times, while she occupied a place at the table where she had
no right to be, she listened to the professor's wife explain how
Miss Atkins had mistaken the date, shown up at the inn in New

.

Bedford wet and confused, accompanied them to the island, and then—"She's been *such* a help!"

Six times she smiled ruefully as the professor beamed across the table and agreed with his wife—and this was, apparently, the closest she was going to get to him. The minute the other students swarmed into the barn she'd felt herself disappear, one minnow among a shoal in dark skirts and striped shirtwaists, mingled with young men in loose jackets, all looking up at him. An honest report to her mother would read: *I see him from the back of the room. From across the field. From the far end of the dining hall.* He was simultaneously genial and boastful, brilliant, confused, brimming with life, half-asleep; unable to remember anyone's name—he'd twice confused her with a woman from Bridgeport, whose dark curly hair resembled her own—yet strangely alert to their inner selves. *I don't understand a thing about him,* she'd have to write. *Any more than I understand if I like it here, or hate it.*

At first either too lonely, or too surrounded by company, she put off answering the letter. On Monday night she was alone in the empty, echoing dormitory; on Tuesday night it was filled with people; by Wednesday night, when she went upstairs after a day that seemed to have lasted a week, she found that the long, open, empty space had been not only populated but partially divided. Three beds along each wall had been enclosed like oysters within tiny planked rooms, which the workmen had built that afternoon. They'd build more each day, she knew. The professor's lessons would be punctuated with the repeated *tap-tap-TAP* of nails being driven home, and each night the common room would seem smaller, the walls advancing toward her own bed until finally she

.

too was enclosed. *I wish,* she might have written to her mother, *that you and Hester were here. Or that I had a friend.*

In the dining hall she ate each meal with different students and compared notes with still others in lectures. *The blind fish of the Mammoth Cave,* she wrote, *thought by some to demonstrate direct modification of an organism by the environment . . .* At bedtime, in the women's wing, she passed soap to the two Marys and chatted with Lily, who slept next to her, and with Laura and Katherine, whose beds faced hers. All of this, the patient rubbing of elbows and the accidental, meaningless intimacy, was familiar from her time at Oswego. But here everything seemed to happen more quickly and some of the students had already formed attachments. Already there were pairs and trios who always sat together at meals, walked together afterward—how had they so swiftly found companions?

By Friday, when the entire class followed the professor, his wife, and two of the assistant teachers to the southwest tip of the island, for a lesson observing and collecting marine invertebrates, she was beginning to think that her days alone with the professor and his wife had done nothing but separate her from the other students. The professor, standing on a rock, said that because the grotto he'd found was accessible only from an hour before dead low tide until an hour after it turned, they would for the sake of efficiency be collecting in pairs. She stood uncomfortably behind a group who seemed at ease with each other, nodding seriously and exchanging glances as he read their names from a list. Her new partner was someone she didn't know, a slip of a girl she'd glimpsed darting down the stairs while the others were still dressing.

On the rocks, where the professor lined them up, they faced

•

a horseshoe of rocky ledges, roofed over by a boulder to form a watery cave. The professor perched on a wooden stool next to the boulder. At his command, the first pair, a high school teacher from Maine and an instructor at Antioch College, scrambled down the weedy rocks toward the grotto, pausing at the entrance.

"Crawl right inside!" the professor encouraged them. He waved his cane and the wind rose, lifting strands of his white hair. "Don't worry about getting wet!"

The men disappeared, leaving visible only the soles of their rubberized canvas boots. Henrietta, clenching her bucket and pocketknife, stole a glance at her partner's tiny feet. Above them the professor consulted his pocket watch. Five minutes later—only by such strict scheduling, he'd said, could they all see the place for themselves—he cried "Time!" and the two young men backed out and stood, grinning, guarding their sloshing buckets as they picked their way back to the shore.

Two more pairs of men entered, and then it was time for the first pair of women. Henrietta realized, as the professor signaled, that she hadn't quite registered her partner's plant-like name. "Clover?" she said tentatively.

"*Daphne,*" her partner responded. "Ready?"

Henrietta nodded and they clambered over the stones. Somewhere in the writings of Ovid, a Daphne turned into a tree. And indeed her partner was as slim as a tree and had pale green eyes. They reached the opening in the rocks and paused.

"Yesterday," the professor said from above them, waving his cane encouragingly, "my wife was able to reach quite a few specimens by kneeling at the entrance and reaching inside."

Yesterday, Henrietta recalled, he'd reminded them all that their previous training meant nothing to him, and that he didn't care what they already knew, or thought they knew. He was interested only in what they could learn by careful observation here. Both she and Daphne balanced themselves on their hands and knees and inched forward, lowering their heads beneath the lip of the roof. Although they'd folded the tops of their skirts around their belts, the hems were already wet and hung heavily around their calves. The sheer bulk of the material kept their lower halves outside the grotto.

"How stupid our clothes are," Daphne muttered.

Henrietta tugged and shifted, but the folds of her skirt, which dragged on the shells and tore at the algae, kept blocking her way. No wonder the professor's wife had stopped where she had. "Ridiculous," she said, trying to fit herself alongside Daphne's slim torso. From the shore they must look like a pair of handbells, stems slipped into the cave. Still, even if they couldn't crawl inside as far as the men had, they could see all around.

As her eyes adjusted to the dimness, she spotted pink algae, red algae, and something that looked like tiny green tomatoes or grapes. Starfish, barnacles, and sea anemones everywhere, *Metridium marginatum*: some fully withdrawn into dull lumps of jelly, others showing a coy frill, the boldest drawn tall and waving their tentacles, purple or pink or white or brown, orange or scarlet, absurdly plant-like yet fully animal. When she touched one, the plumy fringe shrank and disappeared.

Daphne, who had already pried loose several *Metridium* with her pocketknife, fixed her gaze on a patch of seaweed matted over one particular nook. "There is someone," she said, moving like a cobra, "hiding under that . . ." She pounced and came up with a sea urchin. The walls were covered, Henrietta saw; the walls were entirely alive; more of the prickly mounds hid here and there, along with terraces of barnacles, which made room for rows of mussels, which gave way to clumps of sea anemones. Every inch of the rock was used in a way that seemed not random but purposeful, a pattern that, like the tiles on a floor, wasted no space but still allowed each creature access to the nourishing tide. How did that happen? She'd seen clumps of mosses and ferns make similar patterns at the Hammondsport Glen, near home.

"Better hurry," Daphne advised, sliding something from the blade of her knife. "We only have another minute or two."

Quickly Henrietta gathered a starfish, her own sea urchin, two sea anemones with waving white fronds and another mostly orange, three small crabs, a couple of mussels, algae red and green and pink, and a bit of *Fucus* encrusted with a kind of hydrozoan.

"Time!" the professor called from above. The previous day he'd drawn a map of the western hemisphere on the board and then divided it into five zoological regions. Each was inhabited, he explained, by animals perfectly suited to that province, confined to those geographical limits. In each the animals were endowed with instincts and faculties perfectly corresponding to the region's physical character. But because the climate of a country was allied to the peculiar character of its fauna, that didn't mean that the one was the consequence of the other; were that the case, all animals living in similar climates would be identical. Rather, the perfect distribution signified the work of a Supreme Intelligence who created, separately and successively, each species at the place, and for the place, which it inhabits. The animals were *autochthonoi*: originating, like plants, on the soil where they were found.

Henrietta's wet skirts dragged as she lowered her head and began to move back into the sunlight. Did that mean, then, that the creatures in the grotto had each been created to fill its own tiny niche? That they were—did one use the adjective?— *autochthonous*? Wondering about this, trying to remember what, exactly, the professor had said, which had seemed far clearer yesterday, she set her knee down squarely on a patch of barnacles. As she jerked her leg she somehow kicked Daphne, who in an effort to steady herself overturned her bucket, letting out a cry louder than Henrietta's.

The professor leaned over the ledge, nearly falling from his stool as he called, "Are you all right?"

Daphne, grasping futilely at her escaping prey, said something under her breath.

"Barnacles," Henrietta gasped. The sharp plates had razored through her skirt, but she was more concerned at the misery on Daphne's face. "I'm sorry," she said. "That was so clumsy—you'll share what's in my bucket?"

Daphne pressed her lips together. "What choice do I have, now?"

"Take some samples of your assailant!" the professor called genially. "The Cirripedia are fascinating, even if their armor is painfully sharp. God has so ordained that these creatures, who in their second larval stage resemble little shrimps, should swim about until they find a home and then cement themselves head-first in place, transforming themselves into stony lumps that

.

gather food by waving their feathery little legs. As miraculous, if you think about it, as if a creature born in the form of a perch should shed its skin to turn into an eel and then into a robin, only to glue its forehead to a rock and transform itself into a horse waving its hooves in the air." He pointed at the blood staining Henrietta's skirt. "You have been kicked, though. Do take care of that knee."

Daphne, loaning her a handkerchief and then spreading her own skirt wide to block Henrietta's legs from view, said crossly, "If he wasn't going to give us a chance to replace our lost specimens, he might at least have found a more original comparison."

"What are you talking about?" said Henrietta, dabbing at her wounds.

"Comparing the stages of barnacles to a fish that turns into a horse—someone else said that, I read that in an old book about microscopy." Pointing at Henrietta's knee, she added, "You missed a spot." And then, as Henrietta dabbed again, "Swish the handkerchief around in the water when you're done. Then the stain won't set."

Smart as well as practical, Henrietta noted. Not to mention sharp-tongued. Back at the laboratory, where the professor directed them to their workstations, she was pleased to learn that, for the next six weeks, she and Daphne would share not only the contents of a collecting bucket but an aquarium, a table, and a window.

"Lucky me," Daphne said.

Her lips twisted so briefly that Henrietta couldn't be sure she saw the movement. Impulsively, she pushed the bucket across the table. "These are yours now, not mine. Could we start again? I'm not usually so clumsy."

Daphne looked at the bucket, at Henrietta's hand on the bucket, finally at Henrietta's face—and then she smiled, so openly that Henrietta felt a huge rush of relief. Together they decanted their specimens into glass bowls and jars and worked through the afternoon, exchanging quiet comments as the professor talked and strolled between the tables. One mussel they'd collected had a broken shell; they fed it to a hungry sea anemone and watched the tentacles draw it inside. After dinner, they listened to one of the assistant teachers talk about the remarkable ability of the holo-thurians, or sea cucumbers, to escape their predators by ejecting their viscera and later regrowing them.

⁂

THE YACHT CONTRIBUTED by one of the professor's friends from Boston arrived the following week; a colleague at the Coast Survey donated a dredging outfit; by the second weekend the students, grouped into boatloads of eight or ten, had all made at least one excursion, learned to use the implements, and collected some deep-water specimens. On the second Sunday, François spilled from the dredge an excellent example of a basket-fish, which obligingly gathered its five sets of finely branched arms around itself until it looked exactly like woven wicker. Later, as the deck dried and it began to want water, it relaxed into a lacy disk, arms extended around its pentagonal body.

"Oh!" one observant student exclaimed. "It's a kind of starfish!" As indeed it was, the professor explained, back in the laboratory.

•

A brittle star, of the genus *Astrophyton*. He kept to himself the species name, because it was named after him.

Happily exhausted, their hands nicked and scored, the students collapsed on the beach that evening and enjoyed the corn roasted over the fire and the plates of clams steamed in a pit filled with hot rocks and seaweed. Two of the teachers, François and Alpheus, had pitched in to help the kitchen staff organize the feast; another, Arnold, had led a toast; he'd made a little speech himself. Now the work was done, the sky had darkened, the plates were crated and back in the kitchen. The students were talking and laughing quietly, idly drawing shapes in the sand, using the tan husks of tiny horseshoe crabs as finger puppets. Someone's laugh broke into a curious wheeze at the end of each note. Someone knocked over the jar of fireflies someone else had captured. Those who'd already had some experience teaching in high schools and colleges would be sharing what they knew, the professor imagined, with those about to start their first teaching jobs. Alliances would be blossoming, along with at least one rivalry and perhaps a romance or two. Classes all passed through similar stages, which he pretended not to notice although sometimes, as had happened this evening, he caught himself eavesdropping. *She said, he said, I wish I knew, when I go home . . .* All trying so hard to make themselves known to each other. All eager to learn from him and from his dear former students, who loyally continued to follow his teachings despite, as he well knew, secretly leaning in other directions.

François, who'd patiently rigged the dredging equipment and pulled up the prize *Astrophyton*, was considering where he should

take the next expedition. Charles—when had he gotten so bald?—
wanted permission to extend the trench he'd opened in the rise
above the salt marsh, which he was using to illustrate soil forma-
tion and botanical succession. Arnold wanted to show the rest
of them a book a friend had sent him: *The Forms of Water in Clouds
& Rivers, Ice & Glaciers.* Perhaps it might be useful in a class. Odd,
though, to find within it their own exploits from the early 1840s.

"He gives all our names," Arnold said, holding the book close
to his lantern, "and then describes where we worked, the Bernese
Alps and the Rhône Valley, the glaciers of the Grindelwald and
much of course about the glacier of the Aar and what we did
there . . ."

He smiled, and so, after a second, did the professor. Odd indeed
to hear named the places where, after much happy investigation,
he'd grasped the nature of glacial movement and formulated the
idea of an Ice Age. *The surface of Europe,* he'd written somewhere,
*adorned before by a tropical vegetation and inhabited by troops of large elephants,
enormous hippopotami, and gigantic carnivora, was suddenly buried under a vast
mantle of ice, covering alike plains, lakes, seas, and plateaus. Upon the life and
movement of a powerful creation fell the silence of death . . .*

The nearest students, some still munching on lemon cake,
watched the constellations climb over the edge of the ocean. What
stood out, as Arnold read a few sample paragraphs out loud, were
the cunning experiments, the colored liquids they'd poured into
holes to measure the speed of the seepage through the network of
fissures below. The facts but not the feeling of those blissful days.
Once, hearing a sound as loud as a gunshot, he'd held his hand
to the living ice and felt the birth of a new crevasse. Once he'd

built a sturdy tripod over an open well in the glacier, suspended from it a board tied to two strong ropes, and had his friends drop him down the hole, so that he might inspect from his spinning seat the walls' blue laminations. The book described their shelter, built from a boulder at the glacier's edge, but not the feeling of five of them snugged inside like pencils in a tin, talking quietly about someday establishing a permanent summer school for the study of natural history.

"Thirty years late," he said, as if Arnold might have followed his train of thought, "but we finally managed it." Had he already said that, had he and Arnold already told these stories about their work on glaciers to these same students? Always, these days, he repeated himself, his only question—was this a fresh audience?—itself a repetition. Even the worry that he repeated himself repeated.

"It credits you," Arnold announced, "well, us"—he lowered his voice modestly—"with introducing the idea of glaciers as a great geological agent sculpting the landscape. And you with proving, during your visit to Great Britain, that the mountains of Scotland and Wales showed equal evidence of having been molded by an ice sheet."

"A fine trip," the professor said, aiming his voice across the fire. "One of the best."

"A triumph," Arnold agreed, adding, "There's even a section about the parallel terraces of Glen Roy."

"There, at least," the professor said, "I convinced Mr. Darwin of something."

"Tell us," said his wife, who had just returned after helping organize the removal of the plates. Countless times she'd encouraged him like this at dinner parties, watching while the wealthy industrialists from Boston or New York reached for their wallets. So had this very island come to him.

"Mr. Darwin," he said, "when he was young, contended that those terraces represented ancient beaches, left behind from a time when the sea pushed its way farther inland and the valley was essentially a fjord. I simply noted the obvious: that the Scotch Highlands exhibit to perfection all the traces of glacial action. Polished surfaces, striated and marked by grooves and furrows; lateral moraines bordering the valleys and transverse moraines crossing them; boulders sitting by themselves. Anyone could see that a meltwater lake had once filled the area, dammed by a wall of ice and rubble, and that the parallel terraces represented the lake's different levels. Mr. Darwin wrote me, after I published my explanation. He said that as soon as he read it, he knew I was right."

A few yards to his left, the diminutive young woman with the improbably vigorous hair—he'd paired her with Henrietta; was she called Iris?—said, "I didn't know that you and Mr. Darwin were ever friendly enough to talk."

Was she being sarcastic? Perhaps what he heard as an edge to her voice was simply curiosity; after fourteen years of opposing Darwin's theories, his opposition itself had grown famous. "Mr. Darwin and I," he explained, "corresponded when we were younger about our shared interests." Overhead a cloud bit into the edge of the moon. "And indeed I felt lucky to know him, and pleased when he inscribed a copy of his book to me." Which,

•

Darwin claimed in his letter, had not been sent "out of a spirit of defiance or bravado." Although within the book he'd found several places where Darwin had used his own work against him.

Calmly, he continued, "He's widely acknowledged to be one of Great Britain's best naturalists, and I don't dispute that. His work on coral reefs and barnacles shows skill and care and the narrative of his long voyage is a compendium of useful observations. It's a shame he's thrown all that away to chase such a wrongheaded theory."

⁂

THE BOLD QUESTION Daphne asked about Mr. Darwin was, Henrietta knew by then, more typical than not; Daphne was surprisingly self-assured. She spoke to the teachers as if she were one of them, asked questions without raising her hand, rose from her seat in the dining hall and walked calmly to the professor's table to confirm an idea she'd had. In the laboratory, where she and Henrietta worked at the same dissections and experiments, their notebooks looked like they were taking two different courses. Henrietta did as she'd learned at Oswego: neat ruled columns, numbered lists of observations, modest questions framed without any trace of personality, and in such a way that they might be answered. *The "I,"* Mr. Robbins had said, *has no place in scientific study.* Daphne's pages seemed, in contrast, to be filled with everything Henrietta had expunged. Scores of drawings filled the margins, everything from fish eggs to the fringed feelers of the barnacle's waving legs. Describing a beach plum's flowering parts, she broke into unrelated speculations—when an individual polyp of *Laomeda geniculata* dies, does it affect the entire compound creature?—circled these darkly, and then drew arrows from there to cartoons of the professor.

She had grown up, Henrietta learned, on a small farm in a hilly part of central Massachusetts. Her family kept an apple orchard and also some sheep, a vegetable garden, a grove of maple trees tapped for syrup. Her chaotic, lively notebook, in which she wrote down whatever occurred to her, was only the latest in a long series. She'd started writing for a local magazine when she was still in school, little articles about common plants and animals, and although for five years now she'd had a teaching job at a coeducational academy, she continued writing, sneaking back into the empty study room to work after everyone else was asleep. Recently she'd started describing insect pests.

"The potato worm, the pickle worm, the cabbage worm," she told Henrietta. "All those hungry grubs and borers and maggots chewing up whatever we try to grow in our gardens and orchards. Teaching is a perfectly fine way to make a living, but—a person must have a project of her own, don't you think?"

Henrietta nodded, abashed. Until now she'd thought that finding a job was by itself a huge accomplishment. In just a few weeks she would meet her first class, teach her first lessons without supervision. The prospect of simply completing those tasks each day had seemed formidable enough.

"I may try to do a whole book," Daphne said. "Once I dispose of Ezra."

Ezra, Henrietta learned, was a young clergyman from Daphne's hometown, a friend since childhood suddenly grown determined

·

to marry her. Her parents, eager for grandchildren and worried about her age—she was already twenty-six—were pushing her to accept.

"You must have an Ezra, yourself," Daphne added, as they sifted dirt in the potato field near the barn. "Several Ezras, perhaps." Her gaze brushed over Henrietta's face. "Waiting at home to tie you down . . . do you think of marrying?"

"I don't," Henrietta said. There were men she'd been drawn toward at Oswego, men even here she found attractive, but marriage—her mother, with all the miscarriages and stillbirths she'd suffered in the eleven years between Henrietta and Hester, had taught her more than she'd meant. "But what's wrong with *your* Ezra?"

"Everything, really," Daphne said scornfully. She turned over another clump of dirt. "His carefulness, his closed-mindedness. Even if I wanted to marry in the first place, why would I choose a clergyman as backward as the professor?"

"I don't see how you can call the most famous naturalist in the country *backward*."

"He is Mr. Darwin's staunchest enemy," Daphne said. "Which in my opinion makes his own work suspect. Ha!" She plucked out a handsome striped pupa. "Our friend the potato worm."

"Is that its tail?" Henrietta asked. A long, thin tube curved from one end and bent back under the body like a handle.

"Tongue case," Daphne said, sticking out her own pink tongue. "Once it hatches into a sphinx moth, it'll have a tongue that unrolls to be five or six inches long. You must have seen the moths hanging in the air at dusk, lapping up nectar from

•

flowers. Mr. Darwin would say the tongue is a marvelous adaptation, slightly different in each species, selected for over time in response to the shape of blossoms. Whereas our professor would have some rapturous phrase about the elegant contrivances of the Creator."

The two men, Daphne continued, were philosophical opponents, glaring at each other across an unbridgeable divide. Everything the professor taught about the immutable nature of species, Mr. Darwin opposed. Which was the same, Henrietta realized with a shock, as saying that everything she'd been taught, both at her village school in Hammondsport and, later, at Oswego, was in Daphne's opinion purely wrong.

"You," she said, "you think, then . . ."

She stepped over the dusty leaves behind her, suddenly queasy from standing so long in the sun and afraid to finish her question. Surely potato worms were and always had been only, exactly, potato worms. Even when they became sphinx moths. Mumbling something about needing more drawing paper, she left Daphne in the field.

A few days later, though, despite Henrietta's efforts to avoid it, Daphne picked up that discussion again. Another of the professor's wealthy supporters had supplied simple microscopes for each laboratory pair and the professor had shown them how to fashion stands using blocks of wood, metal rods, corks and wire and bits of glass. "Useful," Daphne said approvingly, as they chloroformed bumblebees and prepared to examine the parts. "We could make these inexpensively for our own classes." This sort of practical laboratory skill made the course seem worthwhile; she did not

·

respect the professor's old-fashioned views and she might not, she confided, have signed up for the session had she not needed to see less of Ezra.

She held a dead bee's head as she spoke, waiting for Henrietta to drip a bit of melted sealing wax onto a glass slide. When the wax began to cloud she pressed the head onto the glass and passed the slide back to Henrietta, who positioned it under the lens. Whether he was talking about echinoderms or fossil fish, Daphne continued more quietly, all the professor's lectures circled back to the same essential argument, in her opinion theological rather than scientific.

Henrietta made a careful diagram of the cavity housing the mouth parts, moving the mandibles with a needle and spreading open the sucking apparatus. Instead of returning to the field, Daphne claimed, and gathering actual data, the professor had wasted the last decade opposing Mr. Darwin's theories. He could say as many times as he liked—indeed, he said it here—that the simple structural plans uniting groups of species were actually *ideas*, Divine Conceptions, which existed independent of any material expression of them: but what had he ever found to *prove* that? At home, all the young teachers in her natural history study group were ardent Darwinians, as was she. The professor was nearly alone in his beliefs.

"I think you exaggerate," Henrietta said. She moved the slide clumsily, smearing the wax: spoiled, now. How disturbing it was to hear this! She thought of her mother, back home in Hammondsport, reading aloud to her from the professor's books. "Perhaps not *everyone* agrees with him, but still . . ." Her teachers, two of whom had been his students, admired him enormously. Were they so behind the times?

Daphne fell silent but later, when they were out in the marsh, plucking periwinkles from the eelgrass, she started up again. "He's a wonderful speaker," she said. As persistent as a starfish prying at a clam. "He hypnotizes people. That doesn't make him right."

Henrietta held up a shell. "*I* was taught that science depends on facts, not speculations," she said firmly. "Observations, not wild flights of fancy. It's a fact these are specimens of *Littorina rudis*, also that gasteropods have a radula covered with rows of chitonous teeth. This has a radula, as I do not; it rasps algae from these leaves, as I cannot; these are also facts. The stability of species is a fact. The fossil record, which in no place shows evidence of transitional forms, is another fact. My teachers who read Mr. Darwin's book said it was riddled with fallacies and wild speculations. And that Mr. Darwin departed so far from Baconian methods that his work was not worth reading."

Daphne poked at the tiny turbans in Henrietta's palm. "Why," she said, "don't you just read the book for yourself?"

She loaned to Henrietta her own, much marked-up copy, which she'd brought to the island. Henrietta read it over the next week in secret, hoping to avoid upsetting either the professor or his wife, but it was so absorbing that she began skipping meals and lectures, which made her conspicuous in another way. Soon the professor, who when they first met had seemed so pleased with her, was frowning with disappointment. Twice the professor's wife asked if she was unwell—and still, she kept reading. One sentence locked into the next and the next, the book itself quite different from the ideas as they'd been summarized by her teachers and then dismissed. A gigantic crowd of examples alternately crushed her and then swept her wonderfully, relentlessly along. From variation under domestication—pigeons, who had ever written so much about pigeons?—to the variations found in nature; from the great struggles for existence to the complex modes of finding a place in the natural economy; from natural selection and sexual selection to divergence of character and extinction: she was overwhelmed. Yet she was also troubled by how well the pieces seemed to fit together.

The tide went out as she read about an entangled bank, covered with many kinds of plants. Her legs went numb and the wind stirred up tiny spirals of sand; she missed an entire lecture about clams. The bank was colonized by singing birds and buzzing insects and burrowing worms, each different but all interdependent, produced by the laws Mr. Darwin had earlier described. She looked up and saw the bay gleaming before her. At school, Mr. Robbins had argued this: If species arise by transmutation, then why can we find nowhere in the geological record traces of the intermediate varieties connecting specific forms? We ought to see finely graduated chains; we see no such thing. Indeed we see the opposite: whole groups of allied species suddenly arising in specific formations. The professor had addressed this himself in a lecture about the teleostean fish. Once there were no such things as ray-finned bony fishes. And then there they were, a beautiful array of variations on a single new plan.

Out in the bay, hidden from her eyes but indisputably there, mackerel and cod and bluefish and bass finned swiftly through the water and a question surfaced in her mind: if those fish had been created all at once, in the blink of an eye, what about the creatures they ate, or the creatures who ate them? The whole tangled web of relationships in which each part depended on the others—Mr. Darwin's book, not the professor's lectures, explained this.

The wind blew, the water rippled, an osprey dove and came up with an eel. She worked back once more through certain paragraphs, absorbing what Mr. Darwin called his three great facts. First, neither the similarity nor the dissimilarity of the plants and animals inhabiting various regions could be accounted for by climate or physical conditions: although certain parts of South Africa and of Australia were much alike, the inhabitants were utterly different. Second, wherever significant physical barriers to migration existed—oceans, great deserts, mountain ranges—very different inhabitants existed on either side. Third, and this one struck her most deeply, was what he called the affinity of species inhabiting the same continent or sea: a deep organic bond that was, he claimed, simply inheritance. Affinity, if she understood his argument rightly, had nothing to do with Divine plan but rather indicated simply common descent—which was what her teachers had evaded, and also what the professor denied most vigorously. The mackerel and cod and bluefish and bass were *related* to each other, sharing ancestors as she and Hester shared ancestors with their second cousins, with whom they had little in common except for . . . well, their general shape and size, and their white skins that freckled in summer, their close-set eyes and curled upper ears and a certain curiosity about the world. So obvious, once he'd made her see it. So shocking.

•

Out on the dock on a moonlit evening, bringing up nets coated with luminescent plankton, she and Daphne went through all the arguments again. How tame, Henrietta thought, her schooling had been! The attitudes passed to her by her mother and teachers, a kind of worship, she thought now, which had made her tremble before the professor when she first got off the train, fell away. "You're right," she said. Her mother knew none of this. "Mr. Darwin's right. It changes everything, doesn't it?"

"Everything," Daphne agreed.

THE DAYS ASSUMED a rhythm, and then the weeks. Tuesday and Thursday evenings they sang in the barn; Friday evenings, if the weather was fine, they ate on the beach. Sunday mornings they gathered for services and then students and teachers alike had an early dinner and a few free hours afterward. On Monday, Wednesday, and Friday afternoons they botanized, mapping the distribution of land plants and seaweeds from the land through the littoral zone and into the shallows of the bay. The professor was especially interested in Charles's excavation of the trench, in the rise of grassy land above the salt marsh.

One Wednesday afternoon he climbed down into the trench, aided by the six students who'd done most of the digging and hammered the ladder together. They'd dug cleanly and well: the surface of the meadow was above the top of his head and in the sharp, almost vertical wall, he could clearly see the roots of the grasses penetrating the shallow layer of humus and the lighter brown layer just below that where more sand mingled with the rotted organic material. Farther down, dotted with embedded stumps and bones, were layers of gravel and glacial till.

"Very nice," he said to Charles, who was still loyal, still a fine assistant, but no longer young. What would happen to Charles when he was gone? For months now he'd felt his energy diminishing, and the pains in his eyes, which sometimes brought with them confusion, increased each week. The cerebral hemorrhage he'd had a few years back made him dread the future. To the students he said, "Think about using teaching demonstrations like this with your own classes. There's no substitute for digging through the layers with your own hands and seeing with your own eyes."

One of the young men—Edward?—nodded. "In my part of Ohio," he said, "they'd learn more than geology. You can't dig down more than a couple of feet without finding Indian remains."

"Even better," the professor said, and without quite meaning to started talking about the mound-building Indians of the Ohio. He meant to let them get back to work; he meant only to reinforce the idea, which this trench so beautifully showed, that one set of things lying above another, as fossils lay above each other in strata, did not in any way suggest that the beings of one layer had developed from those of another. One simply lay *atop* the other: succession, not development. Why make such an elaborate hypothesis for what could be so simply explained? And why accept the repulsive poverty of the material explanation? The resources of the Deity could not be so meager that, in order to create a being endowed with reason, he must change a monkey into a man.

But why, if he meant to say that, was he talking about

·

serpent-shaped earthworks and copper tools? And why, while his mouth framed those words, was he thinking again about Mr. Darwin and his theories? He had tried to make sense of them; really he had made an enormous effort. During his last convalescence, while he was stuck in his sickbed unable to walk or even to speak, youngsters had uncovered fossils in Montana and Wyoming that hinted, tantalizingly, at new relationships. They'd used those discoveries to support Darwin's theories, writing papers in which, if he was mentioned at all, he was cast as a kind of dinosaur himself. So upsetting had this been that he'd set off on yet another journey, this time bringing with him all of Darwin's important books. On the ocean, away from the bother of everyday life, he'd meant to consider this question of descent with modification as perhaps—he admitted this only to himself—he had not done thoroughly enough in earlier years.

Down the Atlantic coast of both Americas, through the Strait of Magellan, up the Pacific coast to California. With the new deep-sea dredge he'd planned to sample the ocean bottom, bringing up specimens that might allow him to determine if species in the northern and southern hemispheres were possibly related. Instead the dredge broke again and again, and the ship itself often needed repair. So did he; he was often sick. During long hours in his berth, he flipped through the books but couldn't concentrate. Places he'd hoped to visit had to be skipped; places he visited didn't yield what he'd hoped. The shape of his own mind, he learned, was as fixed as the shape of his skull, a kind of instrument for registering patterns. The spiral of a narwhal's horn like the spirals of willow leaves like the spiral of a snail's operculum, all pointing clearly to a single underlying Mind. He reached San Francisco sure that the real work left to him lay in articulating clearly, to as many people as possible, the flaws in Darwin's arguments and the strengths of his own.

Which didn't mean, he knew, that the students before him were fully on his side. Half or more of those here, he suspected, believed in Darwin's theories even while respecting his own abilities as a naturalist and a teacher. None of them knew, as he did, how the theories seized on with such enthusiasm by one generation might be discarded scornfully by the next. He poked at a round stone embedded in the wall. One might find, layered in such a wall, a whale, a reed, a mackerel, a star-nosed mole, a liverwort. The relics of six discarded theories—or the traces of six young men with their shirtsleeves rolled up, shovels smoothing and scraping the trench while others sketched the section they'd so neatly uncovered.

ON THE MORNING after the August full moon, Henrietta found herself in a little boat with Daphne, Edward, and the professor's wife, who now behaved as if she hardly knew Henrietta. The china they'd scrubbed, the beds they'd made, their arms mirroring each other as they snapped sheets in the air, apparently counted for nothing in the light of the lectures Henrietta had skipped and her obvious absorption in something other than the professor. It wasn't just the book, which Henrietta didn't think the professor's wife had seen. More likely it was the sight of her and Daphne talking so intently outside of class, and the way

Daphne acted as a magnet for the other students interested in Darwin's ideas. In the dining hall the tables were defined, now, by scientific beliefs as well as personal alliances. She and Daphne had places at the far end of the table nearest the door, among a particularly lively group—David, Rockwell, Charles, Lydia, and a few others—swayed by Darwinism. While the professor might not know what bound them, his wife surely did.

Henrietta sat next to Daphne in the stern of their dory, facing Edward, who rowed; the professor's wife sat in the bow, lecturing on the transformations of the Acalephs. "An excellent example of alternate generations," she said in her clear voice. Around them bobbed fourteen other dories, the rest of their little fleet. "To the untrained eye, their different phases appear so distinct and apparently unconnected that previous observers assumed they were separate species."

The sandbar flashed beneath the bottom of the boat. Into the water dipped Edward's oars, the blades slicing the surface, pulling through the depths, rising, and then, with a deft roll of the wrist, flattening to slip through the air. Henrietta tried to visualize the sequence of transformations. "In the autumn, eggs of some species hatch into free-swimming globular bodies, covered with cilia. After a while these attach themselves to a solid surface and then assume a hollow hydroid shape. In early spring, buds appear on the hydroids, each eventually assuming the shape of a medusoid disc that grows and then frees itself. The full-grown medusae of some species swarm together at this time of year, for the purposes of spawning."

One, two, three different stages. The sea was white and shining, the surface quiet but the whole mass undulating in long, slow, shallow swells. Sea urchins too, said the professor's wife, underwent fantastic transformations. A narrow puddle at the bottom of the boat moved forward and back, forward and back, in time with Edward's strokes, while the two buckets awaiting their specimens tilted gently from side to side and the stack of glass bowls clicked together, flashing as the sun hit the rims. The water was glittering too, the jumbled lights making Henrietta drowsy.

"Again and again," said the professor's wife, her words drifting by, "we see one creature seem to change into another." Henrietta touched elbows with Daphne, her friend as fresh and alive as a tree, and for a moment her soul stretched away from her body.

Grub to beetle, larva to barnacle. Now the professor's wife was speaking about the majestic and unexpected paths by which God arrived at the completion of his designs. "The Divine handiwork," she concluded, "exists to remind us always of the greater wonder, the mystery of the moment when God became man."

Henrietta's soul snapped elastically back into place. That wasn't right; those two domains were best kept separate. She turned toward Daphne, who was frowning, and then she bent once more, searching for transparent creatures in transparent water. Her eyes were sore, her head ached, her stomach was announcing, with peculiar clarity, its exact contours.

Splish, said Edward's oars. *Splish, splish.*

The professor, from the dory just ahead of theirs, called out a question to the fleet. "What are the three classes of Acalephs?"

"The ctenophores," said Edward. "And the discophores and the hydroids."

•

Daphne, whose lower back now touched Henrietta's—they were leaning over opposite sides, skirts together, heads and arms far apart—said something Henrietta couldn't hear. The professor's wife told Edward to lift his oars once they rounded the rocky point. The bowls clicked, the edges flashed, and the drops falling from Edward's oars sparkled like broken glass.

"Look," said Daphne, pointing down.

Henrietta swallowed twice and leaned farther over the side. The water had thickened, clotted, raised itself into disconcerting lumps. Suddenly they were floating not on water but on a shoal of jellyfish so thick that the ones nearest the surface were being pushed partially out of the water by those below, and so closely packed that when Edward lowered one oar to turn the boat, he had to force a path between the creatures. All the boats, Henrietta saw, were similarly surrounded; the shoal formed a rough circle fifty feet wide, quivering like a single enormous medusa.

"Pull close together!" the professor shouted from the dory ahead of them. "Now halt! Everyone!" He'd risen to his feet and was standing, his arms held out for balance, looking as though at any moment he might pitch into the sea but too delighted to care. He called out instructions, which his wife repeated more quietly as they stabbed their nets into the shoal. Henrietta worked with Daphne and Edward, trying in the excitement to sort the specimens properly. One bucket for the larger species; the other bucket for the *Pleurobrachia* and the other ctenophores; glass bowls for the most delicate creatures, which had to be kept separate.

As Daphne and Edward were using the nets, Henrietta slid an empty bowl beneath a clear saucer pulsing like a lung: an *Aurelia*, thick and heavy at the center, thin and slippery at the edges, over-hanging the bowl all around. The creature plopped disturbingly as she decanted it into a bucket. "Each of the metamorphoses of the *Aurelia*," the professor was shouting, picking up where his wife had left off, "was once presumed to be a separate species. The hydroid phase was named *Scyphostoma*; the form with the buds stacked up was called *Strobila*. The first stage of the medusa, just after it separates and when it is small and deeply lobed, was called *Ephyra*. Only this stage you are seeing—the breeding adult—had the name *Aurelia*, although we now recognize all four as being forms of the same creature."

Henrietta shifted her canvas shoes, already soaked and stained, away from the wet nets dripping over the floorboards. In the bucket nearest her left foot, a little pink ctenophore mistakenly dropped among the larger jellyfish was presently being consumed. Was the *Zygodactyla* eating it nothing more than an enormous mouth? The other bucket glittered wildly, the sun refracting off the trailing ribbons of the *Pleurobrachiae* and the tiny fringed combs on the *Idyia*, which were darting back and forth. Waves of color, pink then purple then yellow then green, pink again, pinker still.

"Such variety," the professor's wife said, leaning over Edward's shoulder. By now they'd drifted to the edge of the shoal and Henrietta could see water again, the jellyfish scattered more sparsely here and there. "Such beauty."

Daphne, across from Henrietta, had both arms in the water and was struggling with her net. "Ugh," she said, unable to heave whatever she'd found over the side. "What *is* this?"

"Oh," the professor's wife said. "Well done!"

·

As Edward moved the boat a few degrees, Daphne's net shifted astern and then Henrietta could see the gigantic, reddish-brown transparent lump, as wide across as the boat, dangling brown and flesh-colored lobes from a ruffled white margin. A confused mass of tentacles, brown and yellow and purple, trailed behind it.

To the professor, only a few feet away, his wife called, *"Cyanea!"*

In response, he seized an oar from the student rowing his boat and used it to spin the bow around, nosing it into the side of the creature until only the huge disk of jelly separated his boat from Henrietta's. He signaled the remaining boats to nose in similarly, forming a rough ring.

"It's too heavy to bring into our boats with the equipment we have," he said. "And too fragile—its own weight would tear it apart as we tried to lift it. But we can look at it closely from here."

Those who could peered down at the water, some measuring the diameter—at least four feet, they agreed—others inspecting the lumpy ovaries, the mouth parts, the eye specks around the rim. The tentacles, the professor pointed out, were despite their apparent confusion actually gathered into eight distinct bunches. He directed one boat to back slowly away from the circle, following a set of tentacles until they disappeared—which was not, they found to their amazement, for thirty feet. The fair young rower, his face spattered with freckles, lifted his oar and showed the trailing ends draped across the blade. Meanwhile the professor continued to point out the structural similarities between the *Cyanea* and the *Aurelia*.

Daphne raised her head from the mass of blubber and addressed the professor. "That's intriguing," Daphne said. "Those resemblances, those affinities, might well be seen as evidence that the two forms are related, sharing descent from a common ancestor."

The professor shook his head. "You are alluding to Mr. Darwin's theories, I know," he said.

Of course he knew, Henrietta thought. He was tired and old, but he knew what they were reading, as he knew that Daphne was challenging him. Perhaps he even knew he was wrong, but still he had to repeat his old lessons. How wearying this was! She wanted what he himself had told her to seek: the really real world. Before he could say anything else, Henrietta leaned over and thrust her hands into the water, toward the *Cyanea*. The surface felt smooth, surprisingly elastic yet yielding easily to the pressure of her hand. She slipped her left hand from the rounded body into the mass of soft tentacles. Almost instantly her hand began to sting and prickle, and then to burn. With a cry she pulled it out and sat up.

"Oh dear," the professor's wife murmured. "I should have warned you—the name Acalephs alludes of course to their stinging or nettle-like properties. That won't cause any lasting damage, but you're going to be uncomfortable for a few hours."

The professor, looking across the blubber still poised calmly, apparently guiltless, among the surrounding boats, asked if Henrietta was all right.

"Fine," she said unsteadily. The pain was beginning to ebb but so too was all the sensation in her hand. As it grew numb, the pain moved into her head.

"I've done that myself," the professor said. "Just out of curiosity, as an experiment." To the other students he explained that the

.

stinging sensation Henrietta had experienced, and the numbness now creeping over her hand and wrist, had been caused by the myriad tiny cells, called lasso cells, that lined each of the twisting tentacles. "Each of these cells contains within it a tiny, tightly coiled whip, so fine we can hardly see it," he said. "And each whip can be shot out, at the will of the animal, to sting its prey or—as Miss Atkins has so clearly but unfortunately just found—to defend against an attack. In concert, the whips act almost like a galvanic battery, paralyzing small prey and rendering a larger opponent at least partially helpless for a while.

"Now, to address your Mr. Darwin's arguments"—he gestured toward Daphne—"he himself has said that his theory would break down if it could be demonstrated that any complex organ existed which could not have been formed by numerous successive slight modifications. This is a perfect example. How could such a complex mechanism as a lasso cell have developed gradually, in tiny steps, by so-called 'natural selection'? What possible use could half a lasso cell be, a filament that uncoiled but didn't sting, or one that stung but couldn't uncoil? How could such useless half-parts be 'selected'? All the parts have to work in concert for the mechanism to work at all—and they could not work so well and precisely together unless they had all been designed at once by a Divine Intelligence."

As he spoke the *Cyanea* contracted, its circumference shrinking as if it were pulling in its skirts. Deep in the blubber Henrietta dimly saw knotted strands and loops, like the delicate assemblages in the *Aurelia* grown heavy and gross. If the professor was right, the Divine Mind had, for its own pleasure, worked the same pattern on two different scales. If Daphne and Mr. Darwin were right, the pattern repeated because the creatures were related. Affinity represented either descent, on Mr. Darwin's theory, or God's delightful repetition with variety, on the professor's, whereas analogy—did she have these definitions right?—was an accidental correspondence related to function, a bat's wing superficially like a bird's, a whale's tail superficially like a fish's. The sea blubber heaved again, writhed as if it were in pain, and then sank out of sight. Henrietta leaned over and vomited into the water.

⁂

AFTERWARD, THE PROFESSOR was badly shaken. He'd been perfectly calm, as always; his wife had wiped the student's face and wrapped her hand in a damp cloth and they'd carried on with the lesson for a few more minutes before turning the fleet around and heading for shore. They'd acted, he and his wife, François and Arnold and the others, as if nothing surprising had happened, as if there was nothing unusual in a student carelessly poisoning herself. After all, she was known to be clumsy; on their first excursion to the grotto, only she had cut herself on the barnacles. They'd all been frightened, though. And even after her color returned, her evident pain and confusion had made him feel terrible.

Not to François, not to Arnold, not even to his wife had he confided the hopes he'd had during the first few weeks of the session. Back on the mainland, on the rainy evening when she—*Henrietta Atkins*, he remembered, and then forgot—when she had entered the hotel lobby, her hair dripping wet, so young and

•

frightened and eager that, when she introduced herself to him, her voice was shaking, he'd sensed instantly that she might stick by him. Forty years of teaching had given him an instinct for the one or two in each crowd who, not necessarily the most quick-witted or the most skilled manually, learned deeply, thoughtfully, out of an eagerness to please. Eventually most of them turned from the path, they became disloyal, something in them began to doubt as they grew older—but how wonderful they were at first! He'd been longing for a new disciple. During the three days before the other students came, he'd watched Henrietta closely. He'd seen how quickly she adopted his wife's rhythms and movements; how she listened intently to every word about his work. Oh, he could have taught her everything! Then through his own mistake, through pairing her with that Daphne, he'd ruined it all.

With her yellow hair heaped atop her tiny body, and her face all points and lines, Henrietta's annoying partner looked to him like a wizened child. What about sexual selection? she asked, bringing up Mr. Darwin's theories no matter what they were observing. About succession in time and space, variation under domestication, the evidence of embryology? That her dissections were impeccable, her drawings elegant and accurate, only made matters worse. Without her, Henrietta wouldn't have succumbed to Mr. Darwin's theories. Without this very bad influence, she would have listened attentively to him, learned some useful portion of what he knew; gone home after this experience ready to spread his teachings.

Even that night, when he and his wife went to the dormitory to check on Henrietta, Daphne blocked his way. His wife brought cod and roasted potatoes left over from supper and he brought a volume of Mr. Emerson's essays, food for body and soul; his wounded student would be lonely, he thought. Perhaps a little frightened. Instead he found her resting comfortably, propped on pillows Daphne had gathered, eating the supper Daphne had already brought. Listening, in fact, to Daphne read from a book whose title he couldn't see and didn't want to know.

"Excellent!" his wife said, apparently pleased with the scene. "You're feeling better, I see." She set down the plate and smiled at both young women. "I'll leave this in case you want a second helping."

He stood, stiff as a sea fan, unable to say anything to Henrietta in Daphne's presence. His wife murmured some other small politeness, and beneath that cover he retreated down the stairs. Short of breath, oddly addled—when had that happened?—he paused outside in the moon's dull light, herding his scattered thoughts. Then he hurried toward the barn for his evening lecture.

The students were already gathered; he was late. Without notes, without a plan—he could do this in his sleep, and perhaps he was—he spoke about his trip to Brazil and his voyage up the Amazon. Here was evidence, in his opinion, for a continental glacier. All previous travelers had missed these signs of ice filling the valley and choking the river, ice flowing implacably down from the Andes, a continental sheet of ice that had wiped out all the plants and animals, so that there could be no connection of descent between the fossil forms and the living forms found now. Here, once more, was firm evidence that the theories of the transmutationists were mistaken and he had found it, he alone . . .

•

But here, once more, was Daphne, who'd slipped in through the side door to join her usual group of friends. "Could you tell us," she asked, her tone falsely respectful, falsely sweet, "exactly *what* evidence you found of glaciation? Mr. Bates and Mr. Wallace, who spent such a long time investigating the Amazon basin, found no such evidence at all. And I know your colleague Mr. Gray disputes your findings in this area."

In the dormitory, left behind, lay a young woman with a yielding nature, who might have absorbed all he had to give, had this one not interfered. He straightened his back and expanded his diaphragm, lifting his cane as if it were a sword. "I do have evidence," he said frostily. "The fantastic quantities of glacial drift evident at Rio and every place near it, as well as along both banks of the Amazon. The—"

"Then you saw glacial furrows?" Daphne inquired. "Striae? Erratics?"

"None," he said. "For a perfectly good reason. The rocks aren't hard enough, there, to have preserved these traces. Everywhere the rock is friable, decomposed by the burning sun and the torrential rains, and so I have no *positive* evidence. Instead I make a sure assumption, founded on the resemblance of the materials in the Amazonian valley to that found in glacier bottoms elsewhere. Consider the identical deposits of drift at the same level on both sides of what is now the river, the coarser materials settling to the bottom and the finer clays on top."

He turned and picked up the chalk. With his old friends at his side, with the chalk behaving in his hand and the blackboard accumulating drawings as his own voice rippled reassuringly in his ears, he began to feel better. Thirty years ago he'd taken the world by storm with his theory of glacial action; like a young knight he'd gone off to do battle against the established theories and he had triumphed even over Mr. Darwin, convincing everyone that a sheet of ice had descended over Europe and North America, carving the landscape into its present forms. Now he would triumph again.

"Why," he said happily, "is it so improbable that, when Central Europe was covered with ice thousands of feet thick; when the glaciers of Great Britain ploughed into the sea, and when those of the Swiss mountains had ten times their present altitude; when every lake in Northern Italy was filled with ice and these frozen masses extended even into Northern Africa; when a sheet of ice, reaching nearly to the summit of Mount Washington in the White Mountains, moved over the continent of North America— why, then, is it so improbable that, in this epoch of universal cold, the valley of the Amazons also had its glacier poured down into it from the accumulations of snow in the Cordillera, and swollen laterally by the tributary glaciers descending from the tablelands of Guiana and Brazil?"

There. Once more he'd quoted his own writings but let it stand, it was good the first time he wrote it and better now, charged with this night's enthusiasm. Let it stand, and let its meaning shine forth. A sea of ice, God's great plough, periodically reshaped the landscape and extinguished whole sets of flora and fauna, obliterating His living creations so that they might be replaced afresh. *That* was the explanation for the sudden appearances and disappearances in the fossil record. If the younger crowd of scientists seemed more impressed by Mr. Darwin's transmutation theories than with his own vision—well, that was only a tiny disturbance in the sea of time. Nothing changed, really. Beneath the superficial transformations lay the unchanging truth, pure as glacial melt.

❖

IN HER NARROW bed, no longer floating in a vast and airy space but confined now within planked walls and uncomfortably close despite the window, Henrietta lay for another day. When she was well enough to rise, she packed her bag, made excuses to the professor and his wife, and arranged to leave the island early. One last time, before the boat fetched her, she and Daphne sat on the dock together.

"You're sure?" Daphne said. She'd taken off her boots and her stockings and tucked her feet beneath her skirt.

"Perfectly," Henrietta said. "It's a waste of time for me, now. And I don't have any to waste. If I'm not learning things I can use, I ought to be back in Hammondsport, preparing for classes. I have to redo everything. All my lesson plans, everything I meant to teach: all of it's wrong."

She plucked at her own worn skirt, mended clumsily where the barnacles had torn it and stained by blood from her first outing, and by tentacle slime from her last. In the dory, surrounded by lumps of protoplasm, Mr. Darwin's vision of the natural world had finally, completely, pierced her. All she'd read and discussed with Daphne became a part of her; she *saw* what he'd seen, her thoughts followed his. Apparently Daphne had felt this years ago.

•

"I still don't understand why *you* came here, though, if you think the professor is such a fool."

"He's not a fool," Daphne said calmly. "He's a brilliant observer, and he is, or was, the most powerful naturalist in the country. Even now, even a decade after most working naturalists have discarded his views and accepted Mr. Darwin's, his lecture series are packed and we're all still using his textbooks. Look at you—a smart person, trained at a good Normal School: and the place you most wanted to study was here, just as your teachers suggested. I want in my teaching, and in my writing too, to have some real influence. I wanted to see how he did it. Not how he did science— how he spread the word."

"You'll write to me?" Henrietta asked. The boat was moving toward them.

"If you'll write back," Daphne said. "I could use a reader for some of what I want to do this winter. You can tell me how the pieces strike you, and how I might improve them."

Although they exchanged addresses, Henrietta left the island worrying that Daphne's promise had been only politeness. A week after the end of the course, though, the first fat envelope arrived in Hammondsport: ten pages about the tent caterpillar infesting apple trees, complete with Daphne's drawing of a web filled with writhing worms, diligently spinning their common tent before marching out to eat leaves. Henrietta sent back her comments, along with questions about something she'd read, and after that drawings, hypotheses, speculations, and books moved steadily between them. What, Henrietta wondered, would the professor make of this? She retained not his ideas but an image

.

of his shining, enthusiastic face. Of his cane, which he'd held like a trident; of his wife's steady gaze, welcoming as they'd made beds together; guarded—had she known what would happen?—as Henrietta reached for the *Cyanea*.

Her mother, so upset when Henrietta returned home early, and so disbelieving when Henrietta explained how her views had changed, at her urging read Mr. Darwin's book, which had been in the village library all along. When she finished she read it again; then, troubled but not convinced, she began to argue with Henrietta. Hester sat between them at the dining room table, beneath the professor's signed letter, listening to both of them. A deep furrow, Henrietta was pained to see, sometimes appeared between Hester's eyebrows, as if the two sets of ideas were pulling her brain apart. Then Hester would say that her head hurt, and their mother would frown at Henrietta and declare their discussions closed for the day.

On those nights Henrietta went to bed feeling even more lonely than she had during her first days on the island. She reminded herself, and her mother, too, that she was far from discarding all that she had learned from the professor. At her new job, she used his methods—few books, many specimens, constant close observation—to teach Mr. Darwin's theories. And at least once a week, as he would have recommended, she gathered her students for expeditions outside.

In December, she took them to the Glen at the edge of the village, where the waterfall had frozen. Dormant ferns dotted the shale cliffs, which were layered with fossils; the fields rippled with glacial moraines and she could not, she thought, have found a better place to demonstrate the workings of time. They picked their way along the icy rocks, some of the students searching for weathered-out brachiopods while others attacked the gorge wall with chisels. Some collected lichens and frozen mosses and ferns, some inspected the swallows' nests, some looked for tracks in the light snow. She found a frozen mole carcass, which she brought home for Hester.

That night her mother, after admiring the mole, sat her down at the table and passed her a plate of stew with dumplings. There was a folded newspaper near Henrietta's spoon. She glanced at the front page and then looked again and unfolded it and read. The professor had died unexpectedly, she learned, after eating a heavy meal and smoking a forbidden cigar. The article, which filled an entire page, included remarks by many of his students, among them several who'd taught her at the island. No one mentioned disagreements with Mr. Darwin. They concentrated, instead, on his great enthusiasm for natural history, which had never waned, and on his ability to inspire students of all ages and backgrounds. One woman wrote fondly of a class she'd taken years ago, when she was young herself, during which he'd pressed a living grasshopper into each of their hands. They were supposed to follow his lead as he lectured, inspecting a leg joint or a wing, but the grasshoppers kept escaping and popping into the air. What the woman remembered most was the way the professor had laughed and stopped his lecture each time, waiting for them to recapture the runaways.

That was one side, which Henrietta cherished. The other was apparent in the poem Whittier offered, memorializing the professor's last project. Of the endless stanzas, too many to finish, she read these:

On the isle of Penikese,
Ringed about by sapphire seas,
Fanned by breezes salt and cool,
Stood the Master with his school.
Over sails that not in vain
Wooed the west-wind's steady strain,
Line of coast that low and far
Stretched its undulating bar,
Wings aslant along the rim
Of the waves they stooped to skim,
Rock and isle and glistening bay,
Fell the beautiful white day.
Said the Master to the youth:
"We have come in search of truth,
Trying with uncertain key
Door by door of mystery;
We are reaching, through His laws,
To the garment-hem of Cause,
Him, the endless, unbegun,
The Unnameable, the One
Light of all our light the Source,
Life of life, and Force of force.
As with fingers of the blind,
We are groping here to find
What the hieroglyphics mean

•

Of the Unseen in the seen,
What the Thought which underlies
Nature's masking and disguise,
What it is that hides beneath
Blight and bloom and birth and death."

Blight and bloom and birth and death, Nature's mask—there *was* no mask, no underlying thought, only life itself. Behind the garment-hem of Cause, the real skirt she'd torn and stained. In place of sapphire seas, the real, gray, salty ocean, ringing the island—not an isle—where she and Daphne had met.

"I'm sorry," her mother said quietly.

A little black cricket, Henrietta remembered, had leapt into the air that first day at the island, as if presenting itself for the professor's inspection and delight. "I am too," she said.

·

The Particles

(1939)

Once he was in the water, it was easier to see what had happened to the ship. The stern already low in the waves, the empty lifeboat davits and twisted rigging and the blackened, shattered wood on the deck, where the exploding hatches had blown deck chairs and people to bits. They'd been at dinner, spoons clicking on soup bowls, cooks poised over pots, Sam Cornelius thrown from his chair as he pushed aside a bit of carrot. Now it was past nine and fully dark. The searchlight picked out bodies floating near the boat, and when the woman crouched behind him gave her life belt to her wailing son, Sam gave her his and then was even more frightened; despite his age— he was thirty-four—he could barely swim.

In the distance a shape, which might have been the guilty submarine, seemed to shift position. The moon disappeared behind a bank of clouds and then it rained, drenching those who weren't

.

yet soaked; more than eleven hundred people had been on board. When the rain stopped, the moon again lit the boats scattered around the slowly sinking ship. The three of the *Athenia*'s crew in Sam's boat took oars, as did the three least wounded—Sam was one—of the four male passengers. The others, just over fifty women and children, bailed with their shoes and their bare hands, scooping out the oily water rising over their shins.

As the two dozen lifeboats separated like specks on an expanding balloon, one pulled toward Sam's boat to let them know that several ships had responded to the *Athenia*'s call for help. Soon, in just a few hours, they'd be saved. Those hours passed. Not long after midnight, a faraway gleam, which might have been a periscope caught by the light of the moon, caused two women to shriek. A U-boat, one said, the German submarine that had torpedoed them rising now to shell the lifeboats. But the last beam of the searchlight, just before the emergency dynamo used up its fuel and the *Athenia* went completely dark, revealed enough to convince Sam and some of the others that this was a rescue ship.

Steadily, Sam and his companions rowed toward the Norwegian tanker *Knute Nelson*, which, in the light of occasional flares, popped sporadically out of the darkness. A little string of emptied lifeboats tossed in the swell beside the tanker, the boat closest to the stern still packed with people. Some grabbed at rope ladders while the bosun's chair went up and down, hoisting those not agile enough to climb until, in the grip of a heavy woman who pushed off too vigorously, it overturned and left her suspended upside down. The crew struggled to retrieve her, but before they were done another boat nudged in behind the one still being emptied.

·

The man rowing next to Sam muttered, "They should stand out, that's dangerous," and when Sam drew his anxious gaze away from the faces he was searching, he could see how little space separated the last boat in line from the tanker's huge propellers. He turned back to his oars. The sea was rough, the boat's seams were leaking, many of his fellow passengers were wounded or seasick or both, and Sam was working so hard to keep their boat steady that he failed to see exactly what happened a few minutes later. By the time he heard the screams, the broken lifeboat, impaled on one of the propeller blades, was already rising into the air.

"Row!" said the seaman in charge of Sam's boat. "Row, row, row, row!"

Sam, the tallest but not the strongest of those at the oars (he was out of shape), lost his grip and banged into the man beside him, who shouted at him; then all of them were shouting at each other while women wailed and children cried. Unbearable to think about what must have happened to those drawn into the propeller. The boat sped into the darkness, headed, once the assistant purser spotted it, toward an enormous, brightly lit motor yacht that had appeared from another direction. Before they were close enough to hail her, Sam saw two lifeboats tangle at her stern, one crowding the other under the angled counter—the swell had increased, making everything more difficult—which, after rising unusually high, crashed down on the gunwale of the inner boat and tipped it over. Suddenly, struggling figures, too small to identify, also dotted the water.

That was enough for the seaman in charge; Sam's boat pulled away until it was clear of everyone. "Let's wait," the seaman said, "until sunrise, when we can see more clearly what we're doing." The swell grew heavier; dawn finally broke and three British destroyers arrived. The little boy whose mother was wearing Sam's life belt pointed at them, smiled for the first time since the ship had been hit, and said, "Ring around the rosy!" Sam couldn't see what the little boy meant, and then he could: two of the ships were racing after each other, herding within an enormous circle the remaining lifeboats, the tanker, the white yacht, and the third destroyer, which was plucking boatloads of survivors from the water. Twice, he thought it was turning their way, but each time it moved toward another, even more crowded boat.

The sky was red and then pink and then blue; Sam's hands were numb; he hadn't been able to feel his feet for hours. Once or twice he either fell asleep or passed out. Once, he lifted his head just in time to see an old woman in a lifeboat not far away leap toward a lowered rope ladder and miss, slipping into the narrow space between the boat and the destroyer's hull; the boat rose on a swell and the space disappeared. He was barely conscious when, in the middle of the morning, a U.S. merchant ship arrived, cleaned out one boat before taking in a crowd transferred from the motor yacht, and then waved over the boat Sam was in.

The injured and frail went up in a bosun's chair, but Sam, jolted awake by the prospect of safety, scrambled up a rope ladder with the other men. A person reached out for him, grabbed his arm, and heaved him over the side—not a stranger, not a sailor, but someone Sam knew: Duncan Finch. Part of him wanted to jump back in the water. Duncan, here? But there was the ship's name, *City of Flint*, mocking him from the smokestack.

•

"You're all right!" Duncan shouted as Sam dropped onto the deck. "Are you hurt?"

Sam flexed his elbow, which he'd cracked on a thwart but which still seemed to work, and then inspected his shin, where all the blood appeared to be coming from one long scrape. "Nothing serious," he said.

Duncan pulled him toward a dry corner. "Is anyone else with you?"

Anyone, he meant, from the meeting; they'd been at an international genetics congress in Edinburgh, cut short by the situation. Sam shook his head. Families had been broken apart, siblings had ended up in different boats, friends had been randomly assorted: where was Axel? Eight other geneticists had been on the *Athenia* with Sam. One by one, in the thick, dark smoke, they'd climbed into lifeboats, dropped down to the water, and then disappeared.

Duncan said, with apparent enthusiasm, "But at least *you're* here. You're safe."

Omitting, Sam thought, the fact that on their last day in Edinburgh, Duncan had asked Sam grudgingly, and only after Sam had already made his own arrangements, to join the small group he'd finagled aboard this American freighter loaded with wool and Scotch whisky.

"I did warn you," Duncan added now. Still, after eighteen years of annoying Sam, unable to rein in his red-faced, bullying self. "I *warned* you not to take passage on a British ship."

Anyone else would have understood how few choices existed. Sam's booked passage had been canceled, the other ships were quickly commandeered, and on September 1, as he boarded the

Athenia in Glasgow, it had still seemed likely that they'd get away safely. They'd had to pick up passengers in Belfast and then more in Liverpool, both ports packed with Americans and Canadians trying to get home, but by the afternoon of September 2 the ship was heading north up the Irish Sea, rounding the coast early on the morning of September 3. By the time the declaration of war was radioed, they'd almost cleared the most dangerous territory, their ship overbooked but still comfortable and, Sam had thought with a twinge of pleasure, less crowded than Duncan's. Before Duncan left, not only his handful of stranded friends but also a group of college girls caught midway through a European tour had been stuffed into the *City of Flint*, making thirty instead of the normal five or six passengers. Now it bulged with another two hundred people, some freezing and still in shock, and among them—

"Is Axel here?" he asked.

Duncan turned, reached back to steady an elderly woman coming over the railing, and then pointed her toward a man who was giving out fresh water. "Of course not," he said, inspecting Sam more closely. "Did you hit your head?"

For Duncan, Sam realized, Axel was still in Edinburgh, where he'd stayed to visit a friend despite Duncan's frantic urging that he board the *City of Flint*. When the situation grew so dangerous that Axel's friend cut the visit short and delivered him to the Glasgow docks, Duncan had already been at sea.

"He was with me," Sam said. Two teenage boys tumbled onto the deck, their hair matted with oil; a girl in a tidy jacket rushed over to them. "The *Athenia* was the only ship that had a berth." In another situation he would have enjoyed seeing the color drain from Duncan's cheeks.

"He *wasn't*."

"He was," Sam said. "We were eating dinner with that couple from Minnesota when we were hit." One of what should have been many meals; what luck, he'd thought, to have Axel aboard! An unexpected benefit of letting Duncan sail without him. They might walk the decks, share quiet conversations, sit side by side in reclining chairs, and repair what had gone wrong in Edinburgh. At the dock, the sight of Axel's battered gray hat and unmistakable nose had suddenly made everything broken and ruined seem hopeful again.

"But then," Duncan said, "how did you lose track of him?"

The smoke, the darkness, the wounded people, the babble of different languages as passengers crowded boats already full, launched half-empty ones too early. Sam drew a breath. "We went where the crew told us to go, and they assigned us to separate boats. Then the boats scattered. Can you find out if he's here?"

Duncan disappeared with a curse, leaving Sam to be herded down below with the newest arrivals. In a long room lined with barrels, they dripped into a growing puddle, which the crew and the freighter's original passengers tried to avoid as they ferried in spare clothing pulled from their luggage. A plant physiologist from Texas, transferred from the motor yacht, slipped an old sweater over his head as he said that these merchant seamen were a lot more welcoming than the Swedish billionaire who'd originally rescued him. Sam tied his feet into a pair of slippers a size too large, thrilled to find them dry, while his new acquaintance

·

described the smartly outfitted crew who'd handed out soup and hot coffee and blankets and then—the sun was well up, the *Athenia* had gone to her grave, and the destroyers were making their rounds—told the rescued passengers that the owner couldn't interrupt his planned trip and needed to transfer everyone who'd been picked up. "To here," the Texan said, stepping out of his oil-soaked pants and into a seaman's canvas overalls. "Oh, that's *much* better."

Where was Axel, where was Axel? Maybe he'd been on that yacht, or maybe . . . he tried not to think about the huge propeller. Around Sam, coats, blankets, overshoes, shawls flew toward wet bodies, something dry for everyone. So many people, everywhere: bodies racked like billiard balls in every corner and companionway, babies calling like kittens or crows as women tried to comfort them. Among them, Axel might be hidden—or he might be in the water still, or safely headed toward Galway or Glasgow on one of the destroyers. Sam pushed through the mass, some faces familiar from the *Athenia*'s decks and dining room but many not and none the one he most wanted to see, until, when he came out near the galley, he heard his name and looked behind him. Duncan, who'd always had this way of proving himself astonishingly useful just when he was at his most annoying, waved his hand above the crowd. Beside him, his front hair pushed forward into a kingfisher's tuft by a gigantic square bandage, was Axel.

❖

DUNCAN TURNED HIS berth over to Axel, who, after touching Sam's face and saying, "You're here. You're all right," disappeared into the deckhouse and fell, said Duncan later (now modestly moved to the floor of his cabin, where he'd already had two roommates), into an exhausted sleep. Sam, who stayed awake for a while after Axel left, slept that first night on a coil of rope, surrounded by women in men's shoes and torn evening gowns, men wearing dress shirts over sarongs made from curtains, children in white ducks shaped for bulky sailors. A little girl whose parents had ended up in a different boat—Sam hoped they were now on some other ship—lay on a pile of canvas nearby. Earlier, he'd seen the two women looking after her piece together a romper from two long woolen socks, a pair of women's panties, and a boy's sweater. Now the women curled parenthetically around their warm charge.

Sam's trousers were still intact, and between those, his donated slippers, and a wool jacket generously given to him by one of Duncan's cabinmates, an old acquaintance named Harold, he was warm enough to sleep. The next morning, after a chaotic attempt at breakfast, he and Harold, along with everyone else who wasn't injured, helped the ship's crew spread mattresses in the hold, suspend spare tarpaulins from beams to make rows of hammocks, and hammer planks into bunks until everyone had a place to sleep. Harold had helped the captain organize seatings for meals—eight shifts of thirty people—and as he and Sam cut planks to length, they talked about supplies. Harold's friend George, also sharing Duncan's cabin, joined them an hour later and described the list he was making of those who'd been separated from family members and friends; first on it were the seven congress participants still unaccounted for. The captain would radio the list to the other rescue ships, which were returning to Scotland and Ireland—only theirs was heading across the sea, on its original course. But what about allocating medical care and pooling medications? What about basic sanitation? If we had rags, Harold said, we could tear them into squares. If we had a *system*, George fussed, gathering scraps of paper for the latrines.

If, if, if. Sam tried to think of these two middle-aged men as amiable strangers helping to make the best of a hard situation—as if they'd not just been together at a conference where the two of them had looked on blandly as Sam's work was attacked. As if Duncan, elsewhere on the ship that morning, hadn't been the one attacking.

He worked all day, as the ship steamed steadily west and the passengers pulled from the water continued to shift and sort themselves, the sickest and most badly wounded settling in the tiny hospital bay with those slightly better off nearby, the youngest and oldest tucked in more protected corners and the strongest where water dripped or splashed—layering themselves as neatly, Sam thought, as if they'd been spun in a gigantic centrifuge. He claimed one of the hammocks he'd hung himself, glad that at least Axel had a berth and a bit of privacy. Glad too to find, when evening came, that Harold and George had fit him and Axel into their dinner shift, which also included Duncan and the group of college girls.

The big square bandage bound to the top of his head made Axel look unusually defenseless. He smiled at Sam and tapped the spot next to him at the dinner table, but before Sam could get there, Harold, George, and Duncan swarmed in, leaving Sam at the corner. The college girls, already friendly with Duncan's group, filled in the empty seats and introduced themselves to Sam and Axel. One, who had smooth red hair a few shades lighter than Sam's, pointed to Axel's gauze-covered crown. "Is that bad?"

"Not really," Axel said. "A long jagged tear in my scalp, but the doctor said it should heal."

Not nearly enough information. Sam imagined Axel underwater, trying to surface through the debris. An oar cracking down on his skull, a fragment from the explosion flying toward him. When did it happen, who was he with, who took care of him until he reached the ship? He leaned forward to speak, but another of the girls, annoyingly chatty—Lucinda was her name—said, "How do you all know each other, then?"

"We work in the same field," Harold said. His doughy cheeks were perfectly smooth; of course he had a razor.

"Genetics," George added. Also clean-shaven. Briefly, Sam mourned his lost luggage. "The study of heredity."

"These two," Axel said, gesturing first toward Sam and then toward Duncan, "used to be my students."

"Really?" said the one named Pansy. "That wolf-in-a-bonnet disguise makes you look the same age as them."

It was true, Sam thought as the others laughed; the bandage covered Axel's bald spot, his sprouting beard concealed the creases around his mouth, and he was trim for a man who'd just turned fifty. Duncan, ten years Axel's junior, boasted a big, low-slung belly that, along with his thinning hair, made him look like an old schoolmaster. Straightening up, sucking in, Duncan turned to Lucinda and said, "We were all at the genetics conference I told you about."

•

"Where everyone was arguing!" Lucinda said brightly. "See, I *do* listen. Which side"—she turned to Sam—"were you on?"

"Lucinda," said a girl named Maud.

"Actually," Harold said, rubbing his cheek with his thumb, "it was Duncan and Sam, here, who were having a disagreement. But that's all behind us now."

Sam tried but failed to catch Axel's expression, while Duncan changed the subject. But as they were clearing out for the next shift of diners, one of the quieter girls approached Sam and said, "Were you really all quarreling about some experiment while the soldiers were gathering? I would have thought . . ."

". . . that scientists aren't petty? That we're not as childish as everyone else?"

"Something like that," she said, with a surprising smile. "Although I don't know why I *should* expect that. I'm Laurel," she reminded Sam.

Straight brown hair, solid hips, pleasant, but, in Sam's opinion, unremarkable-looking except for her eyes. Up on deck, amid a crowd of people he didn't know and safely away from the ones he did, he watched the water move past the hull and listened to Laurel talk about what they'd heard on the radio. The Germans were smashing through Poland and had occupied Kraków. An RAF attack on German naval bases had gone awry. Each wave took them farther from what was going on in Europe. On the *Athenia*, along with the Americans and Canadians bolting for home, had been refugees from Poland and Romania and Germany who'd managed to get to Liverpool and then fought for berths, only to end up floating in the water before being rescued, if they were among the lucky, by a ship that would bring them back to Britain to begin the process of trying to flee again.

The sky was streaked with mare's tails to the south, dotted with little round clouds to the north; the last edge of the sun had vanished but some color remained. The open deck was so crowded by now that each of them touched at least one other person. Duncan pushed through like a fox through a field of wheat, nodded when he saw Sam, and kept moving. Duncan wasn't stupid, Sam thought; he knew some things, including what it meant to be part of a field of science still in its infancy. But he didn't know the new and enormous thing that Sam and Axel now shared. Sam in one boat and Axel in another, but the same sky, the same rain, the same flares and fears and darkness and dawn. Laurel said something about the windows of a church in London and Sam pretended to pay attention. Why was it, he thought, that even here he couldn't escape Duncan?

❧

IN 1921, WHEN Sam went off to college in upstate New York, he was sixteen years old and six feet tall, trying to conceal his age behind his size and so lonely that he might have attached himself to anyone. His father, an astronomer at the Smithsonian, had died when he was four; Sam remembered his smell, his desk at the observatory, his laugh. Afterward, his mother had moved them to Philadelphia to live with her parents, who seemed to be nothing like her. He slept in a bed his great-uncle had once used, near a shelf on which, between two photographs of his dead father, a mirror reflected back a face framed by his father's thick red hair but otherwise very different. His mother's mouth, her father's heavy lower lids, two moles on a jaw that must have come from someone on his father's side. When he touched that face with hands his father's size but his grandmother's shape, he felt a huge, hazy, painful curiosity he couldn't put into words. Like his mother, he was good with numbers, but otherwise his mind seemed to leap and dart where hers moved in orderly lines. Perhaps, he thought, like his father's? He could only guess.

When he turned eight, his grandfather persuaded a friend to admit Sam to a school so good that his mother, who wrote books and articles about astronomy, was just able to pay the fees. Tearing through his classes, eager for more, he skipped one year and then another. A biology teacher, Mr. Spacek, reeled him in when he reached the upper school, introducing him to the study of heredity. In the empty lab, at the end of the day, he'd enter into Mr. Spacek's fruit-fly experiments as if he were tumbling down a well, concentrating so intently that the voices rising from a baseball game on the field below, or from the herd pounding around the track, shrank to crickets' chirps and then disappeared. From the books Mr. Spacek loaned him, Sam finally gained the language to shape what he'd been feeling since he could remember. Who am I? Who do I resemble, and who not? What makes me *me*, what makes you *you*; what do we inherit, and what not?

Mr. Spacek helped Sam translate his curiosity into hypotheses that might be tested, experiments he might perform. He urged Sam to apply to college a year early, and then got him a scholarship and everything else he needed, including two precious books for the journey up the Hudson River. These, along with the sandwiches Sam's mother had packed him, helped during the bad moment when he confused the motion of the water rushing alongside the train with that of the train itself. Once he arrived at his new refuge, though, he felt fine. The brick and stone buildings were just as handsome as Mr. Spacek had promised, and his room was excellent too, with a big window, two low beds, two desks with lamps and chairs and space for books. Shirts and jackets were already hanging neatly along one half of the closet rod, and these, along with a carton of books and a pair of skis, belonged to a wiry boy who introduced himself as Avery Hayes and asked if he might have the bed away from the window. Sam, who'd never had a close friend, right away liked Avery's smile and his calm, thoughtful movements.

"Of course you can have that bed," Sam said. "But are you sure . . . ?"

"Perfectly," said Avery. "I'm sensitive to drafts. If you don't mind, I'll take this desk then, too."

Which left Sam exactly what he wanted, a view out over the quad, past the beeches and benches and flower beds to the long brick building with limestone lintels, which he'd spotted the instant he arrived: the Hall of Science, the reason he'd come. This was his place, Mr. Spacek had told him, this and no other: because this was the place where Axel Olssen taught.

Mr. Spacek had also arranged for Sam to join Olssen's section of general biology his first semester, and Axel transplanted Sam so smoothly from Mr. Spacek's world into his—soon after the first exam, he hired Sam as a bottle washer, brought him into the lab, and told him to use his first name—that Sam hardly felt

·

the shock. The weeks rocketed by, the work Sam wanted to do crowded by other classes, the regimen of the dining hall, compulsory weekly chapel, and the swimming lessons that were part of the physical fitness requirement. The basement pool was dimly lit, slimy under Sam's feet at the shallow end, where he stood and tried to follow the instructor's motions. He was the only one that year who didn't know how to swim at all, and those first weeks of splashing, coughing, breathing in when he was meant to breathe out, and sinking, perpetually sinking—"You're remarkably *dense*," the instructor said cheerily, trying to support Sam in the water with a hand under his ribs—were humiliating. Thrusting his face back up into the air, Sam lost track of his surroundings and once again was the small, frightened boy who, after his father's death, was sometimes swept away by tantrums. But then, as soon as he crossed the quad and entered the Hall of Science, everything annoying faded away.

Axel was young himself, just a few years out of graduate school, energetic and delightfully informal; he loaded Sam down with his own books, trusting that he could make sense of the material despite being only a freshman. When he discovered Sam's age, he laughed and said genetics was a young man's game—Alfred Sturtevant had been only nineteen, still an undergraduate, when he'd devised the first chromosome map. Calvin Bridges had been an undergraduate too, and a bottle washer, like Sam, when he spotted the first vermilion mutant. Who knew what Sam, the perfect age at the absolutely perfect time, might do? Theirs was a new field, Axel said. A whole new world.

In class, Axel brought new terms and concepts alive with his arms, slicing the air like a conductor, his thick hair sticking up in spikes. They were after more than just the study of vague factors or mysterious unit characters, he said: the gene was not simply an abstract idea; genes were material! Heredity depended on chromosomes, forever splitting and recombining; units of heredity—genes—must be arranged like beads on a string, particles invisible to the eye but visible through their actions, ordered along visible chromosomes. Let the older generation argue about immaterial factors, vitalistic forces, the possibilities of organisms passing on changes caused by will or experience. The truth, Axel emphasized during Sam's first semester, was that the particles of heredity passed from one generation to the next and could not be influenced by what happened to the body. Every living individual had two parts, one patent, visible to our eyes—the me you see, the tree you touch; that was the somatoplasm—and the other latent, perceptible only by its effect on subsequent generations but continuing forever, part of an immortal stream; that was the germplasm. Phenotype, genotype (Sam loved repeating those words). Concepts made visible, Axel said happily, through our own flies.

So Sam couldn't swim; so he hated his history class. When he listened to Axel talk about his work, now *their* work, he was entirely alive. If they helped elucidate the way genes were arranged and transmitted, then they'd begin to understand heredity and variation. If they understood that, they'd begin to glimpse the workings of evolution. And if they could understand evolution, then . . .

"You have a pedigree," Axel said one day when Sam was mashing bananas, sprinkling yeast, and measuring agar: by then he was the food maker as well as the bottle washer. "Just like our flies. You

·

were trained by Charlie Spacek, and now you're working with me. We were trained by Thomas Morgan, who was trained by William Brooks. Brooks was trained by Agassiz himself, at the summer school for the study of natural history he founded on Penikese Island: the ancestor of the Woods Hole labs. One short line: Agassiz, Brooks, Morgan, me, and then you. You're connected to the new biology just as directly as the flies we're breeding in here are connected to the original stocks from Morgan's lab."

Sam didn't share that with Avery, who was as interested in physics as Sam was in biology, but who hadn't yet found the right professor; it would have felt like bragging. But he did love the feel of his own hands linking Mr. Spacek's *Drosophila*, whose ancestors had also come from the fly room at Columbia, to the new generations hatching in the bottles he prepared. Forget the litter, the browning bananas, the morgue filled with bodies drowned in oil. The flies swooned docilely at a whiff of ether, moved easily with a touch from a camel's hair brush, and then—the variations were marvelous. Eye after eye after eye, all red—and then here were white eyes, and there were pink. Wings all shaped like wings, until one fly produced a truncated set and another a pair curled like eyelashes, each mating yielding surprises, a new generation every ten days: how could anyone think of this as work? Work was waiting for frogs to hatch and pass through their stages until they matured enough to mate. Planting corn and waiting for the seeds to germinate, the stalk to grow, the ear to fill and ripen before one could even begin to guess—*that* was work; he couldn't believe the researchers a few hours away at Cornell had the patience. For him it was always, only, flies. In a clean bottle, a courting male

·

held out one wing to his virgin bride and danced right and then left before embracing her: who wouldn't love *that*? Let others fuss with peas and four-o'clocks, rabbits and guinea pigs: for Sam, the flies were the key to everything.

That first Christmas vacation, he returned to school early at Axel's request. As the train rumbled north, he looked up from his stack of journals now and then and noticed the Catskills thick with snow, or a crow flying low above the frozen Hudson, but mostly he kept his eyes on his work. The brindled dog at the train station had to bark twice before Sam stopped to pat him, walking on not to his room—the dorms were still closed—but to a small brick house two blocks from campus, where Axel, unmarried then, lived in happy squalor. Clothes on the floor, sheets on the couch (he always had visitors); Sam was welcome to stay, he said, the ten days until the semester started. A minute after Sam dropped his bag, they headed for the lab, which was warm and stuffy despite the bitter cold outside, electric bulbs glowing inside the old bookcases Axel had turned into incubators. Sam found a path through the tumble of plates and coffee cups and reprints and manuscripts, books lying open everywhere, cockroaches investigating the huge stain—molasses?—on the journal that Duncan, whom Sam then knew only as Axel's senior student, had left at his place.

Axel, Duncan, and two other students, both juniors, worked at desks pushed into an island at the center of the room; Sam's place was at the sink, shaking used food from soiled bottles, or at the counter, filling wooden racks with wide-mouthed homeopathic vials. From there he'd watched Duncan mating virgin females in bottles for which Sam had prepared the food, later shaking the

·

etherized offspring onto counting plates, bending over dissecting scopes, shouting happily when he found something unexpected. In November, he'd discovered a new mutant, which Axel had sent to Columbia, and that had made Sam feel—not that he wanted to be Duncan, not even that he wanted to be Duncan's friend (he was shallow, Sam thought even then, and prone to leap to easy conclusions), but that he wanted a chance to work on his own.

Now he plunged into the clutter, planning to take over Duncan's chair the minute he finished cleaning up. Axel asked if he thought maintaining the stock cultures for the Genetics and Heredity course, even as he was enrolled in it, might be too much.

"I'll be fine," Sam said, bending to his glassware. Everything stank of overripe bananas. "It's no problem at all. I could do more, if Duncan gets too busy . . ."

Axel squashed a fly on the counter and laughed. "You have to sleep sometime," he said. "Although, personally, I think sleep is overrated. Do you want to hear what went on at the meeting?"

"Please," Sam said. "I've been dying for news."

Later—at Woods Hole, in Moscow, every place where, after long days in the lab, he'd end up drinking with fellow geneticists—Sam would try to describe what he felt as he listened to Axel summarize that extraordinary paper from the international meeting in Toronto. As if he'd sprouted extra eyes, which let him see a new dimension. Or as if his brain had added a new lobe, capable of thinking new thoughts. *It is commonly said that evolution rests upon two foundations—inheritance and variation; but there is a subtle and important error here. Inheritance by itself leads to no change, and variation leads to no permanent change, unless the variations themselves are heritable. Thus it* *is not inheritance <u>and</u> variation which bring about evolution, but the inheritance <u>of</u> variation.* Surely the name of the man who'd written that—Hermann Muller—deserved a whole separate shelf in Sam's brain. Whenever he recited those crucial lines, others would chime in with more of Muller's essential insights: that in the cell, beyond the obvious structures, there must also be thousands of ultra-microscopic particles influencing the entire cell, determining its structure and function. That these particles, call them genes, were in the chromosomes, and in certain definite positions, and that they could propagate themselves. Magic, they all agreed. Magic!

For ten dazzlingly cold days that winter, before Duncan and the other students returned from their holiday, Axel and Sam talked about Muller's ideas while they worked together. Then Duncan returned for the spring semester, Axel showed Muller's paper to him—and suddenly they were planning experiments while Sam was sterilizing forceps. The whole semester went that way, until Duncan graduated and, for just a little while, got out of Sam's way.

❄

DURING THE DAY, when trying to move through the mass of people on deck was like being transported through an amoeba, Sam thought often about those early, blissful months in Axel's lab. Here, if Axel wasn't surrounded, he was absent. Reading in his berth, Duncan would say. Or napping, he's exhausted, talk to him at dinner. Each day would end with nothing Sam had meant to say said—and then it was night, when he kept thinking about that night.

•

The night in the lifeboat, the night on the water, which Axel had shared and which Duncan could never know. The night floating under the clouds and the moon, Sam's boat so flooded that it was in the sea as much as on it, everyone packed together as tightly as bodies in a collective grave. Shoulders pressed to others' shoulders, backs to chests, knees to hips; fifty-seven people who, once they were safely aboard the *City of Flint*, avoided those with whom they'd been so strangely intimate. The woman, for instance, who'd worn Sam's life belt: how was it that they didn't stick together? She had given her chance at life to her son, Sam had given his to her; the gesture might have bound them.

Yet she was in one of the bunks near the rear of the ship, nowhere near his cocoon of a hammock, and when he passed her on deck, they nodded politely and kept moving. Each time, he remembered what they'd seen of each other. What that woman— her name was Bessie—had seen of him. Instead of seeking her out, he'd move toward Laurel and Pansy and Maud, who'd turned out to be pleasant company, filled with impressions from their brief time in France and Italy and eager to talk about the news the radio officer relayed.

They kept him company at meals as well, where the questions he longed to ask Axel dissolved in the perpetual chatter. Duncan and Harold and George invariably settled close to Axel, who then would watch, ruefully, Sam thought, as Sam found a separate place.

They were more interesting? They were safer. Harold and George taught at the same little college in Massachusetts, had roomed together at the congress, and, indeed, had come over together with Duncan, yet they gossiped about common acquaintances and speculated on jobs and funding as if they hadn't just had weeks of each other's company. Duncan chimed in with news about colleagues in California, not just from the institute that his former advisor had established and where he still worked, but from Berkeley and Stanford as well. Even Axel, a fixture now at the college where Sam had first met him, offered modest nuggets gleaned from meetings in New York. Whose lab was expanding, who had lost support. Whose marriage had broken up.

What did any of this have to do with science? Or with the reality of what had just happened to them? The meals seemed doubly hard when Sam thought of how much better he'd done recently with his old roommate, Avery. On the inexpensive pre-congress tour, which he'd taken largely so he could see where Avery worked, they'd been scheduled for a day and a half in Cambridge. Sam had skipped all the other sites to visit Avery's lab at the Cavendish, where he'd admired Avery's new X-ray facility and studied his lab notebooks. Together, they'd happily discussed their most recent projects.

By the time the motor coach left Cambridge on Sunday, Sam had felt like he knew his friend again—and it was this, he thought, staring glumly into his pea soup during one particularly trying lunch, that had made him optimistic about what might happen with Axel in Edinburgh. So they had not, before the meeting, seen each other in seven years; so their correspondence had shrunk to an occasional exchange of reprints. His warm meeting with Avery had convinced him that he and Axel would also slip back into their old, easy ways.

•

Through Grasmere and Keswick the following day, on to Edinburgh that afternoon: six hundred geneticists, from more than fifty countries! New work, new ideas; a chance to renew old friendships. He'd been horribly disappointed to find that the Russian geneticists, some of whom he knew from his time in Moscow and Leningrad, had been denied permission to travel. After that, nothing else went the way he'd hoped; the session began to unravel almost as soon as it started. Germany and the Soviet Union signed their pact and the German scientists left. Then the delegates from the Netherlands followed the Germans, and the Italians followed them. In ones and twos the British scientists trickled off to join their military units, while the French left all at once.

By Saturday, when Sam gave his talk, the Poles and others from the Continent were also gone, leaving only a spotty crowd of Americans, Canadians, South Africans, Australians, and New Zealanders to listen. Where was it written that they all had to turn against him? That what he said would actually enrage them? Duncan, who spoke later that day, set his own prepared talk aside and instead spent his time refuting every aspect of Sam's presentation. He was so familiar with the last decade of Sam's work—he had read all of Sam's papers, Sam understood then—that he did an excellent job.

Here on the ship, the sound of Duncan's voice sometimes caused Sam such pain that even if Duncan weren't always blocking his way to Axel, he would have wanted to strike him. He'd come around a corner, find Axel and Duncan, catch Axel's eye, see Axel wave—and then Duncan would turn and smile falsely, and he'd keep moving until he ran into Bessie, which would spin him in yet another direction. Then at night, lying like one of a long row of larvae among his canvas-shrouded fellow passengers, he'd return to his night in the boat, when Bessie's knees and shins had pressed uncomfortably into his lower back. With every stroke of the oar he freed himself briefly from that pressure, only to thump back into her bones. He came to hate her legs, then to hate her. But later, when they stopped rowing and waited for the sun to come up, he grew so cold that he sought her legs on purpose. Her shivering shook Sam's body too, and also that of Aaron, her little boy, who was pressed into the hollow between her chest and her bent knees. Aaron's whole right side—shoulder, arm, torso, leg— over the course of those hours also pressed itself against Sam's back. All the adults faced the same way, unable to see each other's expressions, sensing their levels of misery through the contact of their wet flesh. Bessie's crying passed from her chest through Aaron's side and into Sam's back, and his groans passed the other way, a wave moving through the boat. Her back had to be pressed into someone else's legs, and that person's back to the next and the next and the next. Each time he went over this, he imagined that Axel was listening and that he in turn would describe his own night.

Meanwhile the *City of Flint* kept steaming sturdily through the waves, miles passing but far too slowly: how to get through the days? A grim-faced doctor, still waiting for word of his wife and daughter, busied himself by organizing the ship's hospital, stitching up the survivors' wounds, tending to burns and scrapes. He'd been in a boat that overturned and had spent hours floating alone, clinging to a bit of rudder. What, Sam wondered, did he

·

think of when he stopped working? A Canadian girl, ten years old, had been struck on the head by a falling beam when the torpedo first hit the *Athenia* and, although she'd been conscious during the night in the lifeboats and her first day on the *City of Flint*, had fallen into a coma; the doctor watched over her closely, and Sam would sometimes sit beside her, reading out loud from a novel Laurel had loaned him.

Eavesdropping at dinner, pretending to listen to Lucinda and Maud but actually straining to hear Axel's response to Duncan's questions, Sam learned that Axel, when he wasn't resting, passed the hours reading books he'd borrowed from Harold and George. Harold, meanwhile, kept busy with the little daily newspaper he now posted each morning on a bulletin board, around which people gathered to read his notes of the ship's progress and bits of friendly gossip. The college girls put on a fashion show, herding good-humored volunteers along an improvised runway as others voted for the most outlandish costume. On a day when the sea was very smooth, pierced now and then by leaping fish, Sam wrote letters to his mother and to the woman he was seeing back home, neither of whom knew that his changed plans had put him aboard the *Athenia*. The letters, which couldn't be sent until they reached Halifax, were as useless as curled wings on a fly, but time passed as he tried to describe—not the explosions, not the bodies, not his night in the boat. Not what had happened in Edinburgh, nor what Duncan had done, nor his estrangement from Axel. The shapes the clouds made in the sky, then. The porpoises leaping in sets of three and five. The brave little girl in her improvised romper and the kind women, strangers before boarding this ship, who cared for her.

•

He found a corner where he could wash his face in the morning, and an exercise route—from the open middle deck in front of the smokestack, around the port side of the deckhouse, to the bow, and back down the starboard side—on which, if he rose early enough to beat the crowds, he could pace like a horse in a mine. No matter what he did, or how he arranged his days, he ran into Duncan. When Duncan stopped near the air scoops to light a cigarette, the solid sheet of hair lying over his forehead flapped up and down in the breeze like a lid. Why was he there when Axel, whom Sam so much wanted to see, was always where Sam was not? And when Sam went down below one night to the talent show that Maud and Lucinda had organized, Axel was there, but there with Duncan.

Men sang "Danny Boy" and "Begin the Beguine," children tap-danced, a woman pleated an accordion. Two sailors whacked at fiddles as two more whirled about. Axel came over to suggest that Sam do some little tricks involving toothpicks and gumdrops, which he was good at and used to offer up at parties: two minutes to make a model of a locomotive, a minute—Avery had first taught him this—for a sugar molecule. Sam was almost tempted, remembering how at Woods Hole he'd entertained his companions with models of sea squirts and the polymer backbone of cellulose, but then he looked at Duncan, right by Axel's side and waiting for him to make a fool of himself, and he declined.

Instead, Duncan stepped forward and, in his surprisingly sweet tenor voice, sang a bland version of the song for which, years ago, he used to invent ribald verses, entertaining the students during the summer they'd both spent at Woods Hole. Sam had just finished his junior year at college then; Duncan had been in his second year of graduate school, studying with Axel's teacher, Thomas Morgan. Almost everyone important in their new field was at the biological station that summer, investigating some aspect of genetics or embryology or both. Sam, one of the few undergraduates taking the invertebrate course, paid his tuition by waiting tables at the mess hall and collecting specimens for his teachers. On nights when the moon was in the right phase, he'd bus his tables, drop his apron, and head for the *Cayadetta*'s dock with a long-handled net and a tray of finger bowls. His desire to earn his teachers' approval was as ruthless as the lantern he held over the water, dooming the mating clam worms that spiraled upward.

Afterward, he skipped the gatherings at the ice cream parlor and the visits to the movie house in Falmouth so that he could work on the project that had seized him. A scientist named Paul Kammerer had recently made two American lecture tours; his sensational work—VIENNA BIOLOGIST HAILED AS GREATEST OF THE CENTUR: *Proves a Darwin Belief,* one newspaper blared—was so interesting, and so controversial, that even Sam's mother had interviewed him for one of her articles. Kammerer claimed to have shown that when a change in the environment of his toads and salamanders caused an adaptive change in them—altered skin color, different reproductive behaviors—these changes could be transmitted to subsequent generations. A kind of heresy, Sam knew—the exact opposite of what he'd seen in the lab for himself. Although he'd breathed in his Quaker grandparents' conviction that the world can be improved, first Mr. Spacek and then Axel had trained him out of his unconscious assumptions that when individuals strengthened and developed their faculties, through vigorous use, they then passed that strengthening along. That the ones they stopped using were lost, and lost for good.

At Woods Hole, though, surrounded by interesting strangers pursuing so many different ideas, the truth had begun to seem more complex again, which made him read Kammerer's claims with real curiosity. Axel had taught him to question everything— didn't that include the beliefs that were quickly becoming conventions in their field? At night, roasting oysters on the beach, he and his classmates talked about Kammerer and speculated on the reasons why some biologists attacked him so furiously. Even those opposed to his conclusions were disturbed by that. They were all flirting with socialism then, some more than flirting; they sympathized when Kammerer complained that no one gave him a fair hearing. With the Great War just over, no one wanted to hear that inheritance wasn't everything, or that race and class characteristics passed on through generations might be altered.

Tiny, darkly tanned Ellen Eliasberg, a fellow student in Sam's invertebrate course, was moved by Kammerer's passionate statements about the necessity of man passing on what he acquired in the course of his lifetime to his children and his children's children. Sam was caught up by her arguments—and, at the same time, fascinated by the bad temper Duncan's advisor showed whenever anyone mentioned Kammerer's work.

"The leopard *can* change his spots?" he'd say mockingly. "Fathers *can* pass what they've learned to their sons? Why not just reject every bit of science done in the last century? Why not go right back to Lamarck and his folklore? Cave fishes and deep-sea

·

dwellers lose their eyes because they don't need them in the dark; moles have poorly developed eyes because they're in burrows most of the time; if an organ isn't used, it conveniently disappears, and if it's used often—why not point to the giraffe stretching his neck to reach for higher leaves?—it gets bigger. How long has that been believed? And yet Payne bred fruit flies in the dark for sixty-nine generations, without the slightest change in their eyes or behavior. In my own lab, we've seen well over one hundred new types arise spontaneously, with no environmental influence, each breeding true from the start. Overnight—literally, overnight!—eyeless flies have appeared from normal parents, by an obvious change in a single hereditary factor."

Then he'd say that the popular press was being fooled, once again, and foolishly misleading the public (here Sam thought of his mother; had she sorted this out?); he'd say Kammerer was a charlatan and a publicity seeker and perhaps even a fraud. He ranted so wildly that even Duncan looked uneasy, and Sam saw, for the first time, what might happen when the passion required to defend a new set of ideas went too far.

But he wanted to work, simply to work, and he tried to stay focused on that. The old wooden house where he bunked that summer was less than a block from the lab, surrounded by sand and scrubby pines, but during his first weeks he went there only to sleep. Every minute he could steal from his course and his jobs he spent designing an experiment that might prove or disprove what Kammerer contended. Instead of Kammerer's slow-growing salamanders and midwife toads, Sam decided to use his swiftly reproducing flies. And he'd work with their eyes, not only because variations in eye color had been the first and best-documented of the mutations observed in fruit flies but also because eyes and their development had always been central to these discussions.

He used fly cultures he'd kept for Axel, techniques he'd learned in his lab, a procedure he'd seen Duncan do in a different context. With a needle he ground to a very sharp point and then heated, he touched—just touched—the center of the red eye of a lightly etherized female fly; then he touched the other eye and laid the fly on a dry piece of paper, which he put into a little vial. A couple of hours later, he transferred the treated flies to a food bottle. In the few that survived the procedure he watched how the Malpighian tubules turned deep red and stayed that way. So: injury to one organ, the eye, caused what appeared to be a permanent change in another organ: an acquired characteristic.

Later, he mated the treated females to normal males and proceeded as usual. Amid the next generation he found a few mutants—yellow body, narrow eyes, twisted penis—as expected. And also, unexpectedly, seventeen flies, both male and female, with red Malpighian tubules. This was peculiar, and completely compelling: what did it mean? Immediately, he started breeding these to each other. None of their offspring showed the red tubules, but that might mean nothing; the trait was likely recessive, and he had only a small sample.

Duncan and most of the other students had a sense of what he was doing; they wandered in and out of the open labs and they all talked not only while they worked but also during their outings. Still, no one knew the details until the director asked him to give a presentation at one of the season's last Friday night gatherings. He was nervous when he spoke—undergraduates were rarely asked to speak in front of the whole community—and he referred to earlier work that he hoped might support his own. In particular, a recent symposium that many in his audience had attended and that had examined this crucial question: *could* an injury to one generation cause an effect that was inherited by the next?

Swiftly, he moved through those other researchers' results. One had demonstrated the transmission of acquired eye defects in rabbits, which seemed to have the characteristics of a Mendelian recessive. Others had shown what seemed to be inheritable effects of injury from alcohol, lead, radium, and X-rays. Perhaps, though, this was parallel induction: had a physical agent acted simultaneously on *both* the germ cells and the somatic cells, producing changes independently in each, or had the change induced in the body actually affected the germ cell? Which was the mechanism at work with Sam's flies, and would either case argue for evolution directly guided by the environment? Sam saw Duncan in the audience, listening intently and taking notes, although he didn't ask any questions afterward. Other hands did wave, though, and Sam was pleased with the way he guided the passionate, occasionally contentious, but civil discussion that followed.

In September, when he returned to college and reported all this to Axel, Axel shook his head and said he wished Sam had consulted him before throwing himself at such a controversial issue. He should never, Axel said, have presented this to so many eminent scientists before testing his hypotheses more thoroughly. Then he said that while he didn't yet trust Sam's results, they were intriguing and Sam should push the work forward. He'd supply the flies and the other materials; when the time came, he'd help Sam write up the results. "Although it would have been better," he added, "if you'd done even more while you were still at Woods Hole."

"I should have," Sam admitted.

And would have, he knew, if he hadn't gotten involved with Ellen. Four years Sam's senior, presently working as a biology instructor at Smith, she'd spent the previous year in England, where she'd cut off her hair, befriended several brilliant women, and taken up feminism and eugenics. One opinion she held strongly was that exceptionally intelligent people—"Like you," she said to Sam, during a collecting trip at Quisset, "and me"— should have children together, which would improve the world. Later, she and Sam decanted their specimens side by side, and a few nights after that, when a crowd of students got drunk on the beer two chemists had brewed, they ended up entwined in the dusty wooden attic over the supply room.

The next day, when Sam apologized for what had happened, Ellen calmly claimed it as her own idea and said Sam had only done what she wanted. At the beach, she wore a daring wool-jersey bathing suit that clung to her wiry shape and ended mid-thigh, the white trim disturbingly like underwear, and when she swam she looked to Sam, with her close-cropped hair, like one of the elegant spiraling clam worms he collected at night. He had no idea how he felt about her; he was nineteen, and she let him make love to her. Sam couldn't imagine why.

"Because I want to have several children, starting soon," she

·

told him. "And you're such a good specimen. You're tall"—here she tapped one of Sam's fingers—"big-boned, and bright"—*tap, tap*—"hardworking, sturdy, even-tempered."

By then she was working on Sam's second hand, having thrust the first inside her blouse. His hands on her small, pointed breasts, his mouth in the hollow of her throat, her bony feet on his back. He was completely inexperienced when they met; he was astounded. For the last two weeks of his stay at Woods Hole he was with Ellen every night. "If I'm pregnant," she said the day they parted, "we'll get married. If not . . ."

Not, as it turned out, although they met as often as they could during Sam's last year of college, several times near Sam and twice in Massachusetts, the second time just after Duncan proved him wrong.

What kind of a person would, in utter secrecy, interrupt his own project to replicate a fellow worker's experiments and double-check his results? Duncan published a paper noting that the pre-liminary results of a young student investigator—here he named Sam—presented orally and informally, had sufficiently interested him to push those experiments further. When he did, he found that in flies whose eyes had been burned, the Malpighian tubules indeed turned red, and that a small number of the offspring of those flies also had red tubules.

But he also saw something Sam had failed to see, perhaps because he'd been so absorbed with Ellen. In his early work in Morgan's lab, Duncan had occasionally noticed—or so he wrote; Sam wondered if it wasn't Morgan himself who saw this—fly lar-vae feeding on the eyes of dead adults that had fallen on the food at the bottom of the culture bottle; this had colored the intestines of the larvae red. After seeing the initial data (and this did sound like him; he could test a chain of reasoning like a crow pulling at the weak spots in a carcass), Duncan had suddenly wondered if the pigment might be carried from the larvae through the pupa stage, possibly appearing in the adults.

He crushed the eyes of some flies, mixed them with yeast and agar from a culture bottle, and added larvae; their intestines soon became filled with the red food, and a bit later the Malpighian tubules, visible through the larval walls, became deep red. The larvae pupated; adults emerged; their tubules too were red. Variations with different foods showed clearly that some component of the red pigment in the crushed eyes passed from the digestive tract of the larvae into the Malpighian tubules and remained there into the adult stage. Sam's larvae had eaten the damaged eyes of dead flies and that—not a response to the injury itself—had colored their tubules. Sam had found not an acquired characteristic, but simply a transient response to diet. Acquired characteristics were not—could not be, Duncan said—inherited.

Sam was wrong, he'd been proven wrong, but at first that didn't seem so serious—why would people hold his curiosity against him? He was young, he was enthusiastic; he'd seen a big question in Kammerer's work and explored it open-mindedly, trying to follow the data rather than his own preconceptions; he'd shared his findings honestly. Leaving Woods Hole for his last year of college, he'd sensed that others saw him as a wonderfully promising student, welcome anywhere. Six months later, the recent work he'd done in Axel's lab rendered pointless by Duncan's

·

paper, those same people seemed to regard him as a dubious young man who'd overreached himself. Even Axel, after reading the copy Duncan sent specially to him, a little handwritten note—*I'm sorry*—scrawled at the top, groaned and went for a long walk before sitting down with Sam.

"I should have seen that," Axel said when he returned. "If you'd kept in touch with me over the summer, if we'd been talking about your experimental design . . . I should have seen that before Duncan did." Sam couldn't tell whether Axel was more angry at himself for missing it or proud of having taught Duncan so well.

In the wake of that paper, Sam knew he wouldn't be welcome at Columbia, where everyone had assumed he'd follow Axel and Duncan to graduate school. But with Axel's help he found a place in a small program in Wisconsin, run by a sound but middling geneticist. Not one of Morgan's golden boys, like Bridges or Sturtevant; not even someone at the top of the second tier (which was how Axel disparagingly characterized himself), but a man who knew he was lucky to have a lab and the funding for a few graduate students.

Sam spent that last summer in Axel's lab, maintaining the cultures and leaving everything in order for Axel's next helper, wishing, all the time, that he could be discussing new projects with Axel. But Axel, collaborating with a friend in Texas, was seldom there, and Ellen, who might have helped him settle into his new life, instead did the reverse. If she'd gotten pregnant during his last year of college, nothing, Sam knew, could have wedged them apart—but she didn't, and didn't, and when summer came and she still wasn't pregnant, they didn't see each other for

·

several months. In August, she backed out of her offer to drive to Wisconsin with him and went to Woods Hole instead. Before Thanksgiving, she was gone.

For a long time, Sam was able to avoid her. His luck ran out after seven years, at a big meeting in Washington where Duncan received a prestigious award. Sam was moving toward the back of the auditorium, having just heard a talk by a maize geneticist and hoping to escape before Duncan spoke. He ran into Ellen in the middle of the aisle, herding two boys and a girl, all resembling Duncan in some way, toward the special seats at the front set aside for the prizewinner's family. She introduced the children awkwardly and asked how Sam was doing.

"Fine," Sam said. "Just finishing my thesis." She and Duncan had married before he'd even started that work. After which Axel, as if inspired by them, had married a mathematician he'd met in Texas, moved to a leafy street twenty minutes from the college, and promptly produced a son.

"We miss you at Woods Hole," she said.

"Handsome boys," he said, avoiding their eyes.

Tugging at her younger son's collar, bending to adjust the skirt on her dark-haired little girl, Ellen said that she and Duncan went back every year, always with the children, who loved it. But nothing had ever been as wonderful as her second summer there. When, Sam knew by then, she'd already left him but he didn't know it. When she and Duncan had both returned and Sam, in the shadow of his big failure, had been unable to join them.

ON THE LIFEBOAT, before the sun rose, when the night was at its coldest and the waves were tossing them about and when, having long since thrown up everything he'd eaten the previous day, Sam was retching painfully and Bessie's hand was lightly patting the back of his neck, he had thought about his calm hand bringing the needle's point so lightly, so deftly, to each *Drosophila* eye. How the flies' wounds had sometimes stuck to the food, and to each other; how those that lived were weak for several days, some unable to eat. Here on the ship, shaken about like a fly in a test tube, he too was having trouble eating. One evening he learned that while most of the geneticists who'd been on the *Athenia* with him had been picked up by the British destroyers, two were apparently lost. And on the eighth day of the crossing, while he scored patterns in the oatmeal that was one of the few things left to eat, Sam learned that the little girl who'd been in a coma had finally died.

Gloom spread through the ship as each seating heard the news, and later Sam saw Bessie, near the bow, comforting her son, Aaron, who was crying. He and the girl had been friends, Sam thought, or at least known each other the way children even of different ages do when confined together. He couldn't stop himself from walking over to Aaron and squatting down beside him. He rested his hand on Aaron's back, his fingertips moving gently.

"Shh," he said. "It's all right." Which was what he'd said in the boat, when Aaron was so cold and sick that he was crying. Also this was what Bessie had said to Sam. Now she said, "He's taking this very hard."

"Were they close?" Sam asked. The two geneticists who'd

drowned, husband and wife, had worked at a small Minnesota college and traveled only rarely to international gatherings. Sam hadn't met them at the congress, but he had on the ship, and he'd envied them when they came down hand in hand to what would be their last dinner. Axel had said, at that same meal, how much he'd been missing his wife and son.

"She used to take him for walks around the deck, when she was bored," Bessie said, gesturing toward their own crowded railings, so packed with passengers eager for air—they were expecting rain—that strolling was out of the question. "They played make-believe. You know, the way children will: I'll be the mommy and you be the little boy, and I'll get you ready for school . . ."

"She sounds sweet," Sam said. The figures crowding the railings separated, moved together again, bunched, and dispersed, long lines forming only to condense into shorter segments.

"Not always—once she pinched him hard enough to leave a mark."

Aaron shrugged off Sam's hand and pushed himself more firmly into Bessie's legs. "Do you have children?" she asked, smoothing her son's hair.

"I don't," Sam said, and if Duncan and Harold hadn't joined them just then, he might have told Bessie how pained he'd been when he understood that he likely never *would* have any. Ellen, who couldn't get pregnant with him, had gotten pregnant instantly with Duncan; no woman he'd been with since had had so much as a scare. Sometimes, when he'd had too much to drink (throughout Prohibition, he and his friends had always had access to lab

•

ethanol), he used to joke around with a toothpick-and-gumdrop figure he called Mr. Heredity. *Look at me!* he'd have the figure say. *Interested since childhood in how we inherit traits, but I can't reproduce!* But although he laughed as hard as anyone when Mr. Heredity drooped his gumdrop head, later, when he began to grasp the fact that no one would ever have his hair or his blocky nose, his height or his big hands, he felt quite otherwise. The day his heart stopped, the day he got hit by a bus (the day a torpedo sank the ship that was taking him home), everything that had led to his father and mother and converged in him would be extinguished.

But here were his colleagues, bearing down. He managed a smile as they greeted him and, looking at Bessie and Aaron, asked if they could do anything to help. Sam introduced them only by name, without explaining how he knew them.

"We're fine," Bessie said.

Impossible to focus on her and Duncan at the same time. Instead, Sam kept his eyes on the unusually turbulent sky. Great soft gray clouds piled one atop the other, pushing each other aside like wrestling dogs.

Bessie said, looking only at him, "Margaret's death made Aaron miss his father more than usual. He keeps thinking something's happened to him, that he won't be there when we get home. Those men we saw in the water . . ." She picked Aaron up and left.

Duncan watched them walk away and then turned back to Sam, eyes bright with curiosity. "You were in the same lifeboat?"

Sam nodded. He'd told Duncan nothing about the night in the boat; what Duncan knew of the torpedo, the flames, the boats in the water, he knew from other survivors, not from him.

•

"If you ever want to talk," Duncan said, pushing aside his floppy hair, "I'm happy to listen."

※

AFTER SAM GRADUATED from college, he mostly kept his work to himself. Axel, busy with his new wife and son, also had new students to train and increasingly relied on his connection to Duncan, who was doing very well as part of his advisor's group. Duncan and his colleagues shared fly strains with Axel's lab; Axel and his students collaborated on papers with them, which helped them all. Sam worked alone, steadily and quietly, throughout his years in graduate school, doing nothing without his advisor's explicit approval, choosing a thesis project closer to his advisor's heart than to his own and committing to it entirely. He kept in close touch with Avery, who'd gone to England by then, and Avery helped him modify an X-ray source so he could radiate his *Drosophila* and look for mutations. The experiments he completed were nowhere near as flashy as Muller's work in this area, nor did he and his advisor gather anywhere near as much data—they were working along parallel tracks at first and then, after Muller had yet another big breakthrough, in support of what he'd already shown—but Sam knew it was solid work, a bandage for his dented reputation. By 1930, when he got his degree, he was able, despite the growing effects of the crash, to find a position in Missouri. In between teaching sections of general biology, he worked every spare minute in his own lab, grateful for what he'd been able to salvage and trying not to envy Duncan, who had followed his advisor out to California and had a much better job.

•

Half his salary he sent to his mother, who, in the wake of both her parents' deaths, had taken in boarders but even so was still struggling to hang on to the Philadelphia house. When he lost his job in 1933, he knew she felt the blow too. Although he wrote to everyone he'd ever met, there were no positions to be had. Axel, who temporarily had to close his own lab, could find him nothing, and Duncan couldn't, or wouldn't, help, despite being the protégé of someone who'd just won a Nobel Prize. When Sam had nothing to lose and was on the verge of going back home, he appealed to the man whose paper had so inspired him that first winter at college, and whose field he now shared.

He'd written to Muller a few times during graduate school, sending results that confirmed or extended Muller's own and asking about his latest work. At a conference, Muller had tracked Sam down and inspected his most recent data closely; after that, they'd continued to correspond about interesting questions. If a quantum of light could, as Niels Bohr suggested, trigger photosynthesis, was it also the case that an individual ionization caused a mutation? Did chromosome breaks result from radiation's direct or indirect effects? After Muller left Austin in the wake of a scandal involving his support of a Communist-leaning student newspaper, he went to Berlin, where, he wrote to Sam, he was collaborating with a brilliant Russian scientist who shared his interest in using the tools of physics to explore the nature of the gene. The work was intriguing, the company stimulating, but just as he was settling in, Hitler was appointed chancellor and soon his colleagues began to lose their jobs. Muller accepted his Russian friend's invitation to help set up a research program and

·

most recently had written to Sam from the Institute of Genetics in Leningrad.

Was it possible, Sam wrote him, that given his background and their shared interests, he could be of some use at the institute? Secretly, he thought they also shared a disgust with what was going on in their country, the mad inequities that seemed to be destroying every good thing. In Russia, Sam thought, science might assume its rightful role, and scientists, instead of being separated into little fiefdoms ruled by petty kings, would work under the shelter of the state, free to follow their best ideas. He was thrilled when Muller, so enthusiastic himself about the Soviet experiment, found money for a position in which Sam was, if not quite an independent investigator, more than a student.

Soon Sam was living in Leningrad, exploring chromosomal rearrangements and learning that many of the apparent point mutations caused by X-ray treatment were actually recombinations of broken fragments. Segments were lost, segments were duplicated; he began to get a sense of what size a gene might be, and how it might function when moved to a new position. What if natural mutations were actually rearrangements of the particles in the chromosomes, rather than changes to the particles themselves? Muller proved to be an excellent guide. Not a teacher, as Axel had been; not really a friend, like Avery; he was clearly Sam's superior, but he was accessible and kind, and Sam was thrilled to be working with someone he'd admired for so long.

It hardly mattered that, with housing short everywhere, Sam had to sleep in the corners of other scientists' rooms, for a while in a bed behind a curtain in the laboratory, later in a basement hall.

•

Everything was crowded, everyone was improvising; he was glad to be part of the common flow, and even the struggle to find supplies was worth it—such work, for such a purpose! Surrounded by Russians day and night, he learned the language quickly. And when the institute was moved to Moscow, Sam went too, leaving behind several friends and a woman with whom he'd had a brief affair.

Writing to his mother—he tried to write home twice a month—he described the farmers and engineers he met, the German Jews who'd sought refuge in the Soviet Union as the Nazis rose to power, the ardently socialist Englishmen and discontented Americans. He met men who'd soldiered in several wars, including one who'd fought against Germans at the beginning of the Great War and then later, in the province of Archangel, with the Reds against Americans. *He showed me the white cotton overcoat he'd worn,* Sam wrote, *which had made him invisible in the snow. He claimed that once, as he'd been scrounging for food in the streets, he'd seen an American soldier leap from the top of a gigantic wooden toboggan run and onto the ice below. Really, I am living in the most remarkable place.*

That winter, as the snow fell and fell—he was never warm, no one had enough fuel—Sam thought often of that soldier suspended in the air. Leaping from, or leaping toward? For all the hardships of daily life here, he still felt freer than he had since his time in Axel's lab, and he moved through Moscow with a sense he hadn't had in years of everything being interesting. At the Medico-Genetics Institute he saw hundreds of pairs of identical twins—how eerie this was, each face doubled!—being studied like laboratory mice. He visited collective farms, and he met a geneticist named Elizaveta who'd discovered a remarkable mutant

.

fly a few years before Sam arrived. Walking toward her bench was like walking into Axel's lab for the first time, the air dense with the smells of ether and bananas and flies fried on lightbulbs, the atmosphere of delight. Elizaveta, who had long, narrow, blue-green eyes below the palest brows, said she knew that genes controlled development: but were they active all the time, or did each act only at a particular period of development, and lie dormant otherwise?

At meetings—so many meetings!—he listened to talks about the practical applications of genetics to agriculture and the Marxist implications of the theory of the gene. Once, in a dark room after a day of lectures, he watched a film called *Salamandra*, about an idealistic scientist who'd demonstrated Lamarckian inheritance in salamanders but was then betrayed by a sinister German who tampered with his specimens to make it look as though his results had been faked. Denounced, deprived of his job, he lived in exile until rescued by a farsighted Soviet commissar who proved his work had been right all along. Partway through, Sam grasped that this was a transposition of the life and fate of Kammerer, who'd killed himself after a researcher proved that some of his results had been faked. By then, his own big mistake seemed very far away.

Working all the time, excited by the new experiments in the lab, he ignored what was happening out on the streets until, after a while, even he couldn't avoid knowing about the party members being persecuted and executed, those who disagreed with Stalin disappearing. Intellectuals and scientists from different fields began to disappear as well, including geneticists, some of them

Sam's own colleagues. The director of the twins study vanished and his institute was dissolved. Elizaveta, more cautious than some, gave her flies to Sam and slipped away to her grandmother's village. Geneticists had failed, Sam read in the papers, to serve the state by providing the collectives with new crops and livestock that could thrive in difficult climates and relieve the food shortages. They were stuck in bourgeois ways of thought. If a society could be transformed in a single generation, if the economy could be completely remade, why couldn't the genetic heritage of crops or, for that matter, of man, be transformed as well?

In this context, Lamarck was a hero; and also Kammerer (Sam could see, now, why he'd been shown that film); and also the horticulturist Ivan Michurin, who'd claimed that through some kind of shock treatment he could transform the heredity of fruit trees, allowing their growth farther north. Trofim Lysenko, pushy and uneducated, rose up from nowhere to extend Michurinism beyond what anyone else could have imagined. Lysenko hated fruit flies, he knew no mathematics, he found Mendelian genetics tedious. Even his grasp of plant physiology was feeble. How could Sam take him seriously? Lysenko claimed that heredity was nothing so boringly fixed as the Mendelians said, but could be trained by the environment, endlessly improved. At a big meeting Sam attended at the end of 1936, Muller tried to rebuff Lysenko by clearly restating Mendelian genetics and outlining the institute's research programs. Lamarckian inheritance, Muller explained, could not be reconciled with any of the evidence they'd found.

Sam was amazed when some in the audience actually hissed,

and more so when, after Lysenko responded by dismissing all of formal genetics, those same people stood and cheered. Genetics was a harmful science, Lysenko said, not a science at all but a bourgeois distortion, a science of saboteurs. Muller and his like were wrecking socialism, preventing all progress, whereas he would now completely refashion heredity! His Russian was failing him, Sam kept thinking; Lysenko couldn't be saying this. What should be so, must be so? Yet his friends heard the same thing. Those who doubted him, Lysenko said, were criminal. A theory of heredity, to be correct, must promise not just the power to understand nature but the power to change it.

Muller, after making careful arrangements to protect his colleagues, left the country early in 1937, and Sam followed a few weeks later, first selecting breeding stock from the best of Elizaveta's flies, and then destroying all the papers and letters he'd received from his Russian friends. *Of course I understand why you need me to return to the United States,* he carefully wrote to his mother, who'd requested no such thing but could be counted on to understand that his letters were likely being read. Back in Philadelphia, writing up his last results from the Moscow lab in the small bedroom where he'd slept as a child, the familiar sound of his mother working in the living room complicated by the movements of the two teachers with whom she now shared the house, Sam began another search for employment. This time he had better luck, finding a position at a small college near the western edge of Illinois. For a while, as he was trying to set up yet another lab— how many times could a person order glassware, brushes, ether, drying racks, all the bits and pieces needed to do the smallest

·

experiment?—he thought about changing fields entirely. If science in the United States was controlled by a few powerful people, and science in the Soviet Union was nothing but a branch of politics—then what was the point of doing anything? Perhaps he'd do better at farming, or statistics, or auto mechanics.

Soon enough, though, he got caught up in the life of a place that at first had felt to him like nowhere. His better students were curious and eager to learn, and he found that he had to hurl himself at a problem again, simply to give them something to do. He started a genetics course in addition to his sections of general biology; he bought a little house with two large trees; he met a woman he liked, who planted vegetables in his backyard and taught him how to cook chard. The college gave him an excellent incubator, as well as some other crucial equipment. Through the fly-exchange network he was able to get some useful stock, which in turn put him in touch with many of the researchers trained in Morgan's lab: not only Axel but also Harold and George (that was how he first met them) and, inevitably, Duncan, who immediately mailed to Sam's new address all the papers he'd published while Sam was abroad. Once Sam solved some difficulties with mites and temperature fluctuations, he was back in business and, after hiring a couple of student helpers, began a new set of experiments. For one particular project, he used Elizaveta's flies.

When the fly cultures he'd smuggled in were established, he turned, with a sense of recovering his younger self, to investigating them. Like some of the curiosities naturalists had noticed and collected for years—crustaceans with legs where jaws or swimmerets should be, plants with petals transformed into

·

stamens—Elizaveta's flies shared the property that one organ in a segmental series had been transformed into another. How were those homeotic mutants produced? And were those variations heritable or caused by damage to the developing embryo? An acquaintance of Axel's had discovered a true-breeding homeotic mutant he called bithorax, in which the little stabilizing structures normally found behind the forewings had been transformed into a second set of wings; Elizaveta had worked with that four-winged mutant, and also with an even odder one called aristapedia, which had legs growing where the antennae should be. Endlessly fascinating, Sam thought, and he began to investigate how a mutation to a single gene could cause such massive effects.

Months passed, a year of hard work passed; thousands of cultures and tens of thousands of flies. In the mutant, he learned, the antennal discs developed early, at the same time as the leg discs, allowing the evocator that normally instructed the leg discs to act on the antennal discs as well. *Evocator*: he loved that word. The chemical substance that acts as a stimulus in the developing embryo. How intriguing, how sensible, really, that the mutant gene didn't build a leg-like structure out of thin air. Instead it acted more simply and generally, altering the rate of development so that a whole pattern of growth occurred at a time and place where it ought not to be.

Others were working on this as well, but there was so much to do, along so many branching paths, that Sam had no sense of racing to solve a problem before someone else. Rather, the whole world seemed to shimmer, a delectable feeling he'd first had as a boy, working with Mr. Spacek: the act of throwing himself at one problem, *this* problem, lit up every other aspect of his experience in the world. Legs grew out of a fly's head because of a small change in timing; would his life have been different if his father had died earlier, or later? If he hadn't met Mr. Spacek when he did, or gone to college at sixteen and found Axel willing to teach him. If he hadn't met Avery or Ellen, hadn't met Duncan . . .

In this state of excitement, he'd gone to the congress in Edinburgh, where he presented his results and then connected that work with Goldschmidt's, with work on position effects and the possibility that the particles of heredity might move around, with the possibility that maybe all genetic changes were changes in development. Maybe genes weren't particles after all, weren't arranged like beads on a string, but were more like spiderwebs, susceptible to the influence of events in the cytoplasm; maybe they weren't quite as impregnable to outside influence as previously thought? He aimed his ideas at his former Russian colleagues, who should have been there but weren't; at Axel, who was there but had missed all the groundwork; at Muller, who'd found a temporary haven in Edinburgh and who, although distracted by the responsibilities of hosting the congress, still found time to come and listen to him. He sailed past his notes, avoiding the missteps of Kammerer and Lysenko, which he knew more vividly than most. Carefully, he speculated about the question of timing. When, in the course of development, might a tiny change cause massive later effects? Might inheritance not be far more complex than we'd guessed? When he finished speaking and looked out at the disgruntled faces in the audience—Duncan's face was red, Axel was poking his notepad with a pencil, Muller was gazing at him quizzically—he had a separate thought, which had nothing to do with inheritance. The first big leap he'd taken, with Kammerer's work, had turned out to be wrong. Was it possible that now no one could see the rightness of this second big leap, because of his first mistake?

＊＊

TWO BRIGHT WHITE ships, crisp and military-looking with broad red stripes across the bow, came out of the distance to meet them when they were still several hundred miles from Halifax. Sailors from the Coast Guard cutters transferred food, which they needed badly—oranges! Sam saw, and apples and cheese, potatoes and meat, fresh bread!—along with toothbrushes and hairbrushes, soap, shampoo, donated clothing, more blankets. Two doctors, wanting to examine the wounded to see who might need the alignment of broken bones checked with their portable X-ray machine and who should be transferred to the cutters for care, also came aboard.

For the first time in more than a week, Sam brushed his hair, cleaned his teeth with something other than a finger, and along with everyone else dipped into the new supplies to spruce up for that night's celebration. Officers from the cutters joined them, the captain extracted a case of whisky from the hold, a few passengers did what they could to decorate the deck while others, sensing home not far away, started to relax. All around him, Sam saw groups of people, faces suddenly scrubbed shades lighter, smiling and talking with the friends they'd made on the journey. These women bound to those, these students to those sailors; the college

·

girls—for him, still simply pleasant acquaintances—more closely attached to Duncan and Harold and George than he'd understood.

He felt, for a moment, unusually alone—more so when he saw that Axel, standing only a few feet away as the whisky was handed around, was barricaded by Duncan and Harold and George. Fanning out from them were Laurel and Pansy and Maud, talking to a young man Sam hadn't met; Lucinda, playing cards with the plant physiologist he'd first seen the day they were rescued; and Bessie and Aaron, sitting on one of the hatches, watching the constellations rise in the sky. Sam went over to Bessie's side as Pansy asked the young man what he planned to do when he got home.

"I'm still in school," he said shyly.

Sam looked up, spotting the stars of Pegasus. He remembered sitting on his father's shoulders, following the line of his arm as he traced out shapes overhead. *Look at the horse, do you see the dolphin? There's a whale* . . . Or did he remember those shapes from other evenings, much later, with his mother?

"I'm an art student," the young man continued. "I was traveling on a fellowship. But now . . ."

"You'll go back when the war is over?" Maud asked.

"What's the point?" he said. "Without my friend."

As Sam continued to pick from the glittering sky all the constellations he could remember, the student described how he and a dear friend from their school in Boston had split a traveling scholarship meant for one of them so that they could both see Europe. Despite their pinched budget and the signs of war cropping up everywhere, they'd visited Paris, Amsterdam, Verona, Venice, and even Berlin before returning to London, which they'd reached about the same time Sam reached Edinburgh. They too had found their ship home from Glasgow commandeered and later sailings either booked or canceled; they too had boarded the *Athenia* as a last resort. After the torpedo struck, he and his friend had managed to stay together in one of the last and most crowded lifeboats, which was also the one that had swung too close to the *Knute Nelson* and been crushed by its propellers.

"We dove into the water," the student said. "We dove and then we swam until we found a plank to hang on to. After a while we were picked up by another lifeboat. By then the *Southern Cross* was near us, so we rowed there. And then we got too close to the back of that . . ."

As his voice trailed away, Duncan, who had moved closer, said, "That wasn't the boat . . . ?"

The young man nodded, looking over at Axel and Duncan, then down at the deck, as if embarrassed that others had already heard the story and that some had seen the boat overturned. How could anyone be so unlucky? Not one but two lifeboats wrecked beneath him, his friend by his side through the torpedoing, through the first lifeboat's destruction, only to be lost. Sam closed his eyes. The ship rolled beneath him, a long, slow movement that made him dizzy. A hand touched his: Axel?

Bessie, Sam saw, when he opened his eyes. "Are you all right?" she asked.

"The whisky," Sam said faintly.

"Let me get you some water," she said, burrowing through the crowd. Duncan came up on Sam's other side and poked his shoulder. Jovially, stupidly, looking exactly the same as he had all

.

week—the new supplies had meant nothing to him—he said, "Too much to drink?"

Where had Axel gone?

Duncan stopped smiling. "You don't look very well."

"*Now* you worry about me?" Sam said.

An odd look crossed Duncan's face. "What went on at the congress—that's work. I don't agree with your work; I want it buried. Doesn't mean I want *you* buried. Until you came over the side of this ship, when I thought you might have drowned, I felt—"

"Oh, please," Sam said.

"You're impossible," said Duncan. He pushed past Sam and toward Harold and George. Then, finally, Axel reappeared, his expression concerned and his hand stretched toward Sam.

That night on the water, he'd scanned every boat they approached for Axel's face. Then, it hadn't mattered that they very seldom saw each other, that since Sam's time in Russia—no, before that, even—since Axel's marriage, perhaps, or since Sam had lost his first job and Axel hadn't been able to help him, they had drifted apart. He'd come to the meeting in Edinburgh hoping to repair this, tracking Axel through the corridors and cocktail parties like a devoted beagle, but although they'd had pleasant moments and caught each other up on the trivia of their lives, they'd never had the one, real, deep conversation Sam had been missing for so many years. And when Duncan attacked him so vigorously, Axel had not defended him. He hadn't supported Duncan—but he had not, in public, stood up for Sam. Instead, afterward, he'd pulled Sam toward a bench beneath a holly tree and questioned him closely about his results. Then he said—Sam felt this simultaneously as a blessing and a dismissal—that the work itself seemed promising. But why, Axel scolded, would he expose it to the world at such an early stage! If he would only stop speculating in public . . .

"It's all right," Axel said quietly. "It's all right. It wasn't as bad as all that."

"What wasn't?" Sam asked stupidly.

"When our boat overturned, under the stern of the *Southern Cross*—I saw you turn pale when that young man was speaking, the one we'd pulled from the water earlier, with his friend. I was afraid you might be thinking of what had happened to me and how much worse it might have been. But it wasn't so terrible, not really. I was in the water for a while but I didn't know I was hurt, I couldn't even feel the gash on my head. And I had an oar to cling to, and it wasn't too long before the crewmen from the *Southern Cross* found me and got me aboard. And then once I got here, and Duncan tracked me down, he arranged everything. If you were worrying about me, please don't."

How was he only now learning for sure what had happened to Axel? If they'd had time alone together, if they'd been able to talk . . . why hadn't Axel ever come to *him*?

"That's what happened to you?" Sam said now. "That night in the boat?" It wasn't so much what changed in the environment that altered a living organism; it was the *when*. A question of timing. When in the course of development does the event arrive that initiates the cascade of changes? "That's what happened?" he repeated.

"You knew that," Axel said. "Didn't you? I assumed . . ."

·

That Duncan had told him, Sam understood. That Duncan had relayed to him whatever Axel, stretched out on his berth, the bandage stuck to his oozing wound, had said. Axel must have told the story of his night on the water to Duncan, who lay on the floor in the place where Sam should have been. Perhaps he'd also relied on Duncan for whatever image he had of Sam's own night; he'd never asked Sam. "Duncan," Sam said feebly.

"I know," Axel said. "Really, I *do* know—he can be so exasperating sometimes, he probably told you more than he should have, he's always too dramatic. And he forgets how attached we are. I don't think it even occurred to him that you might be upset by hearing that something bad happened to me. Any more than he seemed to understand, in Edinburgh, how much he'd hurt me by attacking you."

Sam stared at him blankly. "But Duncan," he said, "the way you are with him . . ."

"I do the best I can," Axel said. "You must have found yourself in similar situations with students. You know how sometimes you have to treat the one you actually feel least close to as the favorite, just so he won't lose confidence entirely?"

"I do," Sam said miserably. Not that he'd ever felt treated as a favorite, but he knew what Axel meant: he'd always acted more kindly toward Sam than he really felt, so that Sam wouldn't be too crushed to go on.

"I've always had to do that with Duncan," Axel said. His bandage, unpleasantly stained, had shifted farther back on his head. "I still do, I find, in certain situations. And here—what could I do? He wanted so badly to take care of me."

"You gave him his start," Sam said, not knowing what he meant.

"It's a good thing I can count on you to understand," Axel said. The ship rolled gently, following the long, slow waves. "You're strong enough to go your own way. That's part of what makes your work so interesting. And part of what gets you into trouble."

❄

THE NEXT MORNING, still a day and a half out from Halifax, Axel and five other passengers were transferred to one of the cutters, which had excellent hospital facilities. The wound on his head wasn't healing properly; the Coast Guard doctor wanted to debride and resuture it without further delay. Sam, left behind with Duncan and Harold and George, could do nothing but wave goodbye and hope that they'd find each other later.

At the docks, a huge crowd greeted them, Red Cross nurses and immigration officials, family members of some of the survivors, local citizens who wanted to help, reporters from various papers: they were big news. Theirs had been the first ship sunk and theirs the first Canadian and American casualties; when the torpedo struck the *Athenia*, not even half a day had passed since Britain and Germany had gone to war. Nurses moved in to tend to the wounded; volunteers brought coffee and sandwiches; officials herded them into the immigration quarters, where they arranged baths and offered clean clothes. Scores of reporters moved in as well, eager for stories—what had they seen, what had they felt?—and then all the passengers began to talk at once, a hopeless tangle.

How could Sam be surprised when Duncan stepped forward? Of course it was Duncan who, never having set foot on the *Athenia*, still somehow managed to simplify, generalize, organize the scattered impressions. The reporters turned toward him, relaxing, already making notes: so much easier to follow his linear narrative, spangled with brief portraits of the survivors and vivid details of the crossing! He'd listened closely, Sam saw, to accounts of what he hadn't experienced himself. Bits of Axel's story flashed by, along with elements of the art student's, the plant physiologist's, Bessie's, and more. Bessie looked startled, as did some of the others, but what Duncan recounted wasn't untrue; it just didn't match much of what Sam felt, or what he knew to be important. If Duncan were to tell the story of Sam's working life it would, he knew, be similarly skewed—yet who knew him better than Duncan? Who had been with him for as much of the way?

Only Axel, who, leaving the *City of Flint* for the cutter, had held his hand to his stained bandage, looked crossly at the doctor, and said, "Really, I'm *fine*. I don't know why you want to move me like this. I'd rather stay here with my friends." And then had gestured toward Duncan and Sam, on either side of him.

Archangel

(1919)

❀

The first time she saw him, he was driving a sleigh. Not one of the boxy Red Cross ambulance sleighs, but a rough peasant sleigh with a frame of lashed saplings riding low between the runners. His chin rested on his chest; his hands lay loosely in his lap; the reins looped onto his knees, depriving the little pony of any instructions. The snow in the street was firmly packed, neither icy nor badly rutted, and the pony walked patiently, in a straight line, as if planning to continue past the hospital courtyard to the edge of the White Sea. A long bundle, half buried in hay, lay next to the driver—who must, Eudora realized, be sound asleep.

Already four months had passed since the war had ended for the rest of the world. Four months during which she'd thought, every day, that she'd be leaving North Russia. A bell boomed from the cathedral and caused the pony, who had a particularly

·

thick mane and lovely eyes, to look toward the blue domes. Still the driver let the reins lie slack. Eudora crossed the courtyard and waved, clicking her tongue softly against her teeth until the pony turned between the pillars and brought the sleigh to a stop at her feet. Beneath the usual mountain of garments—knitted vest over olive drab blouse under leather tunic beneath sheepskin-lined overcoat, topped with a thick balaclava helmet crowned in turn by a fur-lined white hat—she could barely see the man. His eyes were swollen, perhaps from failing to use the goggles pushed carelessly up on his hat. His gigantic mittens hung below his armpits from a white twill harness shaped like an A, which made him look like a massive child labeled for retrieval at a rail depot: A for what he was, an American soldier, or for Archangel province, where he, along with the other five thousand members of his regiment, had been sent. She touched his knee.

"What?" he said, waking instantly.

"It's all right," she said. The pony moved its lips and teeth, obviously hungry, and Eudora felt in her pockets for the apple she'd saved. Instantly the pony took it from her hand, chewing while the driver turned his head from side to side. "What are you looking for?" she asked.

"American Headquarters," he said. "Somehow I got turned around." His chunky nose was frostbitten at the tip, above a frozen mustache and raw lips. Undamaged, he would have been handsome. "This"—he gestured sharply toward the bundle beside him—"belongs to them."

"Down the block," she said, pointing toward the big pink building. She stepped closer to the sleigh and the bundle, which was six feet long, sunk deep in the hay, and wrapped in Army blankets blotched at one end. "The hospital's right here, though," she added. "Which you seem to need more than Headquarters. What is . . . ?"

"Havlicek," he said. He peeled back a blanket corner, allowing her a brief glimpse. "Four days dead, a hundred miles east of here. I've been driving ever since."

"You couldn't find an ambulance sleigh? Or a convoy?"

"It's complicated," he said, looking her over. "And you're too young to be here asking me questions. You're a nurse?"

She straightened her shoulders. "Not exactly," she said. "But I work here, my name's Eudora MacEachern. And I'm twenty-two, not that it's your business. I'll get some men to help you with your friend."

He picked up the reins. "Let them figure it out at Headquarters," he said harshly. "Since they did it." The pony began to move again, turning the sleigh in a wide arc.

❖

STORIES ARRIVED AT Archangel in disjointed shards, incomplete, which Eudora like everyone else plucked from the river of gossip. Her sources were Red Cross workers and engineers, ambulance drivers and, most of all, the wounded men who passed through her X-ray room on their way to surgery. Each knew painfully well what had happened right around him, but otherwise—they had no way to grasp the whole disorganized campaign. It was the opposite of France, one officer told her. No real fronts, no lines of battle, thousands of square miles of tundra and swamp and forest dotted by tiny outposts where clumps of men slept in schoolrooms or in the homes of Russian peasants. The wounded soldiers came to her in threes and fours, packed into the boxy ambulance sleighs like eggs in excelsior, or shipped along the rivers and railroad tracks that, on the map in the hospital lounge, showed as red lines splayed like bloody fingers. The fingertips were cut off from each other, able to communicate only with Headquarters, back at the palm. The palm gave orders; sometimes the palm remembered to send supplies. The red lines told her how long the men had traveled back to the palm, hence how much time a bullet or a fragment of shell or bone had had to shift and dig through flesh.

In the dark of her X-ray room, while she waited for her eyes to adjust, the soldiers told her about fighting along a river resembling the lower Mississippi, tundra oozing edgelessly into freezing water, one step on solid ground followed by another that plunged them over their heads. They talked about the lack of supplies and the lack of guns and the lack of ammunition, all piled uselessly here in the city of Archangel; about the British officer who in his panic, and with a quart of whisky in his hand, ordered the shelling of a bridge occupied by their own troops; about the French troops that refused to fight and the Allied planes that mistakenly bombed them and the medical supplies mistakenly left behind. In the dark one soldier told her, weeping, that he'd amputated another's leg with a pocketknife.

Mostly her soldiers were new recruits from Wisconsin and Michigan: boys who'd been drafted last June, trained for a few weeks, and then sent across the ocean. They'd all been expecting to go to France. In England, where they disembarked, they were issued greatcoats, mittens, hats, boots designed by the explorer Shackleton, and rifles designed for the Imperial Russian Army. Then they were shipped toward the Arctic Circle to fight against Russians, with whom they were not at war. Some succumbed to the influenza that swept the transports before reaching Archangel, while more were felled after landing. The soldiers still talked about those horrible weeks before the American hospital opened, when the Russian and British-run hospitals had overflowed and the sick had been crowded into barracks and docked barges.

That part she knew for herself. She'd changed beds and emptied bedpans and sponged soldiers with cool water, simple tasks mastered during her brief training as a nurse's aide. Only after the first battles against the Bolsheviks had she begun to use the skills she'd picked up in France, which had nothing to do with her official training but were what had sent her to a place even colder and snowier than her home in the northern Adirondacks. In the dark, as she worked with the X-ray apparatus to locate the objects that had pierced her soldiers, they asked: What are we doing here? Instead of answers, they got pamphlets and proclamations, which she got too, all purporting to explain the goals of the Allied Intervention. Something about forming a barrier inside which the Russians could reorganize themselves. Something about teaching them, by example and instruction, how to rebuild an army and distribute food.

But she knew perfectly well, as did her soldiers, that the Russian army had split into factions, fighting on opposite sides of a civil war in which the Allies seemed to have chosen a side. The

·

British had claimed that the Bolshevik government was in the hands of the Germans, thus that by fighting the Bolsheviks they were diverting German troops from France. And that this made them guests, not invaders, as the revolutionaries falsely claimed.

Eudora's soldiers, serving unhappily under British officers, following British orders and eating British rations, didn't see it that way. They saw chaos, confusion, peasants who hated them for invading their homes, troops on guard duty in Archangel living high while they starved and froze in the forest. They saw Bolshevik soldiers—Bolos, they called them—who seemed to be fighting with a purpose, and who left, on the snowy forest trails, eloquent pamphlets written in French and English and Russian, pointing out that the Allied soldiers were fighting for the rich, against the working people of Russia. *Come over to our lines, which are your lines!* they wrote. *We are your comrades, friends in the fight against the unprincipled capitalistic class.*

Some first learned about the Armistice from a Bolo armed with a loudspeaker, perched on the riverbank opposite their position and orating in perfect English, under a crescent moon, about the end of this unjust war, which had slaughtered the poor to fatten the rich. And after that, they waited, as did Eudora, for someone from American Headquarters to explain why they were still here. Instead they got another proclamation, which appeared on a wall in the hospital lounge and explained that now they were fighting Bolshevism, which was the same as anarchy, which was destroying Russia. They were here not to conquer Russia but to help her. *When order is restored here, we shall clear out. But only when we have attained our object, and that is the restoration of Russia.* Which object, in the eyes of soldiers, never *would* be attained; which meant they would never leave; which for some few meant that they had to shoot themselves.

That's what had happened, the rumors claimed, with the frozen soldier wrapped in blankets and bundled in that sleigh. Stories spread from Headquarters down through the barracks at Smolny, across the ice-locked river to the supply depot at Bakaritza, finally circling back to the receiving hospital. Eudora learned from these that the driver was one Private Boyd, a member of the ambulance company which, like the medical detachment, had been broken into small squads and attached to the soldiers scattered across the province.

Around the first of March, she heard, the platoons stationed at a tiny village near the easternmost front had been ordered back to Archangel, with the understanding that after a few weeks' rest they'd be sent to a place south of the city where the fighting had recently grown fierce. Boyd and an infantryman, Havlicek, had been held back from the others, ordered to detour ten miles off the route and deliver supplies to a village where a few men were guarding a telephone line. They'd unloaded cigarettes, canned margarine, tea, and tinned beef and then settled in for the night: Havlicek in the back corner of one peasant's house, Boyd near the stove in another, where two other soldiers were already billeted. In the morning, Boyd had woken to the sound of a shot and then a woman wailing from the doorway across the street. Inside, Havlicek lay in the corner, his revolver in his hand, the top of his head blown off and the walls sprayed with blood.

•

❖

SO, AT ANY rate, went the first version of the story's first fragment, which seemed to have traveled by way of one of the soldiers billeted with Boyd. At a Red Cross dance two days later, Eudora heard that the woman had been seen frantically brushing at the air with a broom, sweeping Havlicek's spirit from her house before he could settle in and torment her family. She tried to envision the woman, and then the house as described: peeled logs, sealed double windows, a grandmother sleeping on top of the tile stove, chickens and pigs in the corner, and outside, below the porch railing, a tower of frozen human shit. Had she gotten that right? Every day she was more aware of how little she knew about the world beyond the city, and of how the men at the front felt about the easy life led by the soldiers posted here.

This dance, for instance—a dance! Hundreds of people crammed into a big, warm, handsome room on the second floor of the old Technical Institute, occupations and nationalities as evenly represented as if a giant hand had reached down and gathered samples from across the city. Beyond the windows snow fell, goats wandered the streets, and the frozen river, framed by the pillars on the balcony, gleamed like radium, but in here, portraits of Imperial Army officers in sky blue breeches stared out from gilded frames. Outside people were starving and selling their silverware, their services, themselves, but in here doughboys and Tommies danced with Russian nurses and ward maids, Cossacks in tall gray hats chatted with Serbian soldiers, the six members of the self-appointed Armenian military mission admired each

·

other's epaulettes and polished scimitars. Supply officers made surreptitious deals involving cigarettes while the young editors of the weekly news sheet discussed whether to print the hand-written resolution—an ultimatum, one said; the beginnings of a mutiny, another suggested—drawn up by a handful of doughboys and circulated at one of the fronts. *We the undersigned*, it began, *firmly resolve that we demand relief not later than March 15th, 1919, and after this date we positively refuse to advance on Bolo lines including patrols.*

Eudora, pushed past by a wave of dancers, missed the rest of that discussion. She would have given a great deal to be back in her room, reading quietly; she'd refused the first invitation here, balking until the two Red Cross nurses crushed her resistance. There were nine American women in all of Archangel, they reminded her. Nine, of which she was one; and really only eight because the consul's wife was too sick to come; and how were the soldiers supposed to enjoy themselves if the women refused to do their part? And so here she was, her mouth shaped in a stiff smile, nodding in time to the cheerful sawings of the regimental orchestra.

Food beckoned from the crowded tables, whisky and vodka slopped from glasses. In a corner a middle-aged woman who spoke six languages and had once run an academy was soliciting new recruits for her conversational Russian class. Two YMCA men, glaring disapprovingly at the British Headquarters staff getting drunk on good Scotch whisky, shared the latest gossip about the sergeant who, after stealing enormous quantities of sugar from the American depot, had been caught bartering it for fur and jewels and, disgraced, had shot himself. Near the spread of cakes and cookies, the major despised by everyone was holding forth about the court-martials he organized with such relish. "Not just the murderers," he said, slicing the air as Eudora, impelled by the nurses' words, made her way dutifully forward. "The shirkers have to be punished too, and the ones who wound themselves on purpose."

On the backless benches men Eudora recognized from the hospital sat tapping their feet and staring at the very few women, including her, as if they were starving and she was steak—which was why the nurses had insisted on her presence. The only thing important about her here was that she was single and shaped like a woman. The orchestra played, the glasses clinked, the hum of voices rose and fell, and she danced with two doughboys in from one of the fronts, then with a clerk from the Norwegian embassy, a British medic, a Canadian gunner, a Polish mechanic, an ambulance driver from Lansing. Below her shoulder blades, the spot where the men pressed their hands began to sweat. She could feel them trying to still their thumbs, which wanted to caress her spine. Her right hand, which each man held in turn, was slowly being crushed. A member of a machine-gun crew, looking at his palm pressed against hers, said, "Your hands are huge, aren't they? Bigger than mine," which embarrassed her; at work, where she was most comfortable, her height and strength were assets. The corpse in the sleigh, Havlicek, she remembered as having frozen awkwardly: his arms uncrossed and one large hand bent at the wrist, a foot turned in, a scarf stuck to his skull.

From a supply clerk, who was pleasant enough but whose hands were disconcertingly warm and who was eager to gossip about the incident, she learned more details. Havlicek's platoon and one other had been sent a hundred and fifty miles east in November, to guard the supply of flour held by a little city and also to train Russian troops to fight against the Bolsheviks. Later they were sent still farther east, to attack a gathering mass of Bolos. Havlicek had been hurt during their first battle, heaved into the air by an artillery shell before crashing down on his back. They'd had neither medics nor ambulance men with them and the cuts on his face had been bandaged by a Russian with a first-aid kit. After their retreat to the little city, the medic stationed there had sent three of the wounded men on to Archangel but kept Havlicek, despite his bitter complaints about pain in his back.

He could walk, his captain pointed out, and he could fire a gun; nothing seemed to be broken and they were short-handed. Through December and January, his captain sent him on patrols but he lagged behind or dropped out, infuriating the rest of his platoon. Put on guard duty, he sat; on kitchen duty, he dawdled so long he delayed their meals. He felt, he was said to have said, as if someone had bored a tunnel down his back and buttock and through his thigh, then filled it with salt and flushed it with acid. Why would no one believe him? By February he was taking his meals alone and claiming he could no longer sleep. By March, he'd been utterly despondent.

So it did look like suicide, Eudora heard from several men chatting over drinks—but this was exactly what Private Boyd denied. Before being drafted, Havlicek had never held a gun and he moved and thought like a civilian. Exhausted, made clumsy by the cold, he had in Private Boyd's version been cleaning his gun, or putting it away, and somehow something had happened.

·

But everyone knew, said the driver who repeated that theory to Eudora, that Boyd *had* to say that; Havlicek's family would get no benefits if he were ruled to have killed himself.

Dancing with an engineer in whose hand she'd once located a sliver of steel, Eudora heard further that Boyd had begged a load of hay from the peasants, and then—there'd been no officers at the outpost to stop him—wrapped Havlicek's body in blankets and placed it on top of the hay, where it froze solid. On his own he'd decided to bring the body into the city, in to them.

⁂

IT SNOWED THREE times that week and the sky, despite the approaching equinox, showed no signs of spring. Gray, every day. Gray at breakfast, gray all day, and the snow gray too, especially in the market square and along the plank sidewalks. The rotten ice on the river was littered with garbage. What should have been good news—the Secretary of War had given orders to withdraw American troops from Russia as soon as spring conditions would permit—made no impression; Eudora knew, as all the soldiers knew, that the White Sea was still solidly frozen and that it would be June at least before they were freed. The Peace Conference in Paris was still stalled, as it had been for months and apparently would always be; millions of soldiers were still stuck in England and France; the Bolsheviks had taken over in Hungary and were spreading through Germany and had been arrested by the carload in Seattle. There'd been strikes in Belfast, strikes in Glasgow and Munich, riots, battles, spreading starvation: but half of what she heard wasn't true and she couldn't trust what she read in the odd

•

issues of French and English newspapers that turned up; even they seemed to lie. Astronomers had supposedly just left England, heading for Brazil and the west coast of Africa, to observe an eclipse that was due in May and which would somehow prove Einstein's theories right or wrong; who could have organized such an expedition? Suffragettes had burned copies of Wilson's speeches in an urn across from the White House, been beaten and arrested—had that really happened? Was it true that the man who tried to kill Clemenceau was an anarchist and a Bolshevik? In the dark of the X-ray room, listening to her soldiers and considering all she heard and read, the world beyond the White Sea made no more sense than her world here.

During that gray, discouraging week, she saw Boyd for the second time. He came to the hospital just as she was about to leave for supper—because, he said, he'd heard from someone at the barracks that there was a woman who ran the X-ray facility at the American hospital, and that she was a volunteer, not officially part of the Army.

"Would that be you?" he asked.

"It would," she admitted. The square tip of his nose, sharply defined when she'd first seen it, was now covered with small dark blisters. "But I don't need an X-ray to see what you've done there."

"Forget my nose," he said, plucking at the cloth over his right thigh. "That's not the problem. Can I just show you?"

When she nodded he unwrapped his leggings, peeled three pairs of socks from his feet, discarded his leather tunic and his knitted vest. Then he hesitated. "There's a bathrobe back there," she said, gesturing at the folding screen. He stepped behind it and emerged a minute later, wrapped in the old brown wool robe donated by the major.

She was longing to ask why he'd brought Havlicek's body into the city by himself. Instead she said, "Which doctor referred you here?"

"I sent myself," he replied. His calves were white and strongly muscled, and she saw that the black fur lining his hat had misled her about his coloring; his hair, sticking up in dirty cowlicks, was the color of ashes. Despite that he seemed to be hardly older than she was. He said, "I've done enough first-aid work in the field that by now I can tell when there's something really wrong. But I can't get our doc to pay attention."

"Why not?"

He made a face, which she didn't understand. Then he said, "Some evidence would help. If you could find something . . ."

She put down her clipboard. "You know how this works. Unless we have such a rush of wounded pouring in that there's no time, I have to have a medical officer's order to examine you."

He turned in a half-circle, the brown wool flaring around his knees as he mutely pointed out the obvious: the room was empty, the corridors were silent. Dr. Hirschberg had finished his work and gone up to one of the little cubicles on the second floor where he and the nurses, the cook and Eudora and a few other Red Cross staff were lucky enough to be quartered. The rest of the building, once a meteorological institute, was calm. Downstairs, Eudora knew, two of the Russian washerwomen were boiling linen and one of the nurses was using the same hot stove to sterilize operating room equipment. In a room down the hall another woman—they never had trouble finding help, Russians were glad to work here for food—was using an American sewing machine to make surgical masks and gowns. Behind her the orderlies had finished serving supper in the old classrooms that now served as wards. For the last week they'd had fewer than twenty patients; no one new had come in for three days and all the staff had been storing up sleep and strength. They might have been in any half-empty hospital anywhere, on one of those quiet days when the staff, suppressing sighs of boredom, finally turned to neglected paperwork.

"Who's waiting?" Boyd asked. "What am I taking from anyone else? If you took a quick look, just, you know—it's driving me crazy. Look."

Turning away from her, gathering the bathrobe's hem on the right side and pulling it up and toward the front so that the taut cloth concealed his buttocks and his genitals—a modest man, she noted, marveling at his delicacy—he exposed the outer aspect of his upper right thigh. In the meaty part of his quadriceps was an angry red dot the size of a ladybug.

"Maybe a little infection," she said. "It doesn't look too bad."

"There's something in there," he said. "Way down in. If you could just *look* . . ."

"I can't make a plate," she said. "It wouldn't be right to use the film and the developing supplies. But I can check you over quickly with the fluoroscope."

Fifteen minutes later she had him arranged on the X-ray table in the darkened room. In the glow of the ruby light she'd adjusted the diaphragm and the angle of the screen and positioned him

·

on his back, arms crossed on his chest, with his right thigh sand-
wiched between the tube box, which was below the stretcher,
and the screen suspended from the holder above. She rubbed a
little more paraffin along the ridge that fit into the groove of the
stretcher and then slid the whole thing half an inch, moving the
red dot on Boyd's thigh into better alignment. The movement
startled Boyd and she apologized.

"It's all right," he said. "Just do what you need to do."

She positioned one hand on the screen stand and said, "Okay,
then. I'm going to turn off the red light and let my eyes adjust.
The room will go black, and you won't be able to see me, or any
part of yourself. In about ten minutes, I'll be able to examine you;
we can talk while the time passes, but you need to lie completely
still until I'm finished with the examination. Can you do that?"

"Of course," he said—sounding, as all the soldiers did, mildly
offended that she would ask; unaware, as they all were until it
happened, that these minutes lying utterly still in the black,
stuffy, silent room might cause the most unpredictable reactions.
In the dark, she'd seen men weep silently, cry hysterically, sit up
so suddenly they'd knocked her screen stand askew. Some told
stories about the awful things they'd seen and done; some would
start cursing and be unable to stop; a few, gentle enough in the
ruby light, would after a few minutes in the dark start whispering
obscenities and grab at her thighs and her crotch. One had seized
her hand and pulled it between his legs, then bitten her when she
tried to pull away. She was careful, now, not to let her attention
drift.

So far he hadn't moved. Quietly she breathed in and out,

waiting for her pulse to slow and her eyes to adapt. His voice floated up. "You never asked my name," he said. "I'm Constantine. At home, people call me Stan."

"Constantine," she repeated. Not once had that surfaced in the rumors—always, she heard "Boyd." "Or would you prefer me to call you Stan?"

"Constantine's fine," he said. "We don't know each other yet. May I call you Eudora?"

"Please."

"How did you get here?" he asked.

His tone was perfectly calm; he was fine; this was going to be easy. "The same way you did, I imagine," she said. "Transport, from Newcastle-on-Tyne."

"In September?"

She nodded, before remembering he couldn't see her. "Yes," she said.

Comparing notes, they determined that they'd been on two different ships. More men, nearly forty, he said, had died of the influenza on his ship than on hers. Because he'd been sent down the Dvina to one of the fronts the day after landing, he'd missed the first terrible weeks in the city, which she remembered so sharply: the tiny Russian Red Cross hospital overflowing, men sick on the ships and sick in the barracks, with no place to put them and, until the engineers hastily constructed a cemetery, not even a place to bury them. She'd spent much of her first weeks helping to turn this building into a hospital, installing the X-ray apparatus shipped over from Boston and helping set up the operating suite. Not that any of it helped the soldiers sick with the flu.

.

On the river, he said, ten more men from the infantry company he was assigned to had gotten sick, and two of them had died.

"Did you get sick yourself?" she asked.

"I didn't, somehow," he said. "You?"

"I didn't either."

The darkness had grown soft, almost velvety, which meant her eyes were ready. She lowered the fluoroscopic screen, tapped the floor switch, and adjusted the diaphragm. The coating on the screen began to glow and there he was, his interior suddenly visible, a sight that still astonished her. There were the familiar landmarks and also, suspended among them, an unfamiliar intrusion. What was that jagged, slivery shape? His femur was intact, the hip joint as well, and there were no signs of skeletal injury—yet the projectile she saw, well down from the little red dot on his skin and at an unexpected angle, was neither shrapnel nor a fragment from a shell. Long, slim, pointed at both ends—

"That's bone," she announced. "But I don't see where in you it can have come from."

"Shit," he said. "Sorry. I guess it makes sense, though."

She looked intently for another minute and then, before switching off the power to the tube, inked a small square and a number on his skin directly over the intruder. "You can sit up when you want," she said, moving the screen holder out of the way and turning on the light. Quickly, before she forgot any details, she marked on one of her printed forms the size and position of the sliver. "Why does that make sense?"

"Because it probably *is* bone," he said, "but not mine. Mike's."

In December, he explained, he'd been with a company south

of the city, holding part of a riverbank along with British, French, and Russian troops. If someone actually *was* in charge, the men on the ground couldn't tell. One day they'd get orders from the American colonel at headquarters in Archangel and the next those would be contradicted by the British commander who visited the front. One day they lost four men while fighting to hold a little bridge and the next were told to retreat and burn the bridge behind them; a week later, ordered back again, they'd had to cross on homemade rafts. They slept in the peasants' small homes and ate their food and grew friendly with some; then moved on to a camp in the woods and were told that the peasants were Bolshevik sympathizers. In icy weather, they returned and, so the Bolsheviks would be without shelter, cleared out the families and burned the houses to the ground, watching women who'd fed them a few weeks earlier wail over little mounds of household goods.

Their biggest battle had taken place on what people elsewhere called Armistice Day. For air support they'd had a few Allied planes, Sopwiths fitted with big skis and piloted by former members of the czar's air corps, trained by RAF flyers. One of those Russian pilots, mistaking a group of American and French troops for Bolsheviks, had dropped two 112-pound bombs directly on their position, wounding several doughboys and killing their cook outright.

"I was standing right near Mike," Boyd said. Eudora, who'd listened to all of this without comment, put down her pen.

"The blast tossed me ten feet away but I landed in the snow and at first I thought I'd gotten away with just the cuts on my face and hands. There wasn't anything left of Mike but some little pieces, which we gathered up in a blanket and buried in the crater. That night my leg started killing me and the next day, when I went to the latrine, I found a little hole in my thigh, which wasn't bleeding much but which seemed deep. I cleaned it out, bandaged it, and didn't think more about it. We were so mad about Mike that for a couple of days we wouldn't talk to any of the Brits. Their commanders had trained those pilots, and given them the crummy information—but then the real fighting started up again, skirmishes every day. A patrol went out and lost two men, three more were wounded trying to move supplies across the river. I didn't have time to worry about my leg and anyway the surface scabbed over and the opening began to close. A few weeks later—"

He stopped abruptly and she waited. When he showed no sign of continuing, she said, "Why don't you get dressed?"

He nodded, slid off the table, and disappeared behind the screen. When he returned he looked like a soldier again, whatever else he'd wanted to tell her folded up in the brown wool robe. He tapped his right thigh and said, "So this is from Mike, is all I meant to say—you don't need to know the rest of it. I was standing right next to him and part of him must have blown into me."

"From a long bone, would be my guess," she said without thinking. "Femur, humerus, tibia maybe . . ."

He looked her over and shook his head. "A cold one, aren't you?"

She blushed, something she hadn't done in months.

"That's *Mike*," he said, gripping her arm above the elbow and thrusting his face so close she could see his pale lashes. "My friend.

·

I want that fucking thing out of me, I want *him* out of me. I want the surgeon to fix this and then put me on the sick list and send me to the convalescent hospital and let me work there until I can be shipped home. No fucking way am I going back out there."

Eudora tugged her arm free. "You know it's the surgeon who has to decide that."

"But you can tell him what you saw. That it's infected or whatever it is, and how I'll be crippled if it's not removed."

His eyes were a clear light gray, hard to see because so deeply set. She promised him she'd see what she could do.

⁂

SHE SPENT THAT evening loading film in cassettes, replenishing solutions in the darkroom, and filing two weeks' worth of forms, but despite those dry satisfactions she still felt unsettled when she went up to bed and, although her room was warm and her nightgown was clean, she remained too angry with herself to sleep. When had she stopped seeing below the surface of events, or stopped hearing, beneath what was said, what was really meant? If her hands and eyes, so experienced now, conjured images from the X-ray apparatus, and if the surgeons had come to rely on the accuracy of her readings, that didn't make what she'd lost less crucial. The part of her that had once intuited feelings and responded appropriately had grown as coarse-grained as film meant for use at night, everything delicate sacrificed to speed. Nothing surprised her anymore, only the details differed. This battle, that battle, these wounds, those; shells, shrapnel, airplane crashes, railroad collisions, bombs. Here, they were somehow fighting the

Bolsheviks, not the Germans, with the British, not the French, in charge: so of course it was a British-trained soldier, in an RAF plane, who dropped the fatal bomb, and the friendly cook—why was it never the pig-eyed sergeant who cheated at poker?—who was killed. And of course the sliver of bone lodged in Stan's, Constantine's—*Boyd*'s thigh (after all, she couldn't use his first name) wasn't his own. As that was one of the things that could happen, so it *did* happen, as did everything sooner or later: but she might have remembered what her speculation would sound like to him. *Oh, it must be from a femur . . .*

She folded her limp pillow beneath one ear and pulled her blanket over the other, which muffled but didn't block the sound of the nurses snoring in the cubicles around her. Once she would have thought it odd for one man to be carrying inside of him bone from another, who was dead. But everything here was backwards, including her own presence, which had come about by a chain of events so implausible that she omitted most of them when she wrote to her family back home. Even when she wrote to Irene Piasecka, who had first taught her, she touched only on the surface of her last year. She left out locations, events, the ridiculous journeys between events; Irene, who had made her way from Poland to New York to Colorado, from Colorado to the sanatorium in the Adirondack Mountains where they'd both worked, knew all about sudden, improbable change. Writing to her, Eudora had skimmed over her stay at the mobilization station in New York, her voyage to London, and her shipment to France a few weeks later with a group of Red Cross nurses who, looking on her as a lowly aide, had been consistently unkind. She wrote still less about the British hospital in Paris, where she'd ferried blankets and bedpans through the corridors, brought trolleys of food from the kitchen, held basins while nurses unwound long strips of iodine-soaked gauze—tasks that, she couldn't help thinking, any breathing creature might have done equally well, although she was glad to be able to do them.

And after that—what was the point of describing what she'd seen and heard and done? Searching for something her family could bear to hear, she mentioned that the excellent French she'd learned in high school had finally been put to use when, after the start of the Picardy offensive, she was sent to a French hospital near Beauvais and found, scattered among the French soldiers, wounded doughboys who couldn't communicate with the French doctors and nurses treating them. Couldn't explain that the weights and pulleys holding a shattered leg in traction needed adjustment; longed to write their wives and couldn't ask for paper; hated liver but found it on their trays. They'd been glad to have her interpret for them and to fix what she could.

She had not even tried, though, to describe the insane rapidity with which her duties had been transformed. One day she was writing a letter for a soldier with no hands and the next a French nurse she often saw near the operating room had pulled her over and asked her to hold some sandbags around a *poilu*'s shoulder while he was being X-rayed. The nurse mentioned that she had taken Marie Curie's training course for *manipulatrices* nine months earlier and been practicing ever since, and Eudora in a few words described the machines she'd worked on in the basement of Tamarack State Sanatorium. Briefly, as if appraising a wound, the nurse had looked away from her task and at Eudora's face. Two days later, she began teaching Eudora the difficult, interesting techniques of localization.

A bullet might enter in one place, she learned, but end up in another, after being deflected by a bone. Shrapnel might tunnel this way or that and might, on an X-ray image, seem to be lying over an organ it actually lay under. Fragments of a shattered bone might move like arrows, puncturing viscera or piercing organs which might leak or bleed, undiscovered, were they not able to calculate accurate trajectories. One day she learned something and the next was left to do it alone, which was exactly what she couldn't explain to anyone back home. Out here she saw it happen all the time, to nurses and soldiers and doctors and drivers and engineers alike; no one did what they'd been trained to do, they did what needed doing. She learned more in six weeks than she had in six months of concerted practice at home.

In late May, during the German spring offensive, she was transferred to Auteuil, where she worked surrounded by American doctors and nurses in long white tents spread in rows over the grounds of the racecourse. Orderlies did nurses' work, recuperating soldiers did orderlies' work, nurses acted as anesthesiologists. Wearing rubber boots and a white kerchief over her dirty hair, she changed bandages for two days before an exhausted surgeon heard her say something about her training and promptly moved her into the X-ray room to help the medic struggling with the new equipment. The tube stand broke; she fixed it. She calibrated the tube, loaded the holders, mixed developing chemicals, set up the darkroom efficiently. The medic had trouble using the Hirtz compass to localize projectiles; she taught him how to set the legs correctly. The surgeon, reviewing films with her, said her instinct for sensing how bullets and pieces of shrapnel split after they entered a man's body, and for exposing their peculiar paths, was frightening. Then he invited her to work with him full-time.

All summer, as the wounded men poured into the white tents, she'd continued to work in the X-ray room. Paris wasn't far but she never left the racecourse. She wrote home very seldom, ignored the letters she received, and when she wasn't working either slept or prepared for the next full train. In July she heard that American troops had been assigned to North Russia as part of an Allied intervention; in August, that a small Red Cross unit had left New York on a merchant steamer, carrying food and medicine and other supplies for those troops. Those seemed like pointless facts until September, when she was sent from Paris to London to Newcastle-on-Tyne, where she boarded one of the four ships that at midnight, under a new moon, had floated silently down the river and into the North Sea. As neither the Army nor the Red Cross had roentgenologists to spare, the surgeon at Auteuil had volunteered her.

So that was her preposterous story, which she'd given up trying to explain. No one at home could understand but here almost everyone had lived through something similar, including Boyd. Nothing in his story had been unfamiliar, if the details differed they were only the details; the contradictions and reversals all rang true. Why, then, had she been so insensitive to him?

.

❖

ALL THROUGH THE next day she wrote up a report on a new way to chart the location of projectiles, which she'd developed in France and which Dr. Hirschberg, who'd found it useful, wanted to submit to the Army. He came in several times to check on her but she said nothing to him about Private Boyd's problems, knowing the time wasn't right. At the end of the day she let him leave the building alone, so he wouldn't feel that she was pestering him, and fifteen minutes later she walked by herself to the convalescent hospital. The sky was dark, the moon was hidden by heavy low clouds, and the air was damp and smelled of smoke and garbage. Soon it would start to snow again. People bundled in long dark coats, their faces hidden by hats and scarves, converged in thin columns on the hospital's front door. She joined the back of one column and moved toward the recreation room, where an elderly British professor was giving the fourth of a series of lectures on Russian literature. For a month now this had been her chief distraction: such a relief, to hear someone talk about anything other than the war.

On her way in she stopped to say hello to several soldiers; most of those who'd been operated on and stabilized at the receiving hospital ended up here for a while. Dr. Hirschberg, who'd arrived before her, waved and gestured her over and so she sat at his table, facing the river, in a dark green armchair stained with chocolate and smelling of the horrible cigarettes the British supply officer doled out to the men. The movie screen at the front of the hall was blank; the stage, which most recently had hosted a vaudeville entertainment during which one Viola Grottinetskoff had danced

•

in tights, was now bare except for a small wooden podium. Dr. Hirschberg said, "I'm looking forward to this, aren't you?"

"I am," she said. The gray cardigan he wore every day was neatly buttoned but covered with small spots, and there were specks of skin caught in his heavy dark eyebrows. "I do every week."

"I've been reading Turgenev in French, since the last talk," the doctor said. "I've forgotten—do you read French?"

"Quite well," she said. Although he relied on her films to guide his incisions, she was not sure, sometimes, if he remembered her name. But he was a fine surgeon, calm in the face of the worst surprises, and she was happy to work with him.

"I'm glad you had some quiet time this afternoon," he said. "If it stays like this, maybe we'll try to send your report off later this week."

"It's nice to be catching up," she said. "But I did see one patient I'd like to tell you about."

While the room filled up around them, officers and secretaries and headquarters staff trickling in by twos and threes, she related what she'd learned so far about Boyd. His appearance, half-frozen, with Havlicek's body; his request for an examination; what she'd observed with the fluoroscope. "It's clearly cadaver bone," she said. "And the wound's becoming infected. If you were to operate . . ."

"Then he'd end up here," Dr. Hirschberg said. "Like them." He nodded at the two soldiers guarding the doorway and then at the pair working the refreshment bar. Convalescent soldiers did all the work at this hospital themselves, except for the nursing and cooking, and were also sent out to guard the Headquarters

•

building or work as clerks or typists inside it, to set type for the little newspaper, and even to work as orderlies and kitchen helpers back at her own hospital. If Boyd's surgery went well—

"He wants to have his little operation," Dr. Hirschberg continued, "and then move over here after a couple of days and have a pleasant week in bed, before waiting out the rest of his tour doing light duty in Archangel. Perhaps he'd like to be in charge of making hot cocoa."

Somehow, although that was roughly the same path followed by many soldiers whom she'd examined and he'd treated, his tone was uncharacteristically cool, even mocking. Before she could respond, the professor, dressed as before in his threadbare tweeds, took his place at the podium. While he enthused about Tolstoy and read from his own translations, she puzzled over how she'd offended the doctor.

The professor finished, the applause died down, the room began to empty out. Half the crowd knew Eudora or the doctor or both and stopped at their table to say hello, preventing her from asking him what he'd meant. Only when they had passed through the double doors themselves and were walking outside through the heavy wet snow, did she ask if she'd done something wrong in examining Private Boyd.

"I'm sure you meant well," the doctor said. "And it's not as if we all haven't bent the rules before." The tram clattered past, packed with rowdy soldiers on their way from the barracks to the night-clubs, and he paused, gazing moodily at the men hanging halfway out the windows. "God, I get tired of this," he said. "Them and their bad behavior, us and our bad behavior, the politicians, the

·

people back home—did I tell you what my wife wrote in her last letter?"

"No," she said, uneasily. She located and charted the objects piercing the soldiers' bodies; he dissected them out and closed the wounds: during the worst rushes, they hardly spoke at all, a glance or a gesture conveying all they needed. She ate with the nurses or by herself and he ate with the officers; when they met outside work it was at places like this lecture and they never spoke of personal things.

"According to my wife," he said bitterly, "my continued absence is causing her the greatest inconvenience. My patients have all been taken over by other doctors who've been back home for months, her friends feel sorry for her, my pitiful salary doesn't cover the rises in food and coal, the roof needs work and the garden is a shambles: complain, complain, complain. I can make excuses for her, because she doesn't have any idea what we're going through here. But what's your Private Boyd's excuse? Everyone's suffering, everyone wants to go home—and he's with the ambulance company, he's supposed to be helping *them*. Walking out on them now simply makes him a shirker."

"He's not 'my' private; I hardly know him. But he *is* hurt."

"He's hurt a *little*. But I know some things about him that you don't."

After outlining the same events Boyd had described, the plane mistakenly dropping the pair of bombs, the vaporized cook, the men grieving afterward, the doctor continued, "Half of that company was right on the edge of mutiny; they were so furious with the British officers in charge, and with the fliers, that they burned

.

down a shed they'd been using as a hangar. Two British soldiers were beaten up and no one would admit to it. And someone sent an anonymous letter from the front to Headquarters, demanding that their company be relieved. Did you hear the stories about the driver who lost his mind back in November?"

"Who didn't?" An ambulance driver, without a rifle of his own, had stolen a rifle from a sleeping comrade and then crept through the outpost until he found a British officer. After blaming the officer for starting the war against the Bolsheviks, he'd blown off the officer's head, and then his own.

"Then you can understand why the officers in charge would worry about what was going on after the cook was killed."

Dr. Hirschberg dug his hands deeper into his pockets as they rounded the corner and faced the damp wind blowing off the river. By the water, in the light of a fire, three women with cleavers were dismantling a dead goat. "Jesus," he said. He shook his head, and then continued. At the same time the commanders at Headquarters were considering what to do with those men, there'd been a huge increase in Bolshevik activity far to the east, with rumors of a major attack. More troops were badly needed there. Using that as an excuse, the British commanders had decided to break up the American company, pulling two platoons of infantry and six ambulance and medical men away from the site of the cook's death. Boyd had been in that group.

They passed the sawmill, dimly lit but still running, filling the air with a smell so intense that Eudora was briefly transported to the dark pine and spruce forests of her childhood. She said, "I don't see what that has to do with his injury."

"They should have kept him where he was," Dr. Hirschberg said. "And would have, if he hadn't been one of the ringleaders. The company's supervising medical officer had been shot in the stomach and transported back into Archangel, and besides being shorthanded they had hardly any medical supplies. Boyd's clearly smart, and enterprising; I heard he stitched up someone's leg in the field with a needle and thread from a sewing kit. But he was enough of a wild card that they wanted him out of the way no matter how skilled he was. Your Private Boyd"—there was that phrase again—"did a ten-day march, carrying a full pack, and then he worked at that outpost for three months before the incident with Havlicek. All with the same wound that he's complaining about now. If he wants me to operate on him, you can be sure he has another reason."

※

SHE HAD NOT, before that evening, given much thought to how Dr. Hirschberg viewed his patients. Although he'd had no military experience before the war and left behind a lucrative private practice in New Jersey, he worked long hours uncomplainingly, and she'd fallen into the habit of thinking that he was relatively content. And that despite his increasingly scruffy appearance he was somehow sturdier and stronger than she was: less lonely, less baffled, less consumed by longing to go home. The way he judged Boyd so sharply, though, opened up the possibility that he was judging all his patients—and the nurses, and the orderlies, and her.

Until now she'd believed that he regarded her as simply a component of the operating suite, no less essential, but no more

·

interesting personally, than her X-ray tube. His distant courtesy, which the Russian nurses found insulting, instead made her feel invisible in the most pleasing way. When she'd first learned to use the machines back in the Adirondacks, she'd been alone most of the time and her body had seemed to dissolve in the darkness of the sanatorium basement, leaving her mind directly connected to the wires and the dials. She'd been shocked, in France, to find that the soldiers she tended actually *saw* her. They questioned her passionately about her own life, poured their stories out unasked, returned to the hospital when they were healed and asked her to walk with them, eat with them, marry them. Her only relief had come during the hours she'd spent studying and working with the *manipulatrice*.

Here, Dr. Hirschberg protected her similarly, keeping her busy and hidden. Once he'd said, as she showed him the path a bit of broken rib had traveled, that when he operated it was with her eyes as well as his own, her mind as well as his. They talked about work, and about fluoroscopes and tubes and bones and spleens; about the lectures they both attended when they needed distraction, and about the new books they tried to read. Until his recent outburst about Boyd, that had been all.

She was still thinking about this a few days later when, on her way back from the supply depot, she passed the base of the massive toboggan slide a group of engineers had built to entertain the troops. In Tamarack Lake, the toboggan runs had been built on the lower slopes of the mountains: snow packed into smooth troughs, sometimes iced with buckets of water, acres of softer snow at the bottom ready to slow the toboggans down. Here the run

·

rose straight up from nothing: flat city, flat square, buildings lined up along the wide flat river and, in the midst of them, a huge tower of cross-braced timbers, buttressed by a long wedge and rising three stories into the air. The underemployed engineers had decorated the steps with small spruce trees draped with colored lights.

No wonder the children couldn't stay away from it. At the foot of the wooden stairs, a Russian guard trying to attend to the old woman berating him stood surrounded by a clutch of shrieking little boys and a girl clomping about in what looked like her father's big felt boots. Eudora, stopping among the spectators to see what was going on, gathered, by piecing together their gestures and exclamations, that one of the boys had sneaked past the guard and climbed halfway up the snow-coated treads before slipping and dropping his sled. The sled had clattered down the steps and then crashed into the old woman, who'd dropped her precious bag of flour. Now she was weeping openly, shouting at the guard and flailing at the boy, who had taken refuge behind a doughboy's bulky overcoat.

Private Boyd's coat, she saw when he turned. Her first impulse, which surprised her, was to pull her hood more closely around her face and hope he hadn't seen her. He nodded, though, and she was caught. A small wooden sled piloted by a British soldier whisked down the long, steep curve, iced each night to be savagely hard and fast. Boyd slipped something to the old woman—a coin, perhaps—and then moved toward Eudora. The soldier on the sled leaned back, his feet pressed against the steering yoke and the rope in his hands, his vision blocked by the girl sitting astride his lap with her arms wrapped around his neck and her hair whirling

·

over his eyes. A Russian girl, laughing hoarsely; possibly one of the girls who frequented the notorious café with the dark green roof. The sled shrieked twenty yards across the square, then thirty, leaving behind a wake of startled people. There was nothing to stop the sled from shooting over the steep bank and down onto the frozen river—but just then it hit a bump and tipped both passengers into the snow.

"Interesting technique," she said to Boyd, as the driver raised his powdered head and waved his arm happily at the crowd.

"He got lucky," Boyd said. "And so did I—I've been hoping to see you."

As he spoke, another little boy, sensing a break in everyone's attention, sprinted triumphantly past the guard and up the steps.

"Move back," Boyd said, tugging at Eudora's arm as the boy threw himself down on a flimsy sheet of metal. "He's liable to come flying right over the edge."

"He'll be all right," she said. "The run's been up since January, and the only ones to get hurt so far have been soldiers."

"Figures," Boyd said. "The ones with the cushy guard jobs in the city are so bored they have to go looking for trouble. They should come and change places with us." Then, as she'd been dreading, he asked her if she'd spoken to Dr. Hirschberg about him.

"Just briefly," she said.

"When will he see me? We're going to be sent out again soon."

"I couldn't convince him," she admitted. "He knows of you already, or he thinks he does—he told me about some problems your unit had after your friend was hit by the bomb, and that you'd been sent east as a disciplinary measure."

·

He frowned and stared at the tower, seeming to trace with his eyes the improbably intricate pattern of the timbers. Then he sighed and pulled his collar more closely around his neck. "It's too cold to stand here," he said. "Can I walk you wherever you're headed?"

"If you'd like. I'm going back to the hospital."

He was limping a bit; Eudora matched her stride to his and, as they left the square and began to move along the riverbank, asked how his leg was.

"It hurts," he said shortly, turning to watch a flock of mud-colored crows wheeling toward their roost. "What do you think? If I was a horse—a cow, even—the surgeon would be working on me right now, he'd never risk the damage. When I worked with the calves—"

"You're a farmer?"

He laughed. "Hardly. I grew up in Detroit. But one of my uncles had a dairy farm a couple of hours away, where I worked most summers. I learned early to doctor the sick calves and stitch up wounds, and by the time I was thirteen I was helping out a local veterinarian. He let me read his books and taught me some basic surgical techniques. And I once spent a summer with another uncle, farther away in a little village in upstate New York called Hammondsport. He and some of his friends made me curious about all sorts of things . . ."

An expression she couldn't read passed over his face as he paused. "Anyway," he added, "I got this idea that I might be a vet."

"What happened?"

He shrugged. "Same as what happened to lots of us. I got

·

drafted before I finished my first year of college, and then funneled into the ambulance company because of my little bit of experience. I thought at least I'd learn some medicine, but after basic training all we got was a few weeks of classes. Elementary anatomy, simple first-aid techniques—you know. The dressings go here and you can feel a pulse there. Cover exposed intestines with a damp clean cloth. If blood is jetting out of someone's femoral artery, apply direct pressure. Lice are bad. Hot soup is good. I knew more than that before I was in long pants. Most of it's pointless anyway, the best thing we can ever do for the ones who are hit is to get them back here, to the hospital and you. Which most of the time is just what we can't do quickly enough."

As he spoke he swung his arms in the air, back and forth, more and more briskly. The sun had disappeared below the horizon, replaced by a cheese-colored moon. The market was closing and lights were blinking on in the café windows. "Everything useful I learned on the job," he said, describing the weeks he'd worked without proper supplies. He'd splinted broken bones with sticks, improvised dressings from old rags, gleaned from a Russian doctor essential mortician's skills.

"You don't understand what it's like out there," he said. "None of you here in the city do, not you, not your lazy surgeon, not the officers in charge. You have no idea. We get shot at picking up the wounded, and loading them on the sleighs, and hauling them to the clearing stations and then to the railroads or the sleigh trails. The Bolos cover themselves with white canvas smocks and sneak up on the encampments at night. We can't see them but we feel them out there, and they pick us off one by one. They come up

·

behind us in the woods. Our own supply officers skim off everything good and we end up with nothing, no smokes, rotten eats.
Really," he repeated angrily, "you have no idea."

"I have some idea," she said. "What is it you think I do here?"

By now they had passed the Headquarters building, the place
where she'd first sent him. Her feet were cold and she was hungry but he pinned her with his eyes, still talking. Dr. Hirschberg,
he was saying, had no right to judge what had happened to him.
It was true that after Mike had been killed he'd been angry at
everyone, and would happily have shot the Brits who'd ordered
the bombing, or the Russian pilots who'd made the mistake, but
he and his friends had been *glad* to be sent from that place and the
long hike to the east, which they knew had been meant to punish
them, had actually been glorious. Cold, of course, twenty below
zero, then forty below, so cold he couldn't have imagined surviving
ten days of it, but away from the fighting, away from the crowded,
stifling, stinking billets, he'd been able to see, for the first time,
what was beautiful about this country. Between the tiny villages
ranks of pine and spruce stretched in all directions, marked only
by twisting paths. He'd seen reindeer, and Russian Eskimos, and
wolves; windmills, used for grinding grain, and weirs for trapping fish. Women crouched on the frozen river dunking clothes
through holes in the ice while men, bulky and hairy as bears in
their hooded *parki*, crossed paths with the actual bears, collared
and chained, kept by the Russian soldiers as mascots.

She hadn't left the city once. The surrounding country, flat and
deadly, lacking the ridges and valleys of the land back home, was
almost a blank to her. She imagined rivers in which the soldiers

·

drowned, swamps that sucked at their legs, forests concealing their enemies. Railroads crossing the blankness and bringing them back to her. Her feet, she realized, were numb.

"We trapped rabbits," Boyd said dreamily, as if he'd enchanted himself. Why hadn't she pushed Dr. Hirschberg harder to consider his case? "We fished with grenades and shot deer and ducks and the little wild birds the peasants call *rabchiks*; they make a good stew. One night we stayed in a monastery. Another in a village hidden so deep inside a ravine that we didn't see it until we were in it. At noon the sun was just above the horizon, the rest of the day it was more like twilight, and we had to watch each other constantly for frozen ears and noses. But we were alone, just our two platoons. No British officers, no Russian troops to supervise. No one was shooting at us. We walked all day and ate good meals at night. We watched the sky. The northern lights here make a joke out of those back home, you must have seen them for yourself. Do you go out to watch them?"

"Sometimes," Eudora said. "Not often, though—if I'm not working at night, I'm usually at a lecture, or in my room. I can't..."

Odd, that he didn't understand how impossible it was for her to move beyond the busiest and most public places at night. So many soldiers, from so many countries, and just the tiniest handful of non-Russian women in the city. He looked at her curiously but then started talking again, this time about his leg.

The long hike, he said, was the only time he'd been at peace since landing here, but it had also hurt his leg, inflamed it in some way he hadn't understood until she'd examined him. First a little pain, which he thought had been caused by the weight of his pack, then something more constant and grinding. There'd been nothing to do but endure it. The medic at the tiny field hospital they'd established in a school gymnasium knew no more than he did and couldn't do anything to ease his pain. He'd managed—"Vodka helps," he said—but when he'd met Havlicek, whose pain was so much worse than his own, and who had lost all his friends, he'd felt an immediate bond.

"Couldn't you have asked to be sent back to Archangel? Both of you, maybe?"

He snorted. "You don't get to *ask* for things, in the Army. I didn't choose to be here at all, although I guess you did."

"I didn't either, really," she protested. "I was working in France, I was useful there. Then all of a sudden I got sent here."

The sky had turned an unpleasant metallic shade and a fire flared in the distance, sending up a column of oily smoke. A cart passed, mounded with garbage. Two thin dogs trailed the cart, followed by more little boys—were they the ones who'd been at the toboggan run, or others? She had never seen so many children in the streets. Boyd called something to them in Russian that made them laugh, but when he turned back to her, his face was stern.

"I did try, you know," he said. "To get Havlicek sent back. But the medic who first treated Havlicek took against me right away, maybe because I asked him to look at my own leg. And then I think he heard things about me from a couple of the officers. By the time I asked him to re-examine Havlicek and to put him on the sick list, the whole platoon I'd come east with was under suspicion. People had heard that we complained too much after

•

Mike was blown up, and that we'd been sent to them only because the place was so far away, and because they needed some bodies to stick in front of the Bolos, and they figured we couldn't contaminate anyone else out there. Anything any of us wanted, we got the opposite." He laughed harshly. "I should have asked for Havlicek to be sent wherever the fighting was worst."

They passed a shopwindow in which one small box of sugar sat like a crown on a purple cloth. She said, "But I thought Havlicek's death was an accident."

"Officially an accident, yes. But I didn't think we were talking officially."

Abashed, she shook her head.

"Then, well—I don't guess it was an accident. But if it wasn't, then someone could maybe have saved him. I might have saved him."

She said, as she said to Dr. Hirschberg when he came out of the operating room bloody and pale, a sheet pulled over the face of whomever he'd worked on, "You did what you could. You tried."

"So what?" By now they'd reached the pillars at the entrance to the hospital, and he looked broodingly across the courtyard. "I tried to get people to pay attention to what had happened to Mike, and to pull us out of that stupid place, and that didn't work. I tried to help Havlicek and I failed at that too. That trip into the city—I stopped at a little farm, at the end of my first day, when it was too dark for the farmer to see the bundle on the sleigh. He gave me a place in the house near the stove and let the pony stay in the barn, but when I went out the next morning the whole family was already there, staring at Havlicek's feet, which had come unwrapped somehow. They shooed me away and then the next night, when I stopped at a village, the people seemed to guess right away what was lying under the blankets. They made me leave the sled outside. The third night, I came into a village that was already in the midst of a wake. The men were drunk and when they saw the bundle they unloaded Havlicek without even asking me and carried him into the death house. They stretched him out on a bench next to a body that was already there and they told me I could sleep on the floor. By then I was so tired that I did. The next day I didn't dare stop and so I kept passing all the villages and moving until it was too dark to see and then I got caught out overnight. I couldn't stay warm. Finally I had to unwind one of the blankets from Havlicek's body and wrap myself in it and burrow down into the hay next to him. That's when I froze my fingers and my nose."

She thought back to her first sight of him, hunched and silent, half dead with fatigue. "Why didn't you let me help you?" she said. "Bring you into the hospital then—everything would have been different if you had. Dr. Hirschberg would have seen you frostbitten and hurt from your journey, and he would have taken care of you, he didn't know anything about you then—"

"Because I wanted those lazy assholes at Headquarters to *see* Havlicek. To see him like that, frozen and with a piece of his head blown off. Leave their fancy dinners and their Scotch whisky and make them see what happens to us out there."

"Did they?"

"What do you think? Plus they asked a lot of questions about how he died. If two of the men stationed at the outpost hadn't supported my statement about the shooting being an accident, they would have ruled it suicide for sure. I would have done better to have him buried there. They're all against me, now. Your surgeon, too, I think. Unless you do something to change that."

He turned and she did too, facing him as he faced her, already thinking about ways she might try to convince Dr. Hirschberg to change his mind. The distant pressure she felt next turned out to be Boyd's hands resting on what, through the layers of her thick coat, approximated her waist. The pressure increased; he was tugging her. "We could go someplace," he said. "Do you have a room here?"

She stepped back, beyond his reach. The clouds surged and wavered in ominous patterns and on the river the ice shifted and groaned.

"I'm sorry," he said, his arms still sticking out in the air. "You don't want—well, of course you don't want me. Who would want me?"

"It's not that," she said. "Only . . ." Why didn't he understand how impossible her situation was? It didn't matter, here, what she felt; she was so overwhelmed, surrounded by so many hurt and miserable men, that she couldn't let any one of them get too close.

"Right," he said, pulling sharply away from her. "Only only only *only*. I thought you—never mind. Why don't you get the doctor to *fix* me? What would it cost you?"

"It's not about me, about costing *me* . . ." He knew nothing about the work she and Dr. Hirschberg did together. As indeed the doctor knew nothing about her beyond her work. He might do what he asked, or he might not. "But I'll try again, if that's all you want from me."

"I'd take more," he said.

"So I see," she said, suddenly furious. "Whatever you can get, apparently. I need to go in."

"Now you're angry. I just wanted—"

"Just just *just*," she said. He might accuse her of not seeing him but he was the one who didn't see; he had no sense at all of who she was or what she did, what she felt like or what she endured; for him she was simply an instrument.

AFTER A COUPLE of days she calmed down, convincing herself that Boyd's behavior in the courtyard, at first so upsetting, was a version of what other soldiers experienced in her darkened X-ray room. Something came over them that they couldn't help; she pretended they didn't mean it and so did they. He was no different than the rest of them and what happened to him was no more or less her problem. Of the two paths lying before him, she could influence neither. Either his leg healed and he resigned himself to being sent back to the front—indeed he might already be gone—or the wound became frankly infected and he reported to his medical officer, who'd send him in to the hospital, where she could examine him legitimately. She'd treat him like any other soldier, then, neither better nor worse. Dwell too long on one, she'd learned in France, and many suffer. The lines etched between her nose and her mouth, the weight she'd lost, the nights she spent reading Tolstoy instead of sleeping came from having

·

that lesson forced on her again and again, and from seeing certain soldiers realize that they weren't the only ones she tried to care for. In pain, in the darkened X-ray room, they called for their mothers and girlfriends, then confused her with them, then felt betrayed when she turned to the next in line.

A small rush of patients came later that week, brought in by a train; then four soldiers were hurt in a bar brawl. Busy, usefully busy, she pushed Boyd and his problems aside and didn't immediately think of him when, at the end of March, she first heard about what had happened at the barracks. Another threatened mutiny, one in a string that by this point hardly claimed her attention. In October French troops had put down their arms and refused to fight upon hearing about the pending Armistice; in December a contingent of Russians trained by the British had deserted in the midst of a major battle, bringing maps and plans to the Bolsheviks; in February a battalion of British soldiers had refused to march to the front lines, changing their minds only when the two sergeants leading their revolt were arrested. Most recently, a company of French soldiers who'd refused to board a train heading toward one of the fronts had been confined to their barracks and then shipped back to France. This one involved Americans, though, and the rumors contradicted each other.

It was one platoon, or several platoons; they'd quietly declined to load their sleds until someone explained to them where they were being sent and why, or they'd shouted and stormed away or even, in one version, laid hands on their guns. All the versions agreed that a unit of some size had balked when ordered to leave the city. And everyone heard that the officer in charge had been sufficiently upset to telegraph a report to Washington, and that the news had apparently leaked to some newspapers. On the Friday after whatever had happened happened, Eudora read a stilted, somewhat cryptic account in the English-language weekly paper printed at the convalescent hospital:

> On Monday morning, a company was told that they were being sent to a front south of the city and were ordered out of barracks for the purpose of packing sleds for the trip to the railroad station. The men remained in barracks, and eventually the NCO in charge reported the situation to the officers.
>
> Some of those officers entered the barracks and repeated the orders but the men continued to delay for several more hours. The colonel of the regiment then arrived, assembled the men, and read them the Article of War that pronounces death as the penalty for mutiny, following which he asked if they had any questions.
>
> Although there were no questions regarding this specific Article, one soldier did ask the colonel respectfully: "Sir— what are we here for, and what are the intentions of the U.S. Government in North Russia?" The colonel reportedly answered that he could not answer this question definitively—but that whatever the purposes of the Expedition, it was in danger of being driven to extinction by the Bolsheviks, and that all must now join in successful resistance. Silence followed.

·

The colonel then asked any man who did not agree with his statement, and who would refuse to fight, to step forward three paces from the ranks and explain his position. No one accepted his invitation and the meeting was dismissed with an order to load their packs on the sleds and proceed to the railroad station.

A small group of men, left behind to organize the release from the Supply Company of special rations and medical supplies that unaccountably failed to reach this front earlier, will join the rest of the company next week.

Only then did she begin to wonder about Boyd. Had his company left Archangel right after she'd last seen him, or was it the one that had balked? The following day her question was partly answered when he left a note with the guard at the hospital. *I'm supposed to leave for the front tomorrow,* he wrote. *I'd like to see you before then. Please meet me at 8 tonight, at the toboggan run.*

Of course, she thought. Every place he went he caused trouble; he must have been involved in the incident. A confused man, a difficult man. A man there was no point in seeing, except for the fact that she had failed utterly to help him. After supper, she went to the toboggan run and found him there, pale but apparently cheerful. He thanked her for coming.

"I didn't think you were still in the city," she said. "I was surprised to get your note."

Calmly, quickly, smiling as if it meant nothing, he explained that his had been the company she'd read about. "Everyone boarded the train, in the end," he said. "All but three other ambulance drivers and me. We're supposed to bring more medical supplies down south tomorrow."

Then, instead of confronting her about her failure to persuade Dr. Hirschberg to remove the splinter in his leg, instead of begging her to do something else to keep him from returning to the front, he asked if she wanted to take a run. "This fellow here," he said, pointing to a soldier pulling a toboggan by a rope, "says he'll let us take a ride on his."

What, she wondered, had actually gone on at the barracks? Had he been one of the leaders, or one of those hanging back at the edges, following the tide? "I'd like that," she said.

Up the stairs to the little platform, which was lit by lanterns and was higher than she thought. She could see domes, chimneys, scaffolding, train tracks, the far side of the river. She sat in front, snugged between Boyd's outstretched legs, the steering rope tight in his hands. The moon was up, lighting the scene and accompanied by two bright stars, which perhaps were planets. The wind had dropped and the air was still and cold. At the base of the run soldiers and children and passersby gathered in small knots, chatting and looking up at the toboggan, which eased over the lip, dropped, and then began to gather speed. Music drifted from across the square—an accordion, a violin—and also the smell of potatoes roasting. His legs kept her skirt from blowing as they went faster. What did she know about him, really? That inside his leg was a long sliver of someone else's body. That he'd seen that body shattered before his eyes; that he'd lifted other bodies from the snow and bandaged those who were still alive, loaded them into sleighs and drove them one place and another. That

·

he'd seen a man named Havlicek with his head blown off and had slept, for three nights, in the company of the frozen corpse. But about his life before Archangel she knew almost nothing, other than those summers spent with one uncle or another, on one farm or another. Where had he lived and what were his parents like, did he have brothers and sisters and a favorite friend, had he left behind one girlfriend or a whole string, a ukulele or a camera or a cherished set of chisels? At night, when he'd leaned over a desk to study his schoolbooks, had he done that restlessly or with pleasure? She didn't know whether he liked to fish or swim, watch movies or read, join a gang at the baseball field or lie in a field by himself, dreamily watching a hawk. Even his journey with Havlicek's body remained a mystery; much of what she knew, what she thought she knew, came not from his account but from various rumors.

She leaned back into his chest. All she'd withheld from him and others, all the ways in which, desperately, she'd tried to guard some essential core when she ought to have opened herself—but if she'd done that and let the lives of her soldiers flow in, she would have been unable to work. So she'd been right, then? By denying them one thing, her deepest self, she'd been able to offer all her useful skills. Some, she supposed, would rather have had her feelings. She settled against his chest, she let her back and shoulders flow into him and she felt him pressing back.

The sled shot across the square, slowed when it hit a soggy patch, came to rest near a cart filled with broken branches, which was being investigated by two dogs. She rose, smiling, and brushed off her skirt. "That was nice," she said, as they walked

.

back toward the run. The empty toboggan, which Boyd was tow-
ing, bounced on the rims of their footprints. "I can't believe I
haven't done that all winter."

"You've been busy," he said. "But I'm glad you enjoyed it. To
me it feels almost like flying."

They stepped through the crossed shadows thrown by the
structure's wooden frame, and then they stopped. With an oddly
formal gesture, he handed her the rope. "My friend will be by for
this. But I'd like to do one by myself, really fast. Would you wait
a few minutes?"

Before she could object he picked up a small sled tucked behind
the steps and then headed up. She waited below, enjoying the
feel of the air on her face, watching as he climbed with the sled
under one arm. At the top he stood and tested the rope stretched
between the two ends of the steering yoke. For a second he
paused, looking as if he were about to throw himself belly down
on the sled, hands grasping the yoke—but then he did something
with one foot and kicked the sled into motion with him standing
up on it, holding on to the rope as if on to the bridle of a horse,
leaning back against it, gathering speed. About halfway down the
sled veered left and she could see it was going to bump into the
lip of the run. It bumped and—did she see him, just then, let
go the rope on purpose, raising his hands into the air? Did she
see him look down and, like a diver, twist his hips and shoulders
halfway round, so that he arched gracefully away from the icy
tower and toward a clear spot on the ground? He would fall, she
saw, not on his head or his spine but on his left side, the angle at
which he had poised himself suggesting that his left ankle and

·

knee would strike first; he would shatter that leg, perhaps also his hip; he might cripple himself; he might lose the leg. He probably wouldn't die. He wasn't trying to kill himself, he wanted what they all wanted—which was, she realized as she ran toward the spot where he'd strike the ground, what she too wanted more than anything else: he wanted to leave this place behind and go home, home, home.

Author's Note and Acknowledgments

✿

Most of the characters here are invented, but G.H. (Glenn H. Curtiss), Sir Oliver Lodge, the Professor (Louis Agassiz), and some of the geneticists mentioned are historical figures, and the fiction is rooted in factual events. On July 4, 1908, the *June Bug* flew in Hammondsport, New York, winning the *Scientific American* trophy. Sir Oliver Lodge's objections to Einstein's theory of general relativity continued long after the expeditions observing the May 29, 1919, eclipse. Louis Agassiz founded a summer school for natural history at Penikese Island in 1873; the quoted stanzas are from John Greenleaf Whittier's poem "The Prayer of Agassiz" (1874). Among the passengers aboard the *Athenia*, the first British ship to be sunk by the Germans in World War II, were a number of participants from the Seventh International Congress of Genetics, held in Edinburgh. And the American North Russia Expeditionary Force (also known as the Polar Bear Expedition:

·

the 339th Infantry, First Battalion of the 310th Engineers, 337th Field Hospital, and 337th Ambulance Company) fought in North Russia during the period mentioned here.

Portions of this book have appeared previously, in somewhat different form, in the following publications: "The Investigators" in *A Public Space*, "Archangel" in *One Story*, "The Island" in *Salmagundi*, and "The Ether of Space" and "The Particles" in *Tin House*. "The Particles" will also appear in *The PEN / O. Henry Prize Stories 2013*. My thanks to these publications and their editors. Thanks also to Jill Gilbreth and Jim Shepard, who generously offered helpful readings, and to my husband, Barry Goldstein, whose own work inspired "Archangel" and who helped me throughout.

Margot Livesey read many versions of all these pages; my deepest thanks, as always, for her patience and her brilliant suggestions. Finally, my beloved agent, Wendy Weil, encouraged me before her untimely death with steadfast brilliance and attention. I miss her more than I can say.

·